This Mortal Boy

FIONA KIDMAN

Dame Fiona Kidman OBE, Légion d'honneur, is one of New Zealand's foremost contemporary writers. A novelist, short story writer and poet, she is the author of more than 30 books. She has worked as a librarian, radio producer and critic, and as a scriptwriter for radio, television and film. She lives in Wellington.

Also by Fiona Kidman

Novels
A Breed of Women, 1979
Mandarin Summer, 1981
Paddy's Puzzle, 1983
The Book of Secrets, 1987
True Stars, 1990
Ricochet Baby, 1996
Songs from the Violet Café, 2003
The Captive Wife, 2005
The Infinite Air, 2013
All Day at the Movies, 2016

Short story collections (as author)
Mrs Dixon and Friend, 1982
Unsuitable Friends, 1988
The Foreign Woman, 1993
The House Within, 1997
The Best of Fiona Kidman's Short Stories, 1998
A Needle in the Heart, 2002
The Trouble with Fire, 2011

Short story collections (as editor)
New Zealand Love Stories: An Oxford Anthology, 1999
The Best New Zealand Fiction 1, 2004
The Best New Zealand Fiction 2, 2005
The Best New Zealand Fiction 3, 2006

Non-fiction
Gone North, 1984
Wellington, 1989
Palm Prints, 1994
At the End of Darwin Road, 2008
Beside the Dark Pool, 2009

Poetry
Honey and Bitters, 1975
On the Tightrope, 1978
Going to the Chathams, 1985
Wakeful Nights, 1991
Where Your Left Hand Rests, 2010
This Change in the Light, 2016

Play
Search for Sister Blue, 1975

This Mortal Boy

FIONA KIDMAN

Gallic Books
London

A Gallic Book

Copyright © Fiona Kidman, 2018

Fiona Kidman has asserted her moral right to be identified as the
author of this work

First published by Penguin Random House New Zealand Ltd.

First published in Great Britain in 2019 by Gallic Books, 59 Ebury
Street, London, SW1W 0NZ

A CIP record for this book is available from the British Library
ISBN 9781910709580

Typeset in Fournier MT by Palimpsest Book Production Limited,
Falkirk, Stirlingshire

Printed in the UK by CPI (CR0 4YY)

For Ian,
who believed in this book
and
for E.H.,
the daughter of Albert Black

Chapter 1

October 1955. If Albert Black sings to himself he can almost see himself back home in Belfast, the place where he came from. He begins it as a low hum in his head, but words start tumbling out louder and louder *I am a wee falorie man, a rattling roving Irishman.* He's not sure what falorie means, but his da has told him he thinks it's about sorrow, which at this very moment he is feeling. A falorie man is harmless, just likes a bit of mischief, his da had said. Shut up, Paddy, a voice shouts, and other voices start clamouring in unison, Shut the shite up, Paddy. *I can do all that ever you can,* he sings. Shut up, not really meaning it for him, it's just something to scream about when men are locked in stone cells behind steel doors, they shout and they scream day and night and their voices are the one thing they have, their voices that the warders can't control. *I can do all that ever you can for I am a wee falorie man.* The trains that run past the west wing of the prison have been rattling all night, first the express that runs down south, then the goods trains, their long banshee wails trailing behind them. The morning train passes and

9

he raises his voice louder and louder to drown it out. *I'm a rattling roving Irishman* like it's a yodel now.

'No you're not,' the man in the next cell calls, 'you're a no good ten-pound Pom, why don't you go back where you came from?'

That's me, Paddy thinks, as he straightens his clothes out as neat as he can, for there are no mirrors in this cell. Neither fish nor fowl as far as these men are concerned. He speaks like an Irishman, he calls himself an Irishman, but he's from that No Man's Land that calls itself the United Kingdom. But it's there, Sandy Row, Belfast, the street crowded with shops and life and people going about their business. He's no culchie. There are said to be one hundred and twenty-seven shops in the Row, although he's never counted them. The corner shop with all the items of groceries his mam buys to make their tea, the rag shop, the barber's shop, the pubs where his da spent money they didn't have. There's the picture theatre and the butcher and the sweet shop and the stall that sells double-decker candy apples with coconut on top. Funny how you can go from one place to another in the blink of an eye. There's the chance, in the situation he now finds himself, he could be sent to the gallows. He sees himself standing on a platform, the audience waiting for the last act of the play. The platform will actually be a trapdoor. He will be fit and well, standing up straight, the next minute he'll be down the way, dropped from one level to the next, in a different state, that of the dead. That's what he'll be doing, going from one world to another, his past and his future all rolled into one. All the people in this play will still be alive, but he might not. Who is to know what will happen next?

He allows himself a pace or two back and forth, puts his eye to the slit in the door. The cell, around ten feet by six, consists of a slatted steel bed screwed to the floor, covered by a mattress of canvas and straw that still stinks from the piss of the last man who slept on it; a bench with three shelves where he keeps his notepaper and a book, the cigarettes his friend Peter in the south has sent to him; a bucket to shit in that is due to be taken away, but the man who collects it is always late, as if the task that lies before him must be delayed for as long as possible.

And sure enough, as he sets his eye to the aperture, there's an officer coming, the one called Des, a skinny little man with an out-thrust jaw, keys dangling in his hand. He lets Albert pass through the door, hands him his tie. They haven't given it to him in the cell in case he strings himself up. He's not ready for that, not yet. He fumbles a Windsor knot as he is hurried towards the outside world.

'Good luck, Paddy,' someone calls from the floor above, the rancour gone.

The Supreme Court in Auckland has a high arched dome made of timber, with splendid curved windows on either side of the room. It's said to have been built in the design of Warwick Castle but, handsome as it is, which part of that sprawling edifice it's meant to represent is hard to discern. There is no moat and no tower, although the courtroom is illuminated by a grand chandelier with royal decoration on its rim, like the edge of a crown. Behind the judge's bench hang the flags of the United Kingdom on the left-hand side, and on the right that of the 58th Regiment, presented in 1845 to the inhabitants of Auckland. It says so there on the flag. The dock stands in the centre of the room, almost close enough for the accused to reach out and touch the jurors seated in padded red leather chairs; the jurors sit face to face with the Press Gallery on the other side. There are chairs behind the dock where the public may sit, and above that a mezzanine floor where there is more space for the audience. It's called the Ladies' Balcony, although lately women have been admitted to the main gallery. The whole court is crammed with spectators craning their necks as the moment approaches for the accused to appear. On this day, the lower gallery is brimming with brightly dressed girls, their faces vivid with dark lipstick and blue eye shadow.

The jury has been sworn in and taken their places. Some of them are returned servicemen, others have missed the war because they were too young or too old. The foreman is called James Taylor, a bank manager, dressed in an immaculately pressed charcoal suit, a snow-white shirt and a handkerchief in his breast pocket, his tie striped gold and navy with a crest on it; he sits alongside Neville Johns, a man described as a company director, whose tie appears to bear the same crest, his face shaved smooth as satin. The two men seem to lean towards each other, although it may be that the proximity of Jack Cuttance, a butcher, sitting next to them, is drawing them closer. Jack's thick hands grip the rail in front of him. Beside him sits Ken McKenzie, the youngest on the jury by perhaps twenty-five years, his face bleached with anxiety so that the scars of healed pimples stand out. Then there is an accountant, a tiny man with large black-rimmed spectacles, whose fedora has such a wide hard brim it almost engulfs his face when he puts it on. Next there is a gasfitter with a hard mouth that curls with contempt, as if he had already judged the evidence he is about to hear; a shop assistant who sells men's wear at an upmarket shop in High Street, better dressed in his way than the businessmen, but different, his pale-grey suit jacket slim around his hips, and perhaps the youngest above Ken McKenzie; then a night watchman who has warned them he might have trouble staying awake during the day as he tends to doze off. He and the ticket seller who works shifts at the Civic Theatre along the road have nodded their recognition, as has another man who describes his occupation as a product distributor, which sounds very fancy but turns out to mean he is a grocer. A university lecturer who teaches Classics and wears not a suit but a hairy brown jacket and a tweedy-looking tie, and a high-school woodwork teacher called Frank complete the jury. So that is the lot of them: James, Neville, Jack, Ken, Leonard (not Len, *please*), Wayne, Marcus, Norman, Rex, Roy, Arthur, Frank. The twelve good men and true. Not all of them will invite the others to call them by their first names. Ken McKenzie will call several of them sir when he addresses them.

They glance sideways at the accused as they are seated, and then look straight ahead. After the swearing in, a recess is called where they will get to know each other over morning tea and biscuits. The defendant disappears down a hole in the floor, descending narrow stairs to a holding cell, like a rehearsal for the gallows.

This jury is not the first to have passed judgment on Albert Black, for already he has been indicted by a Grand Jury, a collection of worthy citizens who meet on a regular basis and decide whether a case should go forward to a full trial. The accused does not meet with them, nor are the public admitted, although the press is present. The Grand Jury make their decision in private and offer a recommendation to the judge. There has been no doubt in their minds that Albert Black should confront the full force of the law.

The head of Albert Black, who is also known as Paddy Black, or even as Paddy Donovan when he wants to fool a wee doll into thinking he is someone else, or yet again when he wants to escape the immigration department, rises again through the trapdoor as he ascends, a warder close behind him. Albert is emerging inch by inch, his black hair that is thick and wavy, his green Irish eyes and skin like milk. The jailer, Des Ball, acts as if he would like to have a cattle prod to poke him along, while at the same time he is revelling in a day outside the prison walls. In the blacked-out paddy wagon that has transported them the short distance from the prison to the Supreme Court he'd said, lighting a cigarette without offering one to his charge, shackled as he is by a chain to his leg, 'It's a grand day out there, Paddy my lad. Bet you'd like to be taking a turn or two down Queen Street right now. A nice milkshake at Somervell's, or a rare steak at Ye Olde Barn, that's your favourite trick or treat, isn't it now? Ah yes, remind me now, you don't like people to stand in your way, do you lad? I'm glad not to be standing in front of you, with a knife in the back, that's your speciality, a bit of blood on the floor, never mind the raspberry fizz.'

The Irish boy has said nothing. The moment is upon him as he enters the room head first and all eyes swivel towards him. It's an up-and-down world all right. His trial for the murder of Alan Jacques, the man who called himself Johnny McBride, is about to begin in earnest.

Right at the back of the court sits a pale girl, and he turns his head towards her before he faces the judge. He senses rather than sees her. But she is there.

It's raining, but then it's often lashing down in Belfast. Kathleen sits on a bentwood chair, her hands folded in her lap as she looks out over the slate roofs shining in the wet. A notepad lies on the gate-leg table in front of her, but she can't take up the pen to write in it. There are words swirling through her head. Words like my darling boy, my bonnie wee lad, you will come to no harm, your mother is here waiting to embrace you on your return.

It's a plain room, furnished mostly with remnants from her mother's house. She keeps it clean, but mould festers on the walls up where she can't reach it, even standing on the chair. There is a sofa with wooden arms and a squab covered in a slip made from ends of blue and lemon patterned linen that looked awful nice when it was new, she always thinks. The material was on a small discount from the factory where she works. Perhaps she will get round to making a new cover someday, because her husband and the boys have spilled tea and baked beans over the years. Stains she can't remove; the indelible stains of a life lived within these walls. An armchair and her mother's treadle sewing machine stand in the corner; she has patched many a shirt on that machine. It is what they have; her dowry. It is more than many people round here have to show.

The door opens and her husband comes in. He smells of acrid tar from mending roads, and of dampness from working in the weather. He looks at her and shrugs.

'Dinner not on?' he says.

'I'll fry up some of last night's taters,' she says, 'and a couple of eggs. Clodagh's niece brought some in from the country. There was more than enough for her to use up.'

'There's no good moping,' he says, shifting his bag off his shoulder. 'It'll come to nothing.'

'Our boy's due in the dock. Our Albert. What's not to mope about?'

'It'll have been a mistake. You'll see, they'll sort it out over there in New Zealand.'

But it's three months now since they received the telegram with the terrible news.

He sees the look on her face. 'Worse things have happened.'

'Like what?'

'Like the Blitz you're always reminding me about. Have you forgotten now?'

Kathleen shivers, pulls her cardigan around her more tightly, tucks a frond of her dark hair behind her ear. The fire is low on the hearth. 'The boy was with me then. Not in New Zealand.' Remembering how it was, the explosions and the fire raids, the people dying or already dead all about their street, the way she had put Albert on a shelf in the closet and held the door shut against him, leaning her body in with all her might, hoping not to be thrown off her feet when the next blast came. He was barely six at the time, still small enough to put in a cupboard and keep him safe. Later she had to take him to the air-raid shelters, but by that time the bombing was over, even though the planes flew low overhead at nights.

'You weren't here then,' she says, her voice flat.

'No, you're right, I wasn't here then.' He speaks in a slow way you could take or leave as sarcasm. 'We all have to answer to the Big Fella sooner or later, don't we now?'

So yes, here was her husband who hadn't been conscripted but had gone to the war all the same because it was his duty, the way he saw it, far away on foreign battlefields, while she and their son hid in cupboards and their world fell down around their ears. Even though his grandfather had been killed at the Somme, like those tens of thousands of young Belfast men who had died in the ditches, it was the way it was, to go and fight for what you believed to be right. Never mind that he, himself, had not been so right since he'd come back.

'I'm sorry, Bert,' she says. Their son, the middle one, born between the one who died and the little one in the next room writing his homework, bears the same name as his father, so they are Albert and Bert just to keep them apart. 'You've done what you can.'

She stands and he puts his arms, smelling of tar and sweat, around her, and she rests her head against him, remembering that this was why she, who was once Kathleen McKay, married Bert Black. Through the good times and, now, for the desperate bad. 'I'm at my wits' end. If only I was there with him,' she says. But they have been through all that and it has been to no avail.

'Why did we let him go, Kathleen?' he says, his voice a muffled sob, and now she is the one comforting him. 'We've been up against it since the beginning, that government and all.'

'I've got a few ideas,' she says, and because she is the strong one these days, he listens.

Chapter 2

Mount Eden is a charming suburb. That is how its residents would describe it, and they're right. An extinct volcanic mountain stands at its heart. A mountain road where tourists take scenic tours winds up its side. There are any number of notable buildings to be pointed out, including a residence of the Governor-General, pretty villas and gardens filled with lush trees and roses and dahlias and other pretty flowers, for all things botanical grow well in this area. Tens of thousands of people flock through this leafy suburb every year to watch rugby and other sporting fixtures at the famous Eden Park, the biggest gladiatorial arena of its kind in the country. So it is unfortunate, the residents are inclined to say, that the first thing people are likely to think of, when they hear the words Mount Eden, is Mount Eden jail. It was built to imitate Dartmoor Prison in England, a dark Victorian edifice made from bluestone rock quarried by the prisoners who would live within its walls. Mount Eden jail is surrounded by high stone walls topped with barbed wire, so that the residents can't see what lies behind, neither the walk up the stairs to the heavy doors that clang shut behind a sentenced man, nor inside the prison. It is, if they could see the interior, built on a radial system, the wings built around the central atrium, emerging on several levels with bridges connecting them.

There are always lights on in the passageways of the prison, a dull fluorescent glow that seeps through the Judas holes in the doors, so that even in the deepness of night it isn't possible to be relieved by the forgiving darkness. And even when a degree of stillness falls over the inmates of Mount Eden prison towards midnight, there are still howls that ring through its walls at unexpected moments, bad dreams, sudden rages, the footsteps of warders on the echoing floors. The rock walls of the cells create spaces freezing in winter and like ovens in the summer.

Paddy lies awake, his head aching, longing for some shuteye. The noise is louder than usual. For the past week things have been more subdued, they always are in the days following a hanging. But then the momentum gathers again as if the pent-up rage of those who have survived were being released into the spaces of the night, men banging on cell doors, someone howling like a wolf, and another replying *yap yap yap* like a dog. He had known Allwood, the man they hanged just a few days ago. The prisoners are not supposed to know when a hanging takes place but they always do. You can't miss the sound of the steel gallows being erected. They call it the Meccano set. A few tricks have been tried to distract the men from the event. One night they were sent to the pictures so they wouldn't hear the clank and rattle of the chains that bound the man's feet as he was dragged along the corridors. There had been a near riot after that, the realisation that they had sat there, laughing their heads off at some silly slick American comedy, while a man was being killed just along the corridor. The authorities are getting smarter than that, but they can't hide what's going on. The convicts know when the weigh-ins begin.

'They weigh me every day,' Allwood told Albert when they met in the exercise yard.

'And why would they be doing that every day?' Albert asked. 'They want to put meat on your bones?'

'You don't know, eh? Well, let me tell you how it is. The hangman needs to know the exact weight of the body, so they know how high they need to string you before your neck breaks. You hear that bang every morning? That's them testing the gallows with a sandbag the same weight as myself, to make sure they've got it right.'

'But why every day? I don't get that.'

'So you don't know what day it's going to happen.'

'You mean they don't tell you?'

'Oh, I think they tell you in the morning. I haven't had that pleasure yet of being informed.'

'Perhaps it won't happen,' Albert had said.

'Ha. You cleanskins, you're so innocent. Haven't seen the inside of a prison before. You think they save you at the last minute? Dream on. Mind you, Freddie Foster, they did him in this year, he thought he'd got away with it. He got himself a dose of appendicitis two weeks before he was due. They put him in hospital and took his appendix out and sent him back for the gallows.'

'That's nuts.'

'Ah well, he got to look up a few nurses' skirts at the last. Perhaps he thought his luck had changed. None of us think it'll happen to us. But I can tell you, I'll be taking one of those screws with me. I plan to kill one of them before they kill me.'

Not that Allwood succeeded with his plan. They got him. And a good job done, Des said to Paddy. 'He took a while to go, jerked on the end of the rope for a bit.' It was the second hanging since

Albert had been inside, the third one of the year. The one before Allwood was worse than the others, in terms of the effect it had on the inmates: a young Maori man who had brothers inside at the time. The family of the man stood outside the prison walls, their wailing and sobbing rising in torrents of sound, singing that was strange to Paddy, the brothers inside the walls screaming like wounded animals.

On this morning, the first day of his trial, it's come home to him that he might well be hanged for the death of Alan Jacques, or Johnny McBride, or whoever the man thought he was. The realisation seeps through him, at first a ripple like spring rain starting, then a downpour of terrible knowledge. It's a wonder to him that he hasn't grasped this reality before. What option had he had but to belt Jacques, and how could he have known that it would turn out the way it has? This steadfast belief had carried him through the first months he'd been held in the prison. He couldn't see how it could be perceived any other way. And now he isn't sure. There is a girl who is due to give evidence, and he has no idea what she will say. He thought her a friend but now he knows she is a witness for the prosecution. When he thinks back, the way she might describe the encounter could go either way.

And what of the girl sitting at the back of the court, what will she make of what this girl has to say? Feckless, he is. The drift of life. Feckless and fuckless. It wasn't always like that. The girls appeared, those nights in Auckland, one after the other, always willing; they jived and swung, twisting their hips this way and that in the dance halls, and after, there was always an after, they would like as not swing their way to his bed. He doesn't know anymore what to make of it all, just that it has brought him here. He closes his eyes and sees a dance hall, the girls with their nipped-in waists, whirling floral-patterned dresses flicking out from their knees, or the widgies with their skin-tight skirts that show the cracks in their arses. The Orange Hall in Newton was one of his favourites, a slide and glide place where you pressed your face to a girl's cheek and asked her for the supper waltz, and then the last dance, and when those were over going on, with a girl at his side, drifting along the street to the Maori Community Centre, another world again, and they would dance till two or three in the morning, the music wild, some familiar, some from a different place that sent them all crazy, steel guitars throbbing, a saxophone trebling its notes. There would be a boil-up and a mug of tea. At the Community Centre it felt easier to be an outsider, because he'd noticed that Maori people in Auckland kept to themselves, except here in their own place. They too might have come from another country. Yet when he was among them they didn't question who he was, as if him dancing there was the most natural thing.

He sees himself dancing, his hips rotating, the way he could go on and on and on all night until the morning when he would wake up, spent, a little drunk, the girl he'd met at the Orange beside him, or not, because usually they had to flee home to their parents before dawn. *After the ball*. It makes him think of his mam. 'Dear Mother,' he had written (for he wrote to her in more formal terms than he thought of her), 'life is a bit of a lark. I'm living with a whole heap of mates here in Auckland. I'm just your same Albert, but I've got a pair of dancing shoes. The Teddy boys dress differently from us. Their jackets have wide shoulders and are draped down nearly to their knees, their trousers have very narrow bottoms, and you should see the shine on their shoes. A lot of them are English boys who have come off the ships, they are mostly good sorts, some of them come and stay with me for a night or two when their ships are in port. I have to be a bit careful how many come at once, my landlady is quite strict, but you'll be glad to hear that.'

The day in court hasn't gone how he imagined. The jury took a long time to be sworn in. For much of the day he had sat in the tiny holding cell beneath the courtroom. During a recess he overheard his lawyer, a dark, intense man named Oliver Buchanan, talking to his colleague about the kind of jury he was hoping for: a group of men who might still remember what it was like to be young, and not too biased towards the migrants. That's me, Paddy thought, an immigrant, not one of them, not a Kiwi bloke, as they say. He knew, from what he had been told, that the lawyer can challenge anyone who is called without giving a reason, but he is only allowed four challenges before he has to let the jurors pass. After that he could challenge only if he can show cause. But Paddy got the drift. As he watched the selection take place he saw men with hard eyes, cold stares in his direction, just one or two with a gentler manner, or so he thought. I've done my best, Buchanan told his colleague, within his hearing, but it's still a jury full of old codgers. You know, he added, the sort who believe every word of the Mazengarb Report.

Paddy wondered if Buchanan thought he wouldn't know what the Mazengarb Report is. But he does, because he lived on the doorstep of that government-commissioned document which claimed youthful lawlessness and immoral behaviour was sweeping the country. It was all supposed to have started in the Hutt Valley near Wellington, where the first bodgies and widgies hung out, before spreading to Auckland. The Hutt Valley was where he lived just the year before. He has heard it thrashed to bits, the bickering it started.

It had been late in the day before Paddy reappeared in the dock. The judge seemed like an old man, but then all men over twenty-five look as if they are over the hill. The men on the jury were so close to him he could smell the sweat in their armpits, mingling with the perfume of the girls sitting behind him.

Albert Lawrence Black. His name hung in the air. You are

charged with the murder of Alan Jacques on the twenty-sixth of July 1955. How do you plead? Guilty, or not guilty?

He'd replied, in the firmest voice he could muster, 'Not guilty, your Honour', and they left him standing there for all to see, in his good blue suit and blue-striped tie, while the first of the witnesses for the prosecution was called, a police photographer who took pictures of Ye Olde Barn cafe where, it is claimed, Albert had plunged a knife into the neck of Jacques. The photographer was followed by an architectural draughtsman who had been called to measure the cafe where 'the incident' took place. The draughtsman handed over a scroll of paper containing his drawings, to be passed to the judge.

Albert could describe to them the exact shape of that cafe, but they don't ask him. He sees it in the swimming light of a winter evening, a long room with a bar counter along one side, flanked by six high stools where you can sit and drink Bushells coffee, dark liquid poured from a square bottle, topped up with boiling water from the Zip, eat a steak or a hamburger, or a frankfurter, and, across from there, cubicles that fit six at a squeeze, three on either side of a Formica-topped table lit by low-hanging lanterns. The room leads through a latticed wall adorned with flowering pot plants to the jukebox. Albert closes his eyes again, and for a moment the courtroom ceases to exist. He is trying to play a tune on the jukebox, that's all. He's been beaten up and his body is sore and his head hurts. His hand is on the button of the Wurlitzer, selecting a song. What he wants to play is Slim Whitman singing 'Danny Boy', which will transport him back to Ireland, but someone is stopping him, someone who wants to fight on and deck him again. He is afraid – yes that is it – he is terrified. He opens his eyes and looks at the judge, but he is not allowed to speak. Instead, he must stand there and let them all say what they have to say.

And that is it for the day. He thought there would be more to it than that, that everything would come out and his lawyer would have jumped up and told the judge what was what. But then, he doesn't know whether Buchanan really understands what exactly is what, how it had been. The real business will start happening tomorrow.

After this anti-climax he is back in the paddy wagon being returned to Mount Eden.

And now here he is, lying on his back, staring at the slivers of light from the grating, back in Belfast again, just like every night now, and it's summer, the marley season. He — that is, he who was once Albert — and his mates played their marbles everywhere out on the streets. They had bewlers, the big knuckle-dusters, and dinkies, the beautiful glass miniatures prized by them all; shooters, those were the proven ones, chipped and scarred, but they had a history of straight shooting; and then there were the ballies if you could get hold of them, ball bearings that you had to steal to lay hands on.

Between the Shankill and the Falls area, the Protestant and the Catholic divide, there lay a strip of No Man's Land that had once been a brick field, the hard clay making it the perfect spot to shoot marleys. Albert's mother had told him not to go over there, it was too far away from Gay Street that ran off Sandy Row where they lived. He didn't get it, the reason the Prods and Micks were divided up the way they were. So they went to different schools, and they worshipped at different churches, it was even said they spoke the Our Father in a different way — when he went to St George's everyone said Our Father that art in heaven, but somebody had told him that the Micks said who art in heaven, as if God were a person you might be able to see, a being like them. Well, that was old shite if ever he'd heard it, because God was a creature in the sky that didn't let Himself be shown, you just had to believe He was there. His mother did say, on occasion, that they, meaning the Catholics, were heathens who believed that they truly drank the blood of Christ when they took the communion, when she knew all along that it was wine that represented the blood. It was complicated, she said, but there they were living next door to Clodagh who was a Mick through and through and as good a friend as his mam had in the world. It was only round the Twelfth of July when the Orange Parades were in full tilt and all the Protestants marched along Sandy Row with their banners and drums, across the Boyne Bridge, chanting their slogans, and dressed up in suits and bowler hats, that there was a distance between them. His mother would say not to go to Clodagh's today, she was resting up, but he did anyway, because Clodagh always had a lolly in her apron. She would sigh and roll her eyes. 'You're not such a bad wee one for a sally rod, here take this and be on your way.' Clodagh had had children, it was said, but they'd all died of some fever. It was something you didn't ask about, not even of your mother.

But he remembered a particular day when the sun was gleaming like new coppers, something to recall in itself, a true summer day, and the oak leaves seeming to float on air above the strip, and he and his mates, their gang of three, wee Noel and Rory and himself, were playing marleys and he was winning. It would be something good to tell his da, who had come back from the war and was hanging around the house looking sorry for himself and not too interested in his only son. Only living son, that was, because Albert once had a brother, although that was not exactly as he saw it. Wee William had died before he was born, so that when his mam talked about his brother it was a bit like talking about God in the sky, the same shadowy feeling of someone you had to believe in but would never see. Albert wanted to talk to his da about Belgium where he'd been in the fighting, but his father had said to forget it, that was all over now and they'd all best get on with their lives and he better be good to his mam, now that he was a big boy, ten years old. His da and his mam kept going away to the bedroom and not wanting to talk to him, and his mam was acting strange.

It was this day when the pair of them were off on some secret mission of their own behind closed doors that he and the boys decided nobody would miss them if they took off to the strip to find a spot of their own, the street all around them so filled with games that the marleys were pitching over the circles and knocking out the game of the fellas next door and words spoken between them, a scuffle and a few fists flying.

Albert had brought his special marble that his da had brought home from the war. It was a Lutz that came out of the pocket of a dead German was all he said, the nearest he'd ever come to talking about the action. You don't want to play that one, it's a collector's piece. He had held it up to the light, so that Albert could see the alternating bands of finely ground copper flakes edged by opaque white strands. If he hadn't been mad with his father for distracting his mother the way he was, he would have done as he was told that day and left it in the little bowl on the mantelpiece where it was kept. The Lutz was his lucky marble, he decided. By the end of the day it would have knocked out a dozen of the opposition and, its work done, could be safely restored to the bowl.

At the very moment he flicked it into the circle, a posse of boys, all bigger than them, and none that they knew by sight, came slouching towards them, menace in their eyes. Albert made to gather up the marbles but the boys were on to them and he felt himself freeze with fear. The Lutz glinted in the sun, the copper glowing like molten gold. In a flash it had been gathered into the pocket of the tallest of the marauders.

'It's mine, gimme,' Albert said.

'Gimme,' the boy mocked.

'Please.' Albert heard himself whimpering. 'It's my da's marble.' It sounded stupid cry-baby stuff, but the tears were welling up and he couldn't stop them. 'I'll give you a sprassy if you give it me back.'

'A sprassy for a Lutz.' The biggest boy gave him a push in the head. 'Six pennies for a good 'un like that. Not on your Nellie. What a laugh. Take yourself off and say your Proddie prayers. Tell your da he's got a sooka bubba son. And all.'

When he got home his father was singing away to himself. No, he wasn't, he and his mother were singing. They sang the chorus of 'After the ball is over' which was meant to be a sad song about parted lovers, but they were belting it out as if they were happy

. . . aft-er the ball is over, aft-er the break of morn
after the dancers' leaving, after the stars are gone,
. . . after the ball. Aft-er the ball is over . . . and on and on, a kind of diddle diddle refrain.

And because it was another of the old songs they had sung for years and years, even before the war when he was just so high to his da's waist, they were waiting for him to sing it along with them now. It made him scared *many the hopes that have vanished*, it sounded like the song was all about him and perhaps his da would hate him forever. But at this moment his father's face was shiny and happy and Albert didn't have the heart to tell him what had happened. Instead, he slipped a marble into the bowl on the mantelpiece, a cat's eye, his very best, and hoped that the loss might go unnoticed.

Chapter 3

August 1955. Parliament House in Wellington is an Edwardian neo-classical building built of stone, to the right of a Gothic Revival building that houses the General Assembly Library, all spindly towers like a fairy castle. These buildings sit on a hill facing northward. A grassy lawn separates Parliament House from the street and small dilapidated houses belonging to the poor. A long flight of steps with narrow treads lead up to the reception area. Visitors and politicians alike cross a marbled floor laid out in chequered black and white. The 'tiles', the Press Gallery call it, the spot where they might catch a politician on the run and force an unguarded comment. From there they ascend to the upper chambers by way of more of the sombre solid steps, or in an ornate old-fashioned lift. The Honourable John Marshall, known to his friends as Jack, a major in wartime, likes to take the steps up to his office in the National Party wing of the building. The Attorney-General is spry in his manner, tall and lean-limbed, his mane of hair silvering, his chin as sleek as a seal's backside. Marshall is a lawyer and a firm believer in God. Every Sunday morning he will be found worshipping at the Presbyterian church in the city. He has drafted many Bills, legislating for change. It is a matter of pride to him that under his watch the death penalty has been reinstated. It is not known exactly why he is so enthusiastic about killing criminals, although there has been a rumour circulating for years that a relative of his was murdered in Australia. It is just that, perhaps; a rumour. They swirl around the halls of power, whispers and murmurs that can bring a politician down in the bat of an eyelid. Marshall knows better than to allow his private life to spread into the wider world. Virtue has its own rewards, he believes, and it is a virtuous face he presents to the public.

On the morning of August the fifth, he had received a letter from the New Zealand High Commissioner in London, Clifton Webb. It was an urgent communication, in which Webb outlined an approach he had just received from a Mr Woods, the secretary of the office of the Government of Northern Ireland's agent in London. He had come expressly at the request of Mr Warnock, the Attorney-General in Belfast, asking about legal assistance for Albert Lawrence Black, accused of a murder in Auckland. It seemed that Black's parents lived in his constituency. The mother was clearly in an agitated state.

The telegram had come late in the day when Kathleen was returning home from work at the Jennymount Mill. In the distance, she saw the telegram boy lean his bike against the fence, and for a moment she thought, perhaps Albert is about to spring a surprise on us and come home. But the instant the boy turned around she guessed from the look on his face that it was something awful. Her hand flew to her mouth. It was from a government official on the far side of the world. *Regret to advise*. Like people got when men died at war.

At first she thought, as she read it, it must be some sort of mistake, that his name had got mixed up with that of someone else. The boy on the bike pedalled away as fast as he could, not wanting to be caught up in the drama, knowing when people broke down and wailed and cried. She wasn't going to do that, not here in the street where people knew that a telegram meant something momentous had happened. But her hand had flown to her mouth in an exclamation of horror.

She let herself into the house and re-read the pencilled message. Someone was dead all right. But not her son. Albert was in prison. There was a number to ring, only she didn't have a phone. Soon the post office would be closed. She had to wait for Bert to come home. Oh, she didn't know what to do. The front room was full of late-summer afternoon light, shadows of evening poking themselves through the window. Like cobwebs. Like some strange dust settling in the air. She could hardly breathe. She clung to the table to stop herself falling in a faint.

When Bert finally did arrive it was too late to make the call that night. Her husband had been full of rage, striding around the house. 'The crazy little shite, what's he done?' he shouted, and slammed his fist beside his plate so that his dinner fell off. Not that they wanted to eat. And there was Daniel to consider. He had been sent upstairs. Because Kathleen had said, when she had time to draw breath, that as it surely could not be true, they should keep it to themselves and not go upsetting everybody with this news, not even Daniel. As for her and Bert, they would hear more about it in the morning when they got to phone the authorities in New Zealand. Bert had gone off out, cursing under his breath, just when she needed him most, and she knew that when he came in it would be late, and he would have taken drink.

It would be down to her, she thought. She had yet to work out a plan for what to do, but straight away she decided that if there was a shred of truth in the contents of the telegram she would fly to her boy's side, she must be there with him, make the authorities understand what a good son he was, and a sweet-natured brother, and, oh, that there was no better young man than Albert.

Very early in the morning she and Bert made their way to the police station, where they explained their plight and got permission to make a phone call. They couldn't think of anywhere else to go where there might be a telephone they could use at that hour. The post office didn't open until later, too late in the day to ring a government department in New Zealand. Day and night were back to front on opposite sides of the world. It took a long time to find someone to talk to in New Zealand, where people were packing up to go home from their jobs. Kathleen was put from one department to another and at last she got to speak to the superintendent of the jail where they were holding Albert, and it became clear that the telegram's truth was there in its words. Albert was arrested on the charge of murder.

'It can't be right,' Kathleen said to the man on the other end. 'He wouldn't do a thing like that. He must have been provoked something terrible. Or he was in danger. That must have been it.'

'I can't say, Mrs Black. I'm sorry. It will be up to the courts to decide how it happened. Have you got a message you'd like passed on to your son?' The man, who said his name was Horace Haywood, sounded kind, even sympathetic in an odd sort of way. That was a start.

'Just tell him, oh, I'm sorry, I'm having a few tears here and all, you understand. Just tell him that I love him and that I'm planning to fly to New Zealand.' A grand plan, indeed, but she could be there in less than a week, not a month.

'And how do you plan to get the money for a trip away to New Zealand?' Bert said, back outside on the street. All of the housekeeping money for the week had been handed over to pay for the phone calls. There wasn't a penny left, and here she was talking a hundred pounds or more.

'Perhaps you could ask that mother of yours,' Kathleen said. She saw his hands begin to tremble. Time to back off. His mother had never been keen on her, and as for his father, who had wanted to turn their son into a British gentleman, they hardly spoke from the day she met him until he died. He couldn't forgive his son for marrying one of the girls off his factory floor, not even when his factory was bombed out in the Blitz and he wasn't an owner anymore.

'There's no money left, you know that. He left my mother skint.' Perhaps his sister got some of the money, he had no idea. Kathleen had heard all this before. In some obscure way, he saw her to blame for this state of affairs.

'I'm going straight to Parliament to see Mr Warnock,' Kathleen said. 'Are you coming with me or not?' The Right Honourable Edmond Warnock had been a member of St Anne's, the cathedral church where they had married.

Bert, frowsy and unshaven, looked at her and shook his head. 'You can do better than me, lass,' he said. The way he said it, she knew he was still holding on to his anger, that there was shame ahead for them, and no knowing what was going to happen.

Things would go on like that, back and forth over the next weeks, Bert exasperated and bitter that they had been put in this position, then remorseful that she was shouldering the burden while he stood by helpless. What was a man to do?

Warnock had received her kindly in his office. He sat her down and had his secretary make her a cup of tea while her tears spilled down over her handbag. This was a grave matter and he would do the best for her he could. There, there, Mrs Black, they get things wrong out there in the colonies, he had murmured.

Well, not a colony exactly, but certainly it was a place with a different culture to their own, from all he had heard. Indeed, and he would be getting in touch with the High Commission in London that very day. My people will talk to their people, and who knows but by the end of the week they might have it all sorted out. Money to go to New Zealand, well, that was another matter. Perhaps if she and Mr Black had friends that could help out? No? Well, perhaps it wouldn't be necessary.

A letter arrived for her within days. 'Dear Mrs Black, I'm afraid I don't have very good news for you. I'm advised that the Attorney-General in New Zealand, Mr Marshall, has asked what money you might be able to raise for your son's defence. I know from our conversation that it is unlikely that you will be able to raise the necessary sum, which I anticipate will be several hundred pounds.'

'Several hundred pounds?' Kathleen said. 'They want *us* to pay for his defence?' Her face was bleak. 'Bert,' she said, 'they want our money and we haven't got even enough to fly to New Zealand.'

'We need to think on it,' was all he said.

Their trouble was supposed to be a secret, but mysterious envelopes of money appeared, poked through the letter slot in the door. She supposed that Bert had talked about it while in his cups. Ninety pounds.

'You see,' Bert said, 'we have friends after all.'

'You have done this for me?'

'I've placed a curse on our children,' he said, beginning to weep. 'We've lost one child, not another.'

'That's nonsense,' she said, brisk as she could.

'You need to be with our son. That's still not enough to get you there, but I'm working on it.'

'I'll let Mr Warnock know that we're making progress,' Kathleen said, folding the money, the precious pounds, into a neat bundle and putting a rubber band around them. She would put them in her jewel box, she said. They would be the only thing in the musty little box her mother had given her for her sixteenth birthday. The jewels, a necklace made of amber beads that had been her grannie's, and a pair of pearl drop earrings she had saved for when she first went to work at the mill, had stayed in the pawn shop for a long time now. Perhaps they had been sold. 'When I can talk to Albert, and to his lawyers, God bless them, they will see that there has to be some explanation for all this.'

Though they observe the ritual courtesies and sit at the same Cabinet table of the National Party that governs New Zealand, it could never be said that Ralph Hanan and the Attorney-General are friends. Hanan, from the deep south, the Minister of Health, is a small man with panda-like circles around his eyes and breathing that rasps slightly when he is under stress, the result, it is believed, of his war service in North Africa: at the battle of Minqar Qaim he had had a near-death experience. His other portfolio is that of Minister of Immigration, and it is on account of this responsibility that he arrives at Jack Marshall's door.

'I've been hearing about this boy, Black,' he says, 'the one that's been involved in a stabbing. He's from Northern Ireland.'

'Yes, Mr Hanan, that's correct.'

'I've heard on the grapevine that the judge says he should never have come to this country, that we don't want people like him. Is it true?'

'Mr Hanan, you do yourself a disservice. That's pure conjecture.'

'Jack, don't Mr Hanan me, is it true, or not?'

'I have no idea.'

'This boy stands to go the way of Foster and the others,' Hanan says. Frederick Foster, an Englishman, had been hanged the previous month for shooting his girlfriend in an Auckland milk bar. He had gone to his death protesting his innocence. His mother had come to New Zealand to plead his case, and her desperate pleas had been all over the newspapers. So, too, was an account of her visit to see Jack Marshall.

'Murderers, all of them. And, frankly, if you want my opinion, we could do without these deplorable migrants. You might think about how we could more effectively screen their arrival in New Zealand. The youth who was killed didn't get the benefit of a trial. At least Black gets that. This appears to be a premeditated murder.'

'You don't know the history or circumstance of this incident. You can't pre-judge it.'

'Sometimes I think you chose the wrong party, Ralph. All these liberal left-wing views of yours.'

'You reintroduced the death penalty. I opposed the legislation.'

'I've no wish to re-litigate the matter now, Ralph.' Marshall picks up a file and tidies the papers into a neat pile, placing a blue glass paperweight on top of them. It catches a shaft of light and turns into a burning blue orb. 'We'll get to the truth in due course. The trial is set down for the eighteenth of October.'

'The mother is worried about his defence. They're poor people, they have nothing to send him.'

'Oh yes, I gather from Cliff Webb that they're crying poverty. Warnock's been on his back about getting aid for them.'

'Surely Mr Warnock's recommendation must carry some weight?'

'Oh, Warnock. Well, you know he makes mistakes. They say he could have prevented the Blitz. He didn't believe the Germans could strike that far — he was secretary to the Home Secretary at the time. No precautions taken to provide safe shelter. The Germans toasted them.'

'Jack, that is not the issue now.'

'Look, Black's got lawyers. Buchanan, the chap Black asked for from the duty list roster, and Mr Pearson, will act as senior counsel. I'm told they're prepared to rely on being granted a détente certificate under the Poor Prisoners Defence Regulations of 1934. Both Buchanan and Pearson are content to carry on.'

'His mother is planning to come out to New Zealand.'

'I've heard that, too. And they're crying poor. A little ironic, don't you think? Don't let it worry you, Ralph. You won't have to deal with her and neither will I. Cliff has already seen to it.' He extracts a handwritten note from the file, shifting the paperweight back and forth so that its dazzling light reflects off the surfaces in the room, dancing this way and that, and hands the paper across the desk.

Hanan sits looking at it for much longer than it takes to read. 'I have done my best to protect you from a second interview with a mother of a murderer and hope my efforts will be successful. I hope that I have not gone too far. Beautiful summer weather here. Best regards, Cliff.' His voice is stunned when he speaks. 'You have told her she can't come to New Zealand?'

Marshall shuffles through his papers again. 'Cliff and I have talked it over. I've told him to let Warnock know there'll be no difficulty in finding a prima facie case. This is my last word on the matter. I've written this to him.' He reads aloud from a letter copied in carbon: 'In these circumstances I can only endorse the view which you have taken about the advisability of Mrs Black, the mother of the accused, coming to New Zealand. One cannot, of course, say that she should not come — that is a decision she's free to make for herself. But one can say that the assistance Black will receive from counsel, and the consideration which will be given to this case in the event of his being found guilty, will not be increased or reduced by Mrs Black coming to New Zealand. She may wish to come for personal reasons, but she would have no grounds for feeling that if she didn't come she may have failed to do anything she could have to assist her son so far as his trial is concerned.'

'You bastard.'

'Mr Hanan. Language. Not in my presence.' That is a difference between them — Hanan says what he thinks, and for the most part he is liked the better for it. But Marshall has guile on his side, and an authority that he likes to command.

'In other words, it has been spelled out to her that she is not welcome in this country?'

'I'm not privy to the exact conversation that has taken place between Mr Warnock and Mrs Black.'

'She knows you won't see her.'

'As Mr Webb suggests, one murderer's mother is enough.'

'So there's no point in me going to Auckland,' Kathleen says. 'They won't give me an audience. There's no guarantee I'll even get to see our Albert.' It is close to midnight. The letter from the New Zealand High Commissioner lies in front of her. She has read it twenty times since Warnock handed it to her in his office earlier in the day. He was sorry, he'd said, he had done all he could.

'The superintendent of the prison sounded a decent man when we spoke to him,' Bert says. 'You said that yourself.' Up until now he has sat quietly watching her, his face closed so that she doesn't know what he is thinking.

'But he has to take orders from his superiors. Mr Warnock made it quite clear, they're going to do everything they can to stop me. He told me the Attorney-General in New Zealand said he'd had too many murderers' mothers coming pleading for their sons' lives. They don't know that Albert is a murderer. I said to Mr Warnock, could Albert swing for this? And he said yes, yes, he could. They're a very moral country, he says.'

'Moral? Moral, they say? They still have savages running round.'

'The ninety pounds, Bert. That money doesn't belong to us.'

'It was donated fair and square,' Bert says. 'For our cause. For Albert. We can give the money for his defence. Perhaps that will make them take notice of us.'

She nods then. 'We should go up to bed,' she says.

Drawing a long breath as they stand, she begins to sing against his ear. They are a couple who sing often to each other, as others speak, a running dialogue in song that has been silenced since the day they first heard the news.

> *Now the summer is in prime,*
> *Wi' the flow'rs richly blooming,*
> *An' the wild mountain thyme*
> *A' the moorlands perfuming.*
> *To our dear native scenes*
> *Let us journey together,*
> *Where glad innocence reigns*
> *Let us go, Lassie, go.*

A melody they have sung a hundred times together, one her Scottish father used to sing to her mother and that she taught to Bert when they were courting, a song he took up readily, as if he already knew that love and grief went hand in hand. Kathleen has sung this to the children at nights as she put them to bed, and it's the one she sang the night their little sweet William died in her arms, though he was a boy. She had been surprised that Bert was a man who sang the way he did, because he came from such a strait-laced family who had little music in their hearts, but he had been in a choir at school in England and it seemed like melody just stuck to him. As for her, she comes from a family of singers: it's as natural as breathing.

They stand swaying backwards and forwards.

> *Let us journey together,*
> *Where glad innocence reigns*
> *Let us go, Lassie, go.*

But when it comes to it, they can't sing the last line again, because Kathleen isn't going anywhere. The summer is nearly ended, soon they will be heading into autumn and the heather finished flowering for the season, and next year — they don't have a clue as to what will have happened.

Chapter 4

October 1955. At around the same time as Paddy is being put back in his cell, Ken McKenzie, the farmer's son from up north, is gazing around him with sheer amazement that he can be occupying such an elegant space as the Station Hotel in Auckland. James Taylor, the bank manager who'd put up his hand to be foreman of the jury as if it were natural that he would lead them, has suggested they all meet for a drink 'to get their strength up' in the lounge bar on the hotel's top floor. Nice to be put up for a few nights at the government's expense, he'd said, and winked. Ken looks around at his fellow jurors relaxing in big chairs, drinks in their hands. Only the Classics lecturer looks remote and sour. The judge has asked him to return the next day wearing a dark suit. The lecturer, the judge is sure, must possess one.

Ken is not sure what to do. Conversation flows around him, eddying in and out of the topics of the day. There is an intense dissection of the rugby test against the Wallabies that New Zealand won just weeks before by a precarious five points at Eden Park.

Several of the men had been at the game, and they relived the nail-biting anxiety of the final minutes when the whole series was on a knife edge. The relief of it, not getting licked by the Australians. There had been a few jugs downed that night, they recall. Ken thinks the boy on the stand might have heard their voices raised in rejoicing from his prison cell just along the road from the park. Roy, the grocer, wants to talk about Princess Margaret and whether or not she is going to marry Peter Townsend, that divorced chap, and how the Queen has her hands full with the little minx. The accountant with the owl-like eyes says it would be a terrible sin, a stain on the monarchy, and what a shame the King had died leaving a young Queen in charge. Marcus, from men's wear, says he feels sorry for poor Margaret because anybody can see she is really in love. James Taylor turns a look of such utter scorn on the speaker that Marcus shrivels. Love, Taylor says, and what would you know about that? There is a silence, a nasty pause before someone calls for another round.

Ken walks to the window and looks out. There in the late October afternoon lies the Waitemata Harbour, all a-glisten and shimmering and animated with white caps, a spring breeze filling the sails of yachts. An incomplete structure, not quite meeting in the middle, spans the horizon like a giant coat hanger. Soon one side of the harbour will be connected to the other and people will be able to drive across it in a matter of minutes, a handsome bridge like the one that spans Sydney Harbour. But for now the march towards the new age seems unfinished and stalled, the hulk skeletal against the sky. Outside, trams rattle and shake their way along Queen Street. Across the road stands the railway station, like Grand Central in New York, as proud locals have it. Travellers spill out of its causeways and flood along the street. From here, at the top of the Station Hotel, people seem smaller, grey-clad ants

41

for the most part, scurrying this way and that, although now that it is spring girls are shedding their coats in favour of colourful dresses. Oh, the girls. Ken cranes his neck to see if he can get a better view of them, but they are distant flowers.

He is still marvelling that he has this chance to stand above it all in a top-storey bar, wearing a suit borrowed from his uncle, even if he is pulling the sleeves down every other minute to cover his bony wrists. His aunt had put darts in the trousers the night before.

James Taylor beckons him over to the chair next to him. He leans forward, his manner confidential. 'You're a lad off a farm, young Kenneth, that right?'

'I grew up on a farm, sir. I'm an electrician now.'

'What made you leave the farm, may I ask? It's the future of this country so far as I can tell.' He smiles, a reflective glimmer in his eyes. Ken had noticed straight away what a thick-shouldered man he was, a great head of hair like a springy brush, ash blond as it greys, but he sees, too, that this is a man who doesn't brook opposition. Ken sees him swinging a golf club but, perhaps, never an axe. 'I get to see bank balances, it's my job,' Taylor says. 'Not too many overdrafts in farmers' accounts.'

Ken feels a rising panic. Has the bank manager checked his father's account? Is it possible that his father uses the same bank?

'There were seven of us in the family, sir.' Ken doesn't know why he feels compelled to call the man sir, but there it is, he hasn't mixed with company like this before. 'There were too many of us to stay on the farm,' he explains. 'Some of us had to go. You know, too many Indians.' Trying to turn it into a joke.

The other man wipes his mouth carefully with his napkin, a gold ring on his winkie finger. Your peerie-winkie, Ken's grandmother used to call it. She'd have said, too, that a gold ring on your finger was a bit flash. A flash Jack.

'Indians? Your family were Indian?'

'No sir, of course not, my family are Scots through and through. You know, too many chiefs, not enough Indians; it's an old saying.'

'Yes, of course.' Taylor reddens, annoyed with himself.

'My uncle offered to put me up while I did my apprenticeship. I'm through it now. It's quite hard work, laying cables, climbing around in ceilings and all. A good thing I was used to hard work.' Ken feels himself burbling away, trying to restore the conversation. Of course he was the one to go, the lank, puny one in the family, the weak link in the chain of siblings. It wasn't said that way, but he knew it for what it was when he left the farm, a pimply, nervous youth, not a sociable lad who fitted in at the stock yards or at the local dances in the Returned Services community hall, nor on the rugby field, even when they'd put him on the wing where the team didn't have to pass him the ball if they could avoid it. He'd had a weak bladder as a child; when he is under pressure there is still that old fear that he will lose control.

'I think if you will excuse me now, sir,' he says to Taylor, pushing his chair back, 'I should be getting on my way. I need to ring my uncle, he'll be wondering whether I got called or not.' He has seen the telephone booth in the vestibule near reception.

'Oh well, tomorrow we do the next rounds of the circus, as it were. Tell me, young fellow, what do you think about this case? Are we going to send this bog-trotter down?'

'I need to hear the evidence, sir,' Ken says. 'We need to find out whether Black meant to kill Johnny McBride.'

'But a knife is a knife, surely? C'mon, New Zealand men don't carry knives around.'

Ken glances around the room, catching the eye of the butcher, Jack Cuttance, for a moment. He thinks he has been overheard, and a smile passes between the two of them. 'Have you ever had a pocket knife, sir?' he says, turning back to the banker.

Taylor's eyes have followed his. He grimaces then, as if to say point taken, although he can't bring himself to say it.

At Des Ball's place, his wife has made dinner and put their children to bed. The dinner, roast beef and potatoes, with cabbage on the side, sits in the oven on a plate covered by another inverted one. All the dishes except those that harbour Des's meal have been washed and put away. Marge Ball suffers from an early onset of arthritis. The evening's housework has exhausted her. She had hoped her husband would be home by six, given that he is on a day shift. He has told her he has special duties today, although he hasn't specified what they are. This is his way, not to tell her what he does at the prison. She reads the newspapers with care, and sometimes an item will catch her eye and she will wonder, trying to trace back his mood in line with the events in the news. It isn't hard to put two and two together and figure out that her black eye happened around about the day a man called Allwood was sent to the gallows. Had he been there at the scene; witnessed the man's death? She knows better than to ask. Now and then he might say there is a new smart arse in the cells that he's had to sort out. He isn't a big man, thin as a whip, but wiry, steel in his forearms.

Marge often dreams of leaving Des, but what would she do and where would she go? The world beyond her front gate is a scary place. The women wear bright lipstick and modern clothes. Girls are brazen in their behaviour. They run wild with boys, and smoke and parade in the street. Their little waists are held in with cinch belts, and their breasts are pert in their new Whirl bras. There would be no place for her among the shop girls and the secretaries; she can't begin to imagine where she might find a job, crippled and all as she is.

Now that the time has passed eight, she hopes he might come in much later, so she can limp down the passage and crawl into bed before he arrives. Her knees are the worst, sometimes looking like two pink soccer balls. Like her name since she married Des. His ball and chain, he will say, and laugh. There are nights when she crawls on her hands and knees; she wonders what will become of the children.

There is that ominous click in the door, and she knows she has left her run too late. As soon as she sees his face, she puts the table between them.

'It's in the oven,' she says.

'In the oven, eh? In the bloody oven, what sort of a welcome is that?'

'It's gone eight.'

'So, it's gone eight.' His words slur, his face, with its too-long chin, shiny. She can smell his sour breath across the width of the room.

He opens the oven door and lifts the top plate. The beef has curled at its edges, the cabbage pooled into an amoebic slime.

'They lock you in at the pub?' she says, before she can stop the words from falling out of her mouth.

Des lifts the plate, his fingers curled around its edges, releasing it with force against the kitchen wall.

'Clean it,' he says.

Rita Zilich's house is a long, low bungalow, filled with polished brass and velvet cloths on the tables. It is redolent with the scent of mint and olives and wine. On Fridays her family eat only fish, and her mother has banned her from visiting her girlfriends on that day because you can't trust them not to eat meat. The kitchens in her friends' houses smell of steak and boiled vegetables, and the men drink beer. All that she has come to think of as normal. Her parents' house embarrasses her.

It is an hour before midnight. Rita sits in front of the mirror in her bedroom, practising smoking. The mirror is set in the door of a large wardrobe, an ornately carved piece of furniture that her grandmother brought with her on the ship when she came to New Zealand. It was one of her wedding gifts. Rita hates the wardrobe, which her grandmother left to her as the oldest daughter of her oldest daughter. When she suggested its replacement, her mother looked at her with such sorrowful reproach she had shut her mouth. It is part of an old story: the way Grandma had been a letter bride, her brothers on the gumfields up north asked by a friend for an introduction to a girl back home in Dalmatia whom they might marry, and the brothers, eager to help because they too were looking for wives, had suggested their sister.

'And then,' Rita's mother would say, and her voice would drop almost to a whisper, 'after the brides in the village received a letter with a proposal, they dressed up all in white finery, with a big bouquet of flowers, and had a party to celebrate before they set off.'

'But that's so weird,' Rita had said. 'I mean, getting dressed up in white without the husband. What if he died before she got there, would that make her a widow?'

'Well of course not,' her mother snapped. 'There would be another husband waiting for her.'

'What if she was ugly and nobody would have her?'

'Ah, looks, there is more to it than that. She would make a good wife to any man, have children, make good dinners, wash his clothes, all the things a wife is supposed to do. Like you will do someday.'

'Perhaps,' Rita said.

'You don't understand, my child. Your grandma arrived in Auckland, and made the long journey to the gumfields with all her belongings, with your wardrobe, piled in a cart and pulled over the rough tracks up to the north. All around her was swamp and the stumps of kauri trees. She lived in a little — what do you call it? — a hut, a little shack, the roof thatched from nikau palm fronds. Well, her new husband wanted her to sell the wardrobe.'

'Well, there you are, Mum,' Rita had said, 'he didn't like it either.'

'You make me angry, Rita. She held onto it because someday there would be a girl who deserved a gift as fine as her father had given her when she set out on her voyage. It is a piece of the old world. One day you will know.'

Rita kicks the wardrobe and stubs out her cigarette. The look her mother had given her when she said she didn't like it, and why couldn't she have a pretty little dressing table like her girlfriends had, was nothing to the looks she is getting now. She is, her mother said, a girl who has brought shame on all of them, no wonder they call us Dallies and curl their lip. *They* are the general population of their adopted country, the people who called them aliens during the wars, who took any opportunity to belittle those who came from Dalmatia and to set them apart.

'Nobody knows who I am,' Rita said. 'The lawyer says the judge is sure to give me and Stella name suppression. It won't be in the papers when I give evidence.'

'You think they are fools. The whole community knows who you are. They're talking behind your back already. And when you go into that courtroom and tell them your story about how you lay on the bed with that man, they will know what you did, that you lay down beside a murderer.'

Rita stares at the window, which has been barred for the past three months, ever since the night she climbed out of it and went to the party in Wellesley Street. She looks back at her reflection: not bad, her olive skin glowing with good health, her black hair tumbling over her shoulders. She arches her lips, leans forward to pick up the new lipstick she bought on the way home from work. She traces a deep dark-red curve over her mouth, pouts and smiles. She likes what she sees.

The door handle rattles. Her mother stands there in her nightdress, clutching a candlewick dressing gown at the waist.

'I smelled the smoke,' she says. 'Puff, puff. Only your father smokes in this house.'

'I'm old enough. To smoke. To do other things. To get married.'

'Old enough, eh? Oh Rita, my girl.' She sits down on the bed. 'We were only old enough when we were promised to the man we would marry.'

'I didn't,' Rita says. 'I didn't do that thing.'

'But you would have,' her mother says. 'You have to be very clear when the judge asks you. That it was never in your mind to let this Albert do that to you.'

'I'll just have to tell the truth about what happened, I guess.'

'Truth. Truth is what you tell the priest.'

'Oh yes, and he forgives me, and then if I don't tell the truth in court, I go and tell him that I've lied and he forgives me for that, too. Eh Mum?'

Her mother pulls a handkerchief from the pocket of her dressing gown. There are stains on the garment as if she has washed up the pots while she was wearing it. Rita doesn't know: she's ducked out of dishes of late. Her mother is dabbing at her eyes in a way the daughter hates, so sorry for herself she is and all.

'If you lay on the bed, you were willing then?'

'You're putting words in my mouth.'

'So it's true, you have given yourself to a man before.' When Rita doesn't reply, she says, 'What will I tell your father?'

'Oh for goodness' sake, Mum, my father isn't the priest.'

Her mother makes a gesture, her hands clasping her face. 'Why are you wearing lipstick at this hour of the night, Rita?'

'Just checking the colour. I want to look good for court.'

'For who? For the judge? For the boy?'

'The boy. He's nothing. I've got a steady boyfriend now. He's coming to court with me.'

Her mother slaps Rita's face hard then, and walks out.

Rita clings to the edge of the bed, holding her cheek. She doesn't care. Soon she will be the star of the show.

Her mother can't imagine how hungry she is to feel truly alive.

Chapter 5

Young Albert would find out soon enough what came over his parents that afternoon when they were all daft and singing. Kathleen remembers the day she told him the news, the look of astonishment that turned quickly to red-faced embarrassment. She didn't know if he knew where babies came from, although he had seen more than he should in the air-raid shelter at the end of Sandy Row the night a young woman gave birth in there, her screaming and shouting *sweet Jesus, it's coming, it's coming* and blood and placenta landing up at their feet, and then the squalling infant, its birth membrane glowing in the light of the fires. So he had a fair idea how a baby got out of a woman, but it is how it got put in that he might not know. She had said, placing his hand on her stomach, 'Your da and I have a baby coming. A little brother or sister for you.'

'You *have?*' he said, and seeing the look on his face she guessed someone had told him.

The baby gave a little kick and he pulled his hand away. 'I don't want a brother or sister.' His face was screwed up, fighting tears.

'That's silly. Other children have brothers and sisters, why shouldn't you?'

'I like being your only one.' It had slipped out, little black eels of words making their own truth.

I have spoiled him, she thought at the time, spoiled him for anything but him and me on our own. But he was so precious to her, and she didn't know how to explain this to him. For that matter, it was hard to explain to her husband, when he'd come home from the Front on leave, the way the boy glowered and sulked while he was there, so that his father got cold and unpleasant with him on some occasions. If he had known that the boy, nearly ten by the time the war ended, still climbed into her bed and slept with her some nights, how she'd place her hand on his silky dark hair, her fingers entwined in his, he'd have been baffled, his bewilderment turning to outrage.

She had had to sit Bert down and tell him that, although things were not all grand between them, they could make them good again if they tried. It was the war, she told herself, there were plenty of men like him around the neighbourhood. They looked bruised in their souls. She was lucky: some men never seemed to recover, ones like her grandfather after the Somme, who'd seen his comrades die in their thousands. But Bert listened. After a while things improved and they began to make merry in bed again, like the old days, and to sing the way they had when they first met.

The old days, that was how their courtship seemed now. In her heart, Kathleen sees herself as the stronger of the two of them, though her husband's family saw themselves as superior to hers. When she first knew Bert, his father was a manager at one of the big linen mills, while hers was a man with a horse and cart delivering flax from the fields: one a man of authority, the other a labourer. Bert was sent away to England for his schooling, living with an aunt in Richmond, near London, so that when he came home for his holidays he spoke with a more British accent than the people round about. It didn't last in London; he missed the fishing in the River Lagan, and it was easier to get work in Belfast during the Great Depression, or it was if you knew someone like his father. He had an idea he might get a job on the *Irish Times* as a journalist but they were full up with people who wanted to scribble, as they put it. His father put him to work as a clerk in the mill, *until something better came along*. That's where they met, she and Albert, as she called him then, Kathleen a girl on the factory floor.

'You seem a nice enough girl,' his mother said, when he took her home to meet his family. 'I mean, you're a decent one, aren't you?' That was what she said, straight to her face.

'Kathleen is with child,' her son said.

There was a silence that echoed round the corners of the fancy room with the crocheted antimacassars on the chairs and a picture of King George on the wall.

'I see. In the *family* way.' His mother had crooked her finger above the handle of the bone-china cup she was holding. 'Well, I do see. You're a disappointment to me, Albert. To your father, I'm sure.' His father turned his back so that he couldn't see the pair of them. 'Such shame. You could go away for a while,' she said to Kathleen. 'There are places for girls like you.'

'Albert has pledged to marry me,' Kathleen said. 'My parents are angry too, but they will stand beside me in the church when we're married.'

The mother's eyes filled, two watery saucers of disbelief. 'Marriage. You can't.'

'We're both of age. I think it is our decision, Mrs Black.' It was so, they were both twenty-three, there was nothing to stop them except, she saw at that moment, the danger of his parents persuading him not to go ahead.

'You've seduced him. You tart.'

It was this that gave Bert resolve, she would think later. He moved closer to her, took her hand.

'You'll be poor,' the father said. 'Find out what that's like.'

She wore a lace jacket that had belonged to her mother and her mother before that when she went to St Anne's, the big Church of Ireland cathedral. Her parents came to the wedding, and her aunts and uncles, but her husband's did not.

William was their first-born, a fragile scrap of a boy. He lasted just a year. They lived in Tate's Avenue then, the kitchen slimy with damp, and a tin bath hanging in the back yard. Poor as dirt they were, so she went back to the linen mill to work. They swore to each other they would find a better place to live when the next baby came along. They scrimped and saved those two years until Albert was born. They were able to afford more rent for a half-decent place, buy better beds, still second-hand but clean. And her keeping the house spotless. Albert was the perfect baby, and a miracle one at that, born with a caul, a sign of good luck and high intelligence, hardly ever crying, sleeping all night, and the only one of her sons to take to her breast. The memory of his mouth on her nipple stirred her even now, flooding her like the urge for sex.

She stayed home for a time until the boy started school, making do, making ends meet. If her husband missed his parents, he didn't complain. Now and then he appeared to have a little extra money; she figured that he saw his mother from time to time. After William died, she began to feel a little sorry for her mother-in-law. Her son was as good as lost to her, not that it needed to be that way; it was the way they saw things, or the way they had backed themselves into a corner. All the same, it irked Kathleen that her husband saw his mother on the sly. If he had come straight out and told her, she would have understood. Instead, an occasional fiver that appeared without explanation, put beside her plate at breakfast time, just as he was walking out the door, meaning don't ask.

And then Bert, as she had taken to calling him after the second boy came, left for the war, and there was just the two of them, her and the child, dodging the bombs, watching the cathedral get bombed, and some of the big mills, including the one her father-in-law ran, so she supposed that he might be poor, too.

Wartime wasn't all bad, her and the boy going for picnics on sunny days, taking their walks in the beautiful gardens that lay beside Queen's University, just up the road from Sandy Row. Kathleen tried to imagine what it would be like to be educated. She couldn't see it for herself, but it would be a wonderful chance for a boy. Her son seemed clever to her.

So Daniel was a surprise, ten years younger than his brother, and they were desperate hard up again. But a gift, their Danny, as God is my judge, which is what the name meant and it was the right one for him: they had been judged and found worthy of another boy. That is what her husband said, and it was odd to her that the new boy was, perhaps, the one he preferred, although he kept this to himself. It was just something she knew inside herself. She thought Daniel might have saved her marriage, but it was little Albert she cherished, her companion through the bad years, the one who had survived with her in the hard darkness when the sirens shrieked, her special mortal boy.

And, once Albert got over the gunk of it, the sense of displacement that he expressed when he first learned of Daniel's coming, he was as tender with his little brother as if he were a lass, rocking him when he cried, walking him when she was bushed, singing the songs she had sung to him. Oh yes, he was the perfect big brother. If he sometimes looked sideways at his father when he was ministering to the baby of the family, she pushed away the thought that he was trying to find favour. No, it was real, this love he had for the little one. All of these things.

There are other things she remembers; they run in a loop through her brain, over and again. If she stands at the window she can hear the skirl of bagpipes, the flutes and the drums, see the arches hung with orange bunting and flags of the Empire over the street. In the picture, she has hats for the boys, red, white and blue, which merge with the crowds. It is the day of the Orange Parade when the Protestants show that they own Belfast. There are men in shabby suits like the one her husband wears, men in kilts, thousands of people marching to the sound of the music. The words of 'The Sash' echo in her ears:

> So sure I'm an Ulster
> Orangeman, from Erin's isle I
> came
> To see my British brethren all of
> honour and of fame
> And to tell them of my forefathers
> who fought in days of yore
> That I might have the right to
> wear, the sash my father wore!

Sometimes it doesn't make all that much sense to her, but she keeps these thoughts to herself, and come the day of the march every year she is as excited as everyone.

Young Albert had gone only reluctantly on the last march before he left for New Zealand; hadn't wanted to put on the sash. He was just turning eighteen at the time. She didn't understand his behaviour, not at all, as she said to him afterwards, until they came alongside St Patrick's Church where the Parade would stop to sing

'The Sash' extra loud, shouting the chorus, hoping that those inside would be driven like rats to their holes.

> *. . . if the call should come we'll*
> *follow the drum, and cross that*
> *river once more*
> *That tomorrow's Ulsterman may*
> *wear the sash my father wore!*

You'd see people scurrying out the side doors, barrelling away down the street, though the priests stayed inside.

It was while they were outside that Albert wheeled away from the marchers, and the next thing she knew he was skulking beneath the big tree out front, the leaves awash with summer light, and there was a girl, and they were looking at each other and laughing. The girl passed him the cigarette she was smoking, and Kathleen saw him draw a long drag off it, as if he were all grown up. And then there were two boys alongside of the pair of them, and Albert was ducking for cover, merging with the marchers and not turning to look back. Had she imagined it, or had she seen the flash of steel?

It's all right to have a Taig for a friend, she would say to him afterwards, when the day had turned to night and they were all back at home and Daniel in bed with the door firmly shut on him. 'I stand beside a woman all day at the mill who is of a different cloth. But it is not all right on the Twelfth. You put us to shame with this girl. You're an Ulsterman.'

And his father, who rarely put in a word, said, 'Your mother's right. It is not just now; it's in the future. You walk out with a girl from the other side and before you know it she has you up the aisle and you've become a Papist. They don't come over to our way of seeing things. Their fathers would rather see you dead.'

Kathleen guessed he was thinking that if Albert were to put a girl in the family way, as he did to her, there would be no escaping, but those things were better not mentioned, a private matter between her and her husband. At least she was a Protestant girl. She thinks they have been happy enough. They have weathered grief and hardship, and he is still her man.

'You knew that girl would come after you today, that's why you didn't want to go on the Parade,' Kathleen had said. 'You didn't want us to see you with her.'

'Maureen's just a friend, the sister of Seamus who I fish with at the wharfside,' Albert said, those green eyes blazing and the black swathe of his hair falling over his forehead. Her beautiful boy. Her strong handsome flesh and blood.

'Seamus didn't look too much of a friend today,' his father said. 'They were carrying knives, those lads.'

'Da, everyone carries a toolie. You know that.'

It was true. His father carried one always, strapped inside of his sock. Just in case. You never know what's coming at you in the dark, he would tell Kathleen. A man needs to be prepared.

'So you are carrying a weapon? You'd better hand it over.'

The room had gone quiet, just the ticking of the clock on the mantel. Father and son eyed each other up. The boy didn't move.

'I'll beat the shite out of you, lad, don't think I won't.' He was still the stronger one, his hands hard-muscled from hanging onto the handle of a spade.

The boy reached down to his sock and she saw the slim line of the weapon. He looked up at his father. 'I'll stay away from the girl,' he said. 'She's nothing, just a wee lass who's good for a laugh.'

'Your word on that?'

'Yes, Da, my word on wee Danny's life.'

'Well then. We'll say no more about it.' Dismissing the knife. Or accepting it. Knowing the dangers that lay in dark nights and sometimes in broad daylight. The way things were.

Still, the boy had been more careful after that. If he ran with the Taigs, she didn't get to hear about it.

Kathleen gives a deep shuddering sigh. That is all in the past. He is gone.

Some days she looks at her husband and thinks it is his fault. Then she thinks it is hers for over-loving him, for not wanting to let him go, and her husband seeing that, and thinking he needed the chance to grow up, to go to a land of opportunity.

She thinks of the night before he left, how he'd fooled around, acting the maggot, until it was time for Daniel to go to bed. Later she'd heard him in the room, singing to him the way he had when he was little *oh Danny boy / the pipes the pipes are calling* . . . It had been too hard to resist looking in on them. Daniel had his arms around his brother's neck. 'You'll come back, won't you?'

'I'll do better than that, Danny boy. When I get rich, I'll build a fine house in New Zealand and send for you to come and stay with me.'

'What about Mam and Da?'

'They can come too. They've got miles of beaches where you can swim, and the water's very warm. I've read about it.'

'Will they have fish and chips?'

'I reckon. And telephones in all the houses. They've told me that because I'm going to work for the company, a job waiting and all, not like here.'

'It sounds grand,' Daniel said, the edge of sleep overtaking his voice.

'We'll have a great time, you and me.'

Albert had sat there humming in the dark until Daniel's breathing was slow and even. He looked away from her when he came out into the light, his face smudged with tears.

Just we'ans, both of them. Her two sons.

Chapter 6

1953. As the ship pulled away from the dock, streamers held by passengers on the deck and their relatives on shore began to stretch and break, a tide of singing rolling out *Now is the hour / for me to saaay goodbye*. Around Albert, standing at the railing of the *Captain Cook*, girls began to cry. He was on his own, his family left behind in Belfast. Just as well his mother wasn't there, he thought; it had been bad enough extricating himself from her last frantic hug as it was.

A man alongside him, a tall chap, perhaps four or five years older, leaned over. 'I'm on my own too.' He offered his hand. 'Peter Simpson,' he said, and for some reason they were friends straight away.

He'd have been lonely those first nights on the boat if he hadn't met Peter. The man from Liverpool told him he'd been out of work for a year. With a bit of graft he'd managed to scrape together the ten pounds needed to make the voyage out. What did he mean by graft? Albert wanted to know.

Peter hesitated. He was a clean-cut fellow, what Albert's mother would have called decent to look at. Odd jobs on building sites, rat catching, that sort of thing. Going without dinner two nights a week so he could save his benefit. Yeah, tough, but he reckoned he could make a go of it in New Zealand. He was twenty-three, it was now or never.

When Albert said he was just eighteen these three months past, Peter looked him over, told him to hang out with him. You never knew what was around the corner. There were more than a thousand of them on the ship, men and women and some children — child migrants, Peter said. They were the ones to watch out for. They hadn't asked to be sent, most of them had had it pretty rough. They'd pick your pockets if they had half a chance.

'Not their fault,' Peter said, 'they're kids out of orphanages, most of them, had the shit beaten out of them, abandoned like kids out of a Dickens novel and posted to the other side of the world.' Albert had read *Oliver Twist* in school. His new friend seemed to have a literary turn of mind. A clever man who'd come up through the school of hard knocks. Well, him and himself and all, and goodness knows how many others on the ship, though it seemed he had had it easier than some. During the voyage, these Oliver Twist children appeared now and then, some quite small, barely ready for school, others teenagers. They had closed, tight little faces, as if they already knew all there was to know about life and more.

His father had found the ten pounds that was needed to get him on board, all the family's savings. Ten quid for the passage and a fiver to set you up when you get over there, was what he'd said. His mother had said, with bitterness at the corners of her mouth, that some of the money would have come from his grandmother, the one who lived so close but they never saw. His grandparents, she said, had had money and lost it, but his mother still liked to act as if they'd got the spondulicks tucked away. She didn't want him to leave.

'You need to get out of here,' his father had said. 'There's nothing for you.'

This was not strictly true, for the rebuilding of Belfast since the war was still going on, and there was work on the docks, but that was what it was, labouring jobs and plenty of competition for them. He wondered if his father was reflecting his disappointment at his own situation. The war had left him without a lot of strength, and the doors to a life of words were closed to him. The image of his father, scrawny in his baggy trousers and braces, his hair thinning into mousy strands, would come back to haunt him. There were times when he wondered if his father had sent him away because he thought his wife loved him, her son, more than she did him. One of those things that hung in the air. 'You could perhaps study when you get settled in New Zealand,' his father said.

Albert laughed then. He had no ideas of going back to school. Here he was, eighteen years of age, and that was all behind him. Only the scholarship boys stayed at school that long, and he was not one of those. 'I'll be indentured in New Zealand for two years,' he said.

'Well then, you can do a trade; count yourself lucky.'

'You want me to go, don't you?'

'The Catholics are on the move. They'll take against us sooner or later,' his father said.

'Haven't we taken against them already, Da?'

His father gave him a hard look then. 'Remember you're part of the United Kingdom,' he said. 'Remember, you heard it from me, there's trouble ahead of us here.'

So there was that, perhaps: his father thought he was too close to the Taigs. He would stand, leaning against the rail, trying to make sense of it, watching the sea churn beneath him, or gazing out to a distance so vast it made his eyes ache trying to see a non-existent coastline. Sometimes he wished the ship would turn around, other times it occurred to him that he might jump in the sea and swim back home.

As if he had been reading his thoughts, Peter appeared beside him. 'You coming along to the dance tonight?'

'I can't dance.'

'Some girl will teach you.'

As he stood on the edge of the jiving chaos of the dance floor, shy because he was young and didn't know any English girls, one of them pulled him towards her. He shivered a moment as if an electric current had passed through his body, and his feet found the rhythm of the beat. Dancing came as naturally to him as breathing. The girl wore a tight white blouse and a wide skirt that whirled when he swung her around to the music. Afterwards the pair of them, and a whole bunch of others, went up to the deck and sang along to a guitar a fella had brought to play in the night air. The stars were high in the sky as the ship headed towards the Caribbean Sea and beyond that the Panama Canal. They were singing *I don't want to set the world on fire*, harmonising as if they were The Ink Spots, when he kissed the nape of the girl's neck and felt her breath quickening, starting to kiss him back. 'Paddy,' she said, 'you're the sweetest kid.'

'My name's Albert,' he said.

'Oh, g'won, aren't all Irishmen called Paddy? You're going to set the world on fire, babe.' The next minute she was gone, but that was how it started, his new name, and he liked it, it had an easy ring. He stopped having to explain that he was from Northern Ireland, the divisions within his country, whether he kicked with the left foot or the right, he was just Paddy the Irish guy.

When he went down below, he found Peter sitting smoking a cigarette in the lounge. It seemed that their lives had turned a corner into a place of luxury and expansiveness. The idea of a new country took hold of him and he imagined limitless possibility.

'You found yourself a girlfriend?' Peter asked.

'Nah, I think I was too young for her. She did a runner on me.' But that seemed all right too, because there were so many girls, all as hyped up with excitement as he was, and tomorrow night he would sing along with some other girl at his side.

Paddy, as everyone on the ship called him and he now thought of himself, had seen pictures of the great skylines of the world. There was London, where he had now spent two nights, and Paris and New York with its skyscrapers. He knew that Wellington was a capital city, and he was expecting more of the same. But as the *Captain Cook* sailed into the harbour, all he could see was low white houses huddled on hills, a raw new-looking place in comparison to home.

When they disembarked, he sensed it was a quiet place. Not that there was time to explore. Within an hour or so, he and Peter were despatched on a train to a village called Trentham, way beyond the city limits, part of an area known as the Hutt Valley, a satellite of Wellington, with an Upper and a Lower Hutt. It had just turned out so, that they were to be fellow workers, laying cable for the Post and Telegraph Department. A truck picked them up at the station, driving past military barracks and a racecourse, until they came to a group of small isolated huts set among unrecognisable trees. The very sparseness of their surroundings made Albert, who was now called Paddy, long again for home.

He hung up his coat and unfolded the two blankets lying on the end of the bed. Then he took his coat down and put it back on again and sat shivering on the side of the bed. It was the middle of October and they had been told that it was spring here in New Zealand. If this was spring, it was a cold one. His longing turned to a deep well of loss, a grief so profound he could hardly breathe.

There was a knock at the door. Peter stood there, in his hand a mug of tea that steamed against a frosty landscape, a full moon bouncing across the sky. 'We'll get out of here when we can,' he said.

Something, bird or animal, they couldn't tell, called *honk honk*, again and again, out there in the moonlight.

It wasn't all bad. In the morning they were taken to a training station, where they were shown a model of the top of a telegraph pole and how to find broken insulators. They looked like white china cups. The two of them were allocated to Clarrie's gang. 'I've got a couple of pakehas here for you,' the foreman said. 'New chums.' From now on they would be inspecting the telegraph poles, looking for broken insulators, rotten cross-arms and poles that were in any way unsafe. The weather turned fine and warm.

'Scorcher of a day,' Clarrie would say as one gleaming day of sunlight turned to another.

'Scorcher, my old mucker,' Peter would mutter to Paddy, mopping his brow, a cigarette clamped between his teeth. 'Scorcher, all right.'

They were sent to work amongst pine trees above Wellington Harbour. The trees were so thick, the men could scramble from tree to tree to reach the lines without hauling the extension ladders off the trucks. The clean bristling scent of the pines and the laughter of the others purged Paddy during the daytime at least of what he vaguely understood to be homesickness. In some place in his heart he felt tiredness, and he was too young to have a tired heart.

'What is the creature that goes *honk honk* in the night?' Paddy asked Clarrie. He imitated the sound the way he had heard it.

'Morepork, you've heard the morepork bird. It's an owl, a ruru,' Clarrie said. Clarrie came from up north, a Maori fulla, he described himself, a big man but lithe amongst the tree tops. There were other Maoris in the gang. They whistled a lot and spoke to each other in a language that Paddy and Peter couldn't understand, but for the most part it seemed good-natured enough.

'Is that what it's asking for?' Paddy asked. 'More pork?'

Clarrie laughed and the whole gang joined in. 'Nah, mate, they like a tasty little mouse or a rat. You're too big to get eaten by a morepork.'

Still, he couldn't stop listening to the bird sounding its melancholic haunting notes, as if it were coming for him.

1954. While the fires burned each year in Belfast, books were being set alight up and down New Zealand. Police moved from one bookshop to another, raiding lending libraries and swooping on little corner dairies that carried a small stock of paperbacks, snatching books and comics along the way. Moral panic had seized the country as word spread of an epidemic of loose behaviour by teenagers. Rose Lewis had heard about this because her neighbours talked about it incessantly, and she was bewildered. It all started with the war, some muttered, when the bloody Yanks moved in and corrupted people's minds, never mind their role in the Pacific. They brought candy and flattery and jitterbug dances, petting in the back seat of movie theatres and free love. It was all there in the books. The name Mickey Spillane crept into the vocabulary of the young, a novelist who wrote of violence and sex and degradation. In schools, his books were passed surreptitiously, hand to hand, under the cover of desks, tucked under copies of *En Route* and *History for Everyone*. It was terrifying. The centre of this storm of delinquency was the Hutt Valley. One only had to look there to know that things had fallen apart: that's what the newspapers wrote in their editorials and their headlines. There, in the suburbs of the Hutt, teenagers gathered at milk bars, or sat in the back seats of theatres doing lewd things to each other, or were collecting on the edges of the wide, swift river and having carnal knowledge. Carnal.

The word had an evil ring to it. It was said that the hospitals for unmarried mothers were filling. There was a black market in condoms, so it was whispered. Condoms were banned for the young, although if you knew the right fruiterer to go to you might just strike it lucky. Nestling behind the bananas and pineapples, the dark plums and the rosy apples, the path to the ripe fruit of love might be realised without consequences. Or even at the pie cart. Hot chips and a frenchie, all for five bob.

These were the things Rose was hearing, yet it all seemed a world away from her little house provided by the state in Naenae, one of the new suburbs in the Hutt. Her husband had come home from the war long enough to give her three children, two boys and a girl, before he died during an asthma attack. He hadn't had asthma when he went to the war. She blamed the trenches, the dark winters of the northern hemisphere, rotten rations. There were so many like her, she tried not to be bitter. She had loved that man. She loved him still. Each day she dressed as if he were about to walk in the door, pretty print dresses and a touch of make-up to highlight the warm blush of her skin, her light auburn hair caught up in a roll, small tendrils escaping around her face. She kept herself in this manner not for any other man but to honour the memory of him. Music was her consolation. The rectangular house overflowing with children, or so it seemed, was home to a piano. When the hurt descended, the black moments when it seemed grief would overwhelm her, she would lay her fingers on the keys and the rooms filled with melodies plucked from her past, when she was a star music pupil in the city.

And outside she had begun a garden. So many houses had been built in haste, all looking so much alike, she had wondered where to begin when she first came. The bulldozers that had prepared the land for the construction of all these houses to accommodate the hard-up like her had flattened the ground, leaving swathes of bare clay. There was a rawness about the place that had to be overcome. She had mapped out where the paths would run, and laid down grass so the children had space to play, then she turned over a patch of ground where she planted vegetables — potatoes and carrots, beans and silver beet. The flowers would come later. She knew the soil was good because beyond the houses lay market gardens. The boys worked alongside her, clearing the surface clay in wheelbarrows and spreading fertiliser. They were such good boys, she couldn't imagine they would ever find or make the trouble that was spoken of in hushed voices by her neighbours. The girl, Evelyn, with her curls and her smile, tagged along behind, a three-year-old with her own toy wheelbarrow. She wheeled her dolls, or the kittens, wherever they went in the garden. A stream ran nearby, and it was one of the boys' jobs to make sure Evelyn didn't wander off and get caught in its flow. What they did catch were eels, which Rose learned to skin and cook. Her neighbours despised the fish, citing their poisonous blood when raw, but she knew better than that, frying them and serving them with butter sauce.

The flowerbeds began to take hold, the roses to bloom, the contours of the section to soften. More and more often there were days when Rose could tell herself she was content. One afternoon two young men knocked on her door. At first she couldn't understand what they said, the accents of Liverpool and Ireland thick on their tongues.

They were working in the area laying cables. We're looking for something more like home, they explained, because it wasn't that comfortable in the Post and Telegraph huts where they were living. Naenae appealed to them, kind of cosy-looking, so they'd knocked on a few doors. Someone along the street had suggested she might put them up for a few nights. Mrs Lewis, she's kind, the woman had said.

At first she had laughed. 'Where on earth does she think I'd put you? I've got three kids already.'

'We'd pay our way, give you board money,' said the one she took to be younger, the one with the Irish accent. 'We don't mind bunking in the same room.' One of the cats slid between his ankles. He leaned down and stroked it.

She was about to send them on their way. She had a widow's pension, and had begun to give piano lessons to two or three children in the street for three shillings a lesson — but still she was stretched. The older of her boys was ready for a bike, the second had outgrown his school shoes. And Evelyn really liked sharing her mother's bedroom when she could get away with it.

While she was standing there turning the whole unlikely situation over in her mind, the Irish boy began to recite. *My aunt Jane has a bell on the door / a white stone step and a clean swept floor / candy apples, hard green peas / conversation lozenges.*

'My name's not Jane,' she said.

'Neither is it my aunt's.'

'There are two beds in the sun porch,' she said, the words sliding out before she could stop them. They looked nice enough lads, she thought.

'I'm Peter,' the taller one said, holding out his hand.

'My mam calls me little Albert,' the Irish boy said, and a grin lit up his face. 'You look just like her, like my mam.'

'But I'm not your mother either.'

'I'm called Paddy out here.' His jet-black hair was brushed back from his forehead, his skin tanned from working in the outdoors, a clean white shirt buttoned to his throat.

'Just for a few nights, mind you,' she said. 'Until you find your-selves somewhere more permanent.'

After dinner, when they had all helped her clear away and wash

69

the plates, Rose sat down at the piano and began to play, fingering threads of melodies. Behind her, Paddy picked up the words of 'The World is Waiting for the Sunrise', and as he began the first line, *Dear one*, his voice soared, sweet and true. Rose looked at him, and started humming along with him.

'You're a singer,' she said. 'You have the most beautiful voice.'

'Oh well, it's what we did, my family and all. Song's cheap.'

She figured the young men had come to stay for a while.

Chapter 7

1955. The lawyer for the prosecution is a sleek, fair man named Gerald Timms. He isn't tall, but he has a way of balancing forward on the arched balls of his feet and pushing his head up and down so that he appears to occupy the space of a much larger man. Beneath his gown he is dressed in a charcoal-grey suit with a snow-white handkerchief in his breast pocket. It is October, just two years since Albert Black came to live in New Zealand, almost to the day.

A girl stands in the witness box. She is wearing a black suit and a black beret slanted over dark and lustrous hair tumbling past her shoulders. She glances briefly at the man in the dock; their eyes lock for an instant, then she drops hers, straightening herself.

'Miss Zilich,' Timms began. 'Will you please tell us your name, address and occupation.'

'My name is Rita Zilich,' she begins. 'I'm sixteen years old. I live with my parents in Anglesea Street, Ponsonby. I'm a shorthand typist. I passed my exams with top marks in School Certificate, you know. At my school, that is.' She turns to a youth seated in the gallery and gives a little wave. He's dressed in tight black trousers and a red windbreaker that is unzipped all the way down the front, showing a white tee-shirt. He waggles one finger at her

'Miss Zilich,' the judge says sharply.

'Oh sorry,' she murmurs, and composes her face into the semblance of great attention.

'Yes, thank you, Miss Zilich,' Timms says. 'That's very good. If you could just tell us about what happened on the night of Monday, July twenty-fifth of this year, it would be a help. You knew the accused?'

'Oh yes, you couldn't help but notice him. He's pretty good-looking, if you go in for those kind of looks.' In spite of herself, she throws a cool appraising glance in the direction of Albert.

Timms breathes deeply and makes a steeple with his fingers. 'Very good. I'd like you to tell the court in your own words what happened. How long you knew him, whether you knew the deceased, what occurred on the night in question.'

'I've written it all down in shorthand.'

'Just tell the story, Miss Zilich, never mind the notes.'

Rita flicks her mane of hair back from where it has encroached across her shoulder, and launches into her account, the witness box becoming her stage. 'I knew the accused for about three months before the twenty-fifth of July. I knew him as Paddy, that was the only name I'd heard. I knew the other guy too, Alan Jacques, only of course that's not what we called him. He was Johnny McBride. But I'd only known him about, oh, maybe two weeks. I wasn't keeping company with either of them. Actually, I'd been to the pictures on the night in question. I'd been to see *Calamity Jane*, you know the one where Doris Day sings "My Secret Love", it's an amazing picture. And I'm crazy about the song.'

'Yes, of course. We appreciate your good taste, Miss Zilich.

But you went to Ye Olde Barn cafe after you'd been to the pictures?'

'Yes, this was about seven thirty, I suppose. I didn't mean to, it was just that I was walking past, planning to go home, and there was a crowd there. Somebody called out, I don't know whether it was Paddy or Johnny, but I think it was one of them, and said come on over. So I went over, and Paddy said come on up to the house, we're having a party tonight. I knew where he meant, it was at 105 Wellesley Street. I'd been to a party there before. Well, I thought, why not? I hadn't arranged to meet Paddy or anything like that, but it sounded like a bit of fun. Actually, Paddy's girlfriend was in the cafe, now I come to think of it. Bessie Marsh, that is, so obviously I didn't mean to meet Paddy. I shouldn't think she's his girlfriend now, not now he's gone and stabbed Johnny. He wouldn't be mine, I can tell you that.'

'So you went on to the party instead of going home?'

'Well. Not exactly.'

'Why not exactly?'

'I'd told my parents I'd be home. Well, they're not so keen on me going to parties. So I went home, and when they'd gone to bed I hopped out the window and went back to town. This was about quarter past ten.'

'So what happened at the party?'

'Well, Johnny and Paddy were both there, and Bessie, and one of my girlfriends called Stella, and a whole bunch of others, I guess about ten altogether at that stage, mostly guys, you know. Someone was playing a guitar, everything seemed normal. A normal party, that is. You know?'

'We're happy that you're enlightening us, Miss Zilich. Please go on.'

'Well, Paddy was sober. And Johnny was sober, is about what I'd say. Then Bessie said she had to go home because she had exams or something early the next day. She's a student of some kind, I think.

She'd gone off to the library after I first saw her. I think Paddy went and collected her later on while I was off seeing my parents.'

'Misleading them?'

'Um, yes.'

'Never mind.' Timms appears annoyed with himself.

'Myself, I don't have to be at work until nine, I'm a secretary at the Council, they have very regular hours. I mean, I wouldn't start at eight unless I had to, but with my qualifications I can pick and choose. I got eighty-five per cent for typing, you know.'

'Indeed.' Timms was tapping his fingers on a folder, his eyes willing her to get to the point.

'Well then, I think Paddy must have walked Bessie home, or to a taxi, I don't really know, but he was gone a while, and when he came back he asked me to sleep with him that night. At first I said no, but then he asked me again, and I said I'd think about it. I was just putting him off, of course, trying to be polite.'

'But he thought you meant it?'

Rita hesitates, pushing a strand of hair away from her face as it escapes from under the beret. 'I didn't want to give offence. I said it in a nice way.'

'And you say the defendant was sober?'

'I'd say so. Well, I didn't know what he was like when he was drunk.'

Listening to her, Paddy thinks I can tell you what I'm like when I'm cut. But you wouldn't want to know. Staggering, that's what he is. He is back in Trentham and it's late Friday afternoon. On Fridays the Post and Telegraph gang knocked off early so they could put in a few hours at the pub, a barn of a place, nothing like the pubs at home. They close at six o'clock of the evening, just about the time men are heading for their local back home in Belfast. The trick here in New Zealand is to drink as much beer as you can down in the least possible time. At first Paddy couldn't bring himself to go in. He'd tasted ale before, just a glass or two with his da at the Sandy Row Arms, a quiet enough place, with low ceilings and carpet underfoot, a handful of men leaning against the bar, telling yarns. Here the bars are long counters, the walls sloped for easy cleaning because men vomit like fountains of spaghetti, the crush of men so dense the service is just the bartender pointing a pistol-shaped spigot at out-held glasses. The beer shoots out a white cuff of foam. The six o'clock swill, he'd heard it called, and looking at men lurching out of the bars he'd found himself disgusted. He shouldn't be, because his da has come home two sheets to the wind often enough, but somehow this was different. Besides, here in New Zealand he was still an under-age drinker. His shoulders had filled out, his face darkened in the sun, and he'd grown a couple of inches since he landed. He passed for being older, but he still wasn't legal to enter the pub.

There came an afternoon, the sky a high bird's-egg blue above the Naenae hills, and their throats as dry as old bones, when the New Zealanders in the gang called him and Peter out. What are you? Wowsers? they asked as they prepared to drop the two of them off at the huts. They had to make a detour to get back to the pub, which all took up time.

'Okay, all right then,' Peter said on this summer afternoon, 'we'll go with you today. Just one drink, mind you.'

The first beer slid down Paddy's throat so easily it was like cool lemonade, with about equal an effect, he thought. Peter and he grinned at each other: this was no roaring Guinness, you could drink it like tap water. Phew, they joked, nothing to it, and held their glasses out to the spigot. After the second drink, Paddy felt warm fuzz in his head, his body dissolving. This drinking lark was easy. He found himself telling Peter and anyone who'd listen bad Irish jokes. Any moment he would be singing them all a song. Perhaps he did sing. 'My Aunt Jane'. Rose liked that one; maybe he sang it to the men or maybe he went home and sang a verse to her, the one that made her and Evelyn, the wee cutie, laugh:

> My aunt Jane she can dance a jig
> Sing a song 'round a sweetie pig.
> Wee red eyes and a cord for a tail,
> Hanging in a bunch from a
> crooked nail.

Yes, he must have sung that one, because now he remembers everyone laughing and singing along with him.

He remembers that he and Peter had their arms around each other, holding each other up. 'My old mucker,' Peter said, 'you're a bit of a laugh all right.'

My old mucker. His best friend. It felt grand that he had one.

After that he and Peter went with the men every Friday afternoon, until a day when too many beers slid down too fast. After the fifth or sixth, he lost count of them, the barman called time, meaning they had to be through in fifteen minutes. 'Drink up,' someone shouted, 'time for another round.' So that was part of the trick too, to order another drink before the pub closes, swallow it down and get another one in, in the last five minutes, because the barman can't throw you out while you're still drinking.

Paddy felt his vision blur, his knees tremble. And then it was over, and he and Peter were holding themselves up on a lamp post outside, and he was singing 'Danny Boy' at the top of his voice, and then, just as suddenly, he began to cry. 'Oh holy shite,' he said, 'don't mind me, it's my little brother Danny I have in my mind right now.' Some of the gang were shovelling him and Peter onto the back of the Post and Telegraph truck that had to be returned to the depot, and soon it began to weave its way back towards Trentham. A military band was playing, the brass making yellow noise; soldiers marched down the road, some special parade from the army camp. It reminded him of the Twelfth of July. He tried to stand up on the back of the truck and salute, was pulled back by the ankles just as he was about to topple over the edge.

'So,' he shouted above the noise of the truck, 'you heard the one about the Black and Tans?'

'Who are they?' Clarrie asked.

'Soldiers. Irish soldiers,' Peter said. He was drunk too, but not as drunk as Paddy.

'British soldiers *ac*tually,' Paddy said. 'Because you see we're part of the UK.'

'Nah, Paddy, you're an Irishman,' Clarrie said. 'So go on, what happened?'

'Well you see, there was your man called Murphy, the rain's pissing down, and the Black and Tans are going to hang him. Murphy says to the hangman, it's an awful day, wouldn't you say? And the hangman, he says, wait for it, he says, you're lucky, Murphy, I've got to walk home in it.'

'Oath, that's a bad story,' Clarrie said.

Back at the huts, Paddy threw up in the grass. Peter stopped him collapsing in his vomit. 'Jesus, Pete,' Paddy said, 'do people ever die from getting drunk?'

'You won't die, Paddy.'

'You promise?'

'Yeah, sure, I won't let you die.'

'I reckon you'll last longer than me, Peter. You'll live longer.'

'That's drink talking. Stop, Paddy, stop it.'

'Pete,' Paddy said, 'I want to go home. I want my mam.'

In the morning, Peter said, 'I said we'd get out of here. I reckon it's time, Paddy.'

Gallows humour. Bad jokes, they come flooding back to him. That is what he is like when he's cut, Rita. You don't know at all.

So no, he wasn't particularly drunk that night. What is the girl in the witness stand going to say next? Has he ever wanted to sleep with her? He supposes so. She had a jaunty air about her that night and a come-hither look. He sees the way the eyes of some of the jurymen follow her. Yes, probably most men would get into her knickers if they could. Not him, not anymore.

He knows the pale girl is not far away. He can almost catch her scent or what he remembers of it, a fragrance like fresh Irish linen airing on a summer's day.

'Well, anyway,' Rita Zilich is saying, 'round about eleven o'clock, Stella and I went to the toilet. You have to go outside and round the house to get to it out the back. We saw Johnny McBride outside the house, he came out after us. I mean, I don't think he was actually following me, it just so happened that he came out at the same time. Johnny stood there and talked to us for quite a while, and then Stella went inside. Johnny and I stayed outside for about five minutes, and then Paddy came out from the room where they were having the party. He wanted to know what we were doing. We both said we were just talking. He didn't seem to believe us. Not that he said so in so many words, but you could sort of tell. Well, as a matter of fact, Johnny McBride had kissed me, but that didn't seem like Paddy's business.'

The judge, a man who looks very old indeed to Albert, pushes his spectacles further up the bridge of his nose. At times he looks as if he is being swallowed by his wig. He has a pale, pinched look around his mouth. His tongue hovers around his lower lip as Rita continues.

'Anyway, they began to fight. I was going to go inside but they'd started this fight.'

'Who struck the first blow?'

'I can't tell you that. I didn't really see. I didn't stay and watch the fight. I went inside and told the boys inside to go out and stop it, so they did. Paddy and Johnny didn't seem too friendly after that. One of them said something about continuing the fight the next day. I don't know who said that, honestly, I don't. I saw that Paddy had a cut over his eye. After that he went and lay down on the bed. There was a boy called Mack who'd been trying to break up the fight. Paddy called him over to the bed, and all of a sudden the fighting started up again. I don't know what that was about. Everybody joined in the fight and it spilled right outside onto the footpath. They were all mixed up in it. Johnny McBride was part of it. So then we tried to get Johnny into one of the boys' cars, which he did do, and I got in too and so did Stella, but Paddy said I was to get out. I got out. Paddy was pulling at my arm.'

'I see,' says Timms, 'so you were resisting. You were being dragged from the car by the accused?'

Buchanan bounces to his feet. 'Objection, your Honour. The witness is being led to this conclusion.'

'Objection sustained. Please continue, Miss Zilich. In your own words.'

'Well, it might have been Paddy, or perhaps it was one of his friends, because Paddy was in a pretty bad way at that stage. Perhaps it was his friend Pooch Quintal.'

'Why, what had happened to Paddy? To Albert Black?'

'Prior to me getting in the car, Johnny kicked Paddy in the stomach. That affected him pretty bad. While I was standing by the car, somebody, I think it was Paddy, had a bottle in his hand, and he went for Johnny's face with the bottle, so Johnny kicked him in the stomach and he doubled up.'

'So Black attacked Alan Jacques with a broken bottle?'

'Objection, your Honour.'

'Objection overruled. Miss Zilich?'

'Well. I'm not sure. It was in somebody's hand and I presumed it was Paddy's, because that's who Johnny kicked.'

'What happened next?'

'Everybody went home, and there was just Paddy and me. I told Paddy I wanted to go home, and I started picking up glasses and bottles and things, tidying up the room. I put them in a beer carton, and also I put a knife in the carton. Paddy lay down on one of the two beds in the room. He asked me to pass him a mirror. I got one down off the wall and gave it to him. It was a big mirror. He looked at his face in the mirror and then he threw it on the ground and it broke. I said to him, what's the matter Paddy? He said he was going to kill Johnny McBride. I told him not to be silly, if he did that he'd go to jail and get hanged, but he said it didn't matter. He said he'd probably be dead in a year anyway. So I said to him, you've just had too much to drink. He asked me to stay the night but I said no, then I asked him to lend me some money for a taxi and he walked me a little way along the street, down towards the Civic where I caught a taxi.'

'But he said he would kill Johnny McBride?'

'Yes, he said that he'd kill Johnny. I didn't see him again the next day.'

Chapter 8

Juvenile delinquency, the words spread like a stain through the Hutt Valley, like ink spreading on blotting paper. Elbe's was a milk bar in the centre of the Hutt. At the weekends, boys wearing leather jackets congregated on motorbikes, young girls flocking to meet them. And if the girls weren't up to tricks with the motorbike riders, they were with the boys from their school. Or so it was said. Bodgies and widgies, comic books and Mickey Spillane, suggestive American songs on the hit parades. The bodgies wore stovepipe trousers and thick-soled shoes, and hair greased with Brylcreem touching their collars. And coloured socks. Lime green or red or pink, colour manifesting itself after the drab years of the war. The widgies wore their cardigans back to front with the sleeves pushed up to their elbows, one of the sure signs a girl was going off the rails. Or, pedal-pushers, tight three-quarter-length pants, another sign of degradation. The Prime Minister, a craggy, thick-browed man called Sid Holland, had ordered a report be drawn up so that this delinquent behaviour could be stamped out. Some years before, he'd used strong-armed tactics during a waterfront dispute. A man not to be crossed. What he said went. He had a heavy head and prominent sparkling dentures, the people's man, going by the results on one election night after another. Sex, he made clear (although he preferred the term carnal knowledge), was not something polite people talked about, and young people had no right to get up to it. Young girls needed protecting from themselves. (It wasn't so bad for boys.) They would never get husbands if they got up to tricks beforehand. If a girl fell pregnant, she got sent away, out of sight, or hastily married in her parents' front room if the father could be captured. That is, and here voices lowered even further, if the girl knew for sure who the father was. Or if she was even old enough to get married. The moral scandal smouldered up and down the country, but it was the Hutt Valley, with its long, straight rows of plain state houses, beneath the bush-clad hills, beside the wide and swirling river, that was seen as the place where vice had been ignited.

Oswald Mazengarb was Holland's friend, a man with a long face not unlike the Prime Minister's, and they were frequent visitors at each other's houses. Sid Holland did magic tricks after dinner at the Mazengarb house, disappearing things beneath handkerchiefs, doing shadow play with his hands, it was reported. It was Mazengarb, his God-fearing Baptist friend, whom Holland had called upon to chair a committee of inquiry into the morals of teenagers all over the country. The report that Mazengarb wrote would be spilled into public view, posted to every household in the country, just before the next election. Meantime, the inquiry progressed with revelations that increasingly shocked the older generation and troubled anxious parents. All this was unfolding in the year that Peter and Paddy went to live at Rose's house.

Rose had known from the start that she wouldn't turn away the two young men who arrived on her doorstep. As far as she was concerned, they were there to stay. The children were entranced by them, the boys trying to imitate the way they talked, the little girl Evelyn staring at them with rapt attention, as if she had two fathers rather than none at all. The first few nights Peter and Paddy stayed, they bunked down, as she put it. She couldn't get her head around calling Paddy by the name Albert; it just wasn't a name that New Zealanders went in for much these days, one of those names reserved for monuments and parks. When she had sorted her head out about this change in the family's circumstances, she took down the striped brown and orange curtains in the enclosed sun porch and washed them on a sunny day, watching them blow on her clothesline like tiger lilies, suddenly feeling happier than she had since her husband died. At the back of her linen cupboard she found some unused pillow slips that she had had since her wedding day, waiting for goodness knows what, and it was silly to keep them when they could be put to good use now. Into the wash they went, then she pegged them on the line too, so that the sky seemed to be billowing with colour and extra clouds. Later, down at the second-hand mart, she found a pretty rug that scrubbed up well, and a basket-weave chair. She'd keep her eye out for a second one. When the two beds were made up side by side, the room looked homely and just right.

While she was picking through the goods at the mart, a woman she knew only slightly, a plump, short woman, one of the Naenae crowd who were regulars at the Cosmopolitan Club, or the Cossie, as they called it, came up to her. Rose knew about the Cossie, because she heard it mentioned when she went to parents' night at the school. The Club had a bar, and cheap meals, and pool tables. It was a place women could go with their husbands, not like the pub, but as she didn't have a husband it wasn't a place she could or even wanted to go. Her life was outside of all that. It was the way it had to be.

The woman, whose name was Sally, said, 'I see you've got some young men, Rose. That should keep you busy.'

Rose felt herself flush. 'They're kids,' she said. 'They need somewhere to stay for a bit.'

'Big kids. Teenagers more like it.'

Rose felt compelled to respond. 'One of them is,' she said. She wasn't the only widow out here in the Valley, but most of the others were war widows, which, strictly speaking, she was not because her husband had died later. For the children's sake she wanted to avoid a quarrel. It was on the tip of her tongue to tell Sally to mind her own business. Instead she said, knowing it sounded awkward, 'The older one's in his twenties.' Straight away, she saw that this was the wrong thing to have said.

Sally raised her eyebrows, a smile tweaking the corner of her mouth. 'Golly, that's corker, Rose. A real bloke.'

'They're from the United Kingdom,' Rose said. 'Two boys who came on the same boat, they're mates.'

'I didn't say a word, Rose,' Sally said. 'But you want to keep an eye on them. You know what they're saying about the kids out here, they're out of control.'

'Yours might be, I wouldn't know.'

As if she hadn't heard this, Sally circled the forefinger and thumb of her left hand, using the forefinger of her right to poke back and forwards through it. 'At the pictures, down on the river bank. There's that big report everyone's talking about.'

Rose averted her eyes. She had heard the rumours, of course. The shadow of Oswald Mazengarb hung heavily over the Valley. The world, according to him, might be all shook up with madness, but he was going to put it right, write a blueprint to set it straight.

'Third Form kids, they meet at Elbe's. They're up to things

all right,' Sally said. 'Petting and stuff. You know, below the waist and all that.'

Rose turned her back on the woman with her vulgar gestures. In her opinion, the committee was doing more harm than good, titillating people's imaginations, making them think more about sex than before. It wasn't that she had forgotten the pleasures of her past. There were days when she sat on the step of the house provided by the state in Naenae and looked out over the market gardens that stretched along the valley floor, lettuces, sharp green and crisp in their rows, tomatoes on the vine, strawberries in summer, and thought that life in all its abundance was passing her by. But now she had the children to consider, and it was unthinkable that they be touched by scandal. She knew of children who went to school with Ned and Harry who had new 'fathers' every weekend, men who emerged wearing next to nothing at their mother's bedroom door and told them to hop off now, their mother was busy. None of this was what she wanted to discuss with Sally with her bright, excited eyes.

The woman, sensing her distaste for the conversation, sniffed and said, 'Well, if it's not one thing it's another. The country's full of foreigners these days. Wogs everywhere. Spicks. Jews. Chinamen. All sorts, if you ask me. We were better off before the war.'

Rose knew this was directed at her boarders. As far as Sally was concerned, they were foreigners too.

The happiness she had experienced while choosing items for their room ebbed away as she steered Evelyn in her pushchair along the street that led to home. Surely the young men who had come to live with them wouldn't harm others? She thought back again to the evening of their arrival. Her own two boys, just a year between them, were kicking a ball in the back yard. Peter, the older man, had walked over to them, flicking it between them with an expert move.

'How did you do that?' Ned asked, and before they knew it, Peter was demonstrating stopovers and scissors and drags. Every evening he taught them new tricks that he said he had learned at school in Liverpool. Nothing special, he'd said, I never made the team, but I always wanted to.

As for Paddy, he had squatted in front of Evelyn, his face level with hers, and asked her name. When she replied, he'd said, gosh, if I had a sister I'd like her to be called that. It's a beautiful name.

But however Rose defended them, the young men were different. They might be from the UK, but their accents gave away their backgrounds. She had chosen to accept them as they were.

One afternoon, when Peter was playing soccer with Harry, Ned hung back.

'What's the matter, don't you want to play?' Peter called to him.

'Can you teach us some rugby passes?' Ned said.

Peter stilled the ball with his foot. 'Rugby. Not sure about that.'

'My mate says soccer's for sissies.'

'Rich sissies,' Peter said, his voice even. 'Rich boys play rugby where I come from.'

'Everybody plays rugby here,' Ned said. 'We've got the All Blacks. They can beat the Poms.'

'That's enough,' Rose called, tapping at the kitchen window.

For a day or two the games stalled, Harry wanting to play while Ned sulked. By the weekend it was game on again.

On some Saturday nights her boarders changed into jackets and good grey flannel trousers and caught the train to Wellington. Going dancing, they said, and sometimes they didn't come back until the next day. Paddy stayed out more than Peter. She didn't ask, although now and then they would refer to dance halls they'd been to. The Realm in a suburb called Hataitai was one of their favourites. She knew the ballroom, tucked away in a village near the sea. She and her husband danced there when they were courting. Just thinking about it stirred up a yearning she would rather forget, for now at least. She imagined the young men sleeping over in one of the little wooden houses on the hillsides, perhaps in a girl's bedroom, but she hoped it might be on the sofa. Perhaps she had made a terrible mistake. When she got home she would phone the mart and cancel the delivery of the chair she had found. And when the time was right she would calmly tell the boarders that their time was up; it was never her intention that they stay for long.

As she rounded the corner of the street, Rose saw a van stopped at her gate. A man was unloading timber, supervised by Peter and Paddy.

'Surprise,' they shouted.

The timber was for building a play shed for the children, an early Christmas present. They had marked out a patch of ground at the back of the house. The next weekend, and the one after that, were spent sawing and hammering. Peter had designed the building, there seemed no end to his skills, although there were mistakes and lengths of timber sawn too short, hammered thumbs, muffled curses. But the shed was built, high enough for the children to stand up in, and Rose too if she bent her head. Evelyn moved her dolls in, and Ned and Harry had shelves for their soccer gear. The season was over, but they carried on with the practices, honing their skills. There wasn't another kid in Naenae who could match them now that they had an in-house coach. The boarders went to the dances again, but for a time they didn't seem as keen, now they had a stake on her territory. It was as if her house was as near to home as they could get, although Rose noticed that Paddy rushed to the table by the door where she put the mail as soon as he came in each day. Almost every week there was a letter postmarked from Belfast, and his name, Mr Albert L. Black, written with a soft flowing hand and a small curl at the end of each word. She guessed the letters were from his mother.

When Christmas came around, she sewed herself a new dress, made from polished cotton with a floral design, with small cap sleeves and a fitting bodice and a skirt that whirled around her calves. The boarders said they wanted everyone to have a good Christmas, and insisted on each donating an extra pound on top of their board money so she could get food with trimmings — ham and roast chooks, freshly dug potatoes from the market-garden stall, and trifle and pavlova and everything. It was their second Christmas in New Zealand; the first had been spent at Clarrie's place. They knew what should be on the table.

'You can't do that,' she protested. 'You put all that money into the play shed.' They gave her the money anyway.

Just before Christmas a parcel arrived for Paddy. His mother had sent him a white shirt, and a woollen scarf each for him and Peter, and a linen tablecloth for Rose. She fingered the heavy cream fibre, patterned with pale blue flowers, with its perfect hemstitching. 'She shouldn't have. This parcel must have cost her the earth.'

'I told her about you,' Paddy said.

Rose was embarrassed; she had bought each of the boys a box of chocolates. The beautiful cloth was an heirloom, something to be passed on to Evelyn one day.

Paddy read out his Christmas letter. Kathleen Black had written: 'My dear son Albert, another Christmas passes and I will lay a place at table for you, our absent one. I hope you are doing well in your life. We miss you but wish you well. Daniel has grown another two inches this year, you would hardly recognise him. I will get his photograph taken soon so I can send it to you and you will see for yourself. I bless the people who are taking such good care of you. God bless you, son, be sure you live a good clean life until you return to us. Your father sends his love, as I do mine. Mother.'

Rose would never forget that Christmas Day. They all dressed up and, as if there hadn't been surprises enough, Peter and Paddy had one more, a music box that they had got a shop in the city to order from London. On top of it stood two miniature figures of a prince and princess who twirled in unison as the box tinkled 'The Blue Danube Waltz'. Evelyn stood clapping her hands with delight, and Paddy lifted her by her hands and stood her on his feet, waltzing her around the room in time to the music.

In the afternoon, when they were drowsy and sated with all the food, they went onto the front lawn and took it in turn to take each other's photographs with Peter's camera. There were no pictures of all six of them, because someone had to take turns behind the camera. When Rose looks at them in years to come, she finds herself missing in almost all of them, although she thinks Paddy took one with her in it to send to his mother. She will find one of Paddy cradling his favourite of her three cats in his arms, and Evelyn clinging to the leg of his trousers. His skin is deeply tanned from working in the sun, his shoulders broad and packed with muscle. The roses are in full bloom, the sun shining, and she will think that they looked a happy prosperous bunch, like one of those English families you saw in magazines. Or, like a summer afternoon at her parents' house in Thorndon, in a time before the Depression when her family still had money, and pretty dresses and music lessons were taken for granted. In the evening she sat at the piano, and at Peter's request she played 'White Christmas' and Paddy's voice soared, just as if Bing Crosby was in the room recalling the Christmases he once knew, and everyone sang along and clapped their hands.

'Actually,' Peter said, 'I don't care if I never see another white Christmas; I just like the song.'

Rose saw an expression flicker over Paddy's face. He doesn't agree, she thought, and it occurred to her, not for the first time, that he was pining for home. She called for quiet then as she began to play 'Silent Night', and this time she could have sworn a tear slipped down his cheek, but it seemed best not to let him see that she had noticed.

The next day, Boxing Day, Paddy came into the house, his hands cupped around a spiny brown bundle. It was a hedgehog. 'His leg's hurt,' he said, his voice agitated. 'I think one of the cats got it.'

'A cat wouldn't hurt it, it's too prickly.'

'It would, I've seen it at home. I saw a cat go after one. They can't run, you know, that's why they keep getting run over. We see them all over the place when we're out on the truck. Splat. We should be looking after the little blokes.'

'What do you think we should do about it?'

'Have you got a box I can put it in?'

Rose dug around in the laundry cupboard and came up with a shoebox that had held Ned's school shoes. 'How about that?'

Paddy found some newspaper and made a nest for the animal. That night he put the box in the room he shared with Peter. The arrangement was a failure. Peter looked irritable and sleepless in the morning. The hedgehog, it transpired, had snuffled and scratched against the walls of the shoebox most of the night.

'Hedgehogs have fleas,' he said. 'He who lies down with the dogs rises with the fleas.'

'Oh shut up your face, it's just a little fella,' Paddy said. He volunteered to sleep in the play shed with it the next night.

'You can't do that,' Rose said.

Paddy seemed childlike in his devotion to the creature and wilful in his determination to protect it. The matter was resolved in the evening. It was clear the hedgehog had died. At first Paddy insisted that it had just curled up as if hibernating, and refused to accept the death. After a while he retreated to the play shed, still holding onto the box with the dead animal inside. The children could see it would be a bad idea to follow him. Eventually, Rose went out to him, holding a mug of tea. She found him sitting inside, his expression morose, his knees drawn up under his chin. He looked big, filling up half the shed; she reminded herself that he was only nineteen.

'Paddy,' she said, 'what's bothering you?'

He turned his face away from her. 'The bloody hedgehog died, that's all.'

'You missing home?' When he didn't reply, she said, 'Why don't you phone your mother and talk to her. I'd pay for it. I didn't give you a proper Christmas present.'

He rested his eyes on her, puzzled, as if she couldn't see a thing. 'My mam doesn't have a phone,' he said. 'My folks, they don't own much, you know.'

So she saw how it was, her in her little state house, giving music lessons to make money stretch and taking in boarders — because, yes, the money they brought in was helping, no doubt of it — seemed rich in comparison to where he'd come from. And yet, the mother had given so generously at Christmas. She saw how so much was invested in the faraway son, what his absence was costing her.

The school holidays passed, the weather flickering in and out of summer, the heat interrupted by storms, Wellington's wild windy weather sweeping up through the Valley, making the house shudder and creak at night, but it was always short-lived and for a while the heat abated. The linesmen returned to their jobs, busier than ever after the holiday break and the high winds that had brought lines down. These school holidays had that endless quality that came around every year in late January. The boys got tired of eeling and swimming, and started hanging around the house. In the market garden the corn had grown *as high as an elephant's eye*, just like the song.

Only, Paddy had stopped singing. Three weekends in a row he went off to Wellington by himself, or so he said. Peter, the more homely-looking of the two, and more of a homebody in himself, looked anxious. He and Rose listened to the request sessions on the radio after the children had gone to bed, or sometimes a talk on the concert programme. In October he and Paddy would be free to take up jobs of their choice, their indenture to the government over. He confided that he had visited the hospital laboratory to see what sort of training he needed to become a technician. Medicine had always interested him. He wasn't ready to settle down and marry, not just yet. When the time was right he'd find a *decent* girl. The emphasis was his. If could stay here while he got his career sorted out, it would make a difference to his future. Neither of them mentioned Paddy in these conversations. The last time he had come home, late on a Sunday, he was wearing stovepipe trousers, his hair slicked back from his forehead.

At the grocer's shop one afternoon, Rose ran into Sally. 'See your lad's spending a bit of time at Elbe's,' she said. 'Turning into quite a ladies' man, I hear.'

'They sell very good ice-cream sundaes at Elbe's, I've heard,' Rose said, as if it was of no consequence. But she knew straight away that Paddy hadn't been telling her where he went. He was changing before their eyes and she didn't know what to do about it.

As she walked up her path, she heard shouting inside the house. Her pace quickened.

Ned was dancing around in front of Paddy, holding a letter in the air. 'Paddy's got a girlfriend, Paddy's got a girlfriend,' he chanted.

Paddy leapt on the boy. 'Give it here. I'll fucken do you.' His hand was raised in a fist. Rose stood transfixed by what was unfolding before her. She moved forward to stop him as Paddy's fist descended, and then he stopped himself, perhaps because he sensed her there, or maybe he understood just in time that it was something he couldn't do.

'Ned,' she said. 'Stop it. Give Paddy his letter at once.'

'Paddy's got a girlfriend,' he said, his face a knot of defiance.

She recognised the writing on the envelope. 'If he does it's none of your business,' she said. 'As it happens the letter's from his mother, which is not your business either. Go to your room. Now.'

Rose turned to Paddy. The possibility of violence was not something she had calculated inside the four walls of her home when she took the young men in; she felt ashamed. 'Would you have hit him?' she asked her boarder.

He stood, smoothing the envelope against his work overalls. 'I don't know.'

'You need to think about it.'

'I'm thinking of leaving,' he said.

'You don't have to. We can sort this out. I'll speak to Ned. You just need to remember that he's a little kid and not lose your temper.'

He shook his head. 'I couldn't live in a better place.'

'Then what? Peter doesn't want to leave. Is it a girl? Have you met someone?'

He gave a half-grin. 'I've met a few of those,' he said. 'I reckon I just don't fit in here. In New Zealand, I mean. It's not like home.'

So there it was again. Home. Belfast. 'Of course it's not. But you're like another son to me.'

Paddy shook his head, his smile apologetic now. 'And you're young enough to be my girlfriend.'

'That's enough,' she said, more sharply than intended. 'I won't have that sort of talk.'

'I want to go to Auckland.' He leaned his elbow against the

mantelpiece, fingering the casing on the old black clock, with its gold gilt numbers and hands, which had once belonged to her father. It still chimed on the hour. 'I reckon I could earn more money there. You see, I've been looking into going home. Do you know, I was a ten-quid Pom but it costs twelve times that amount of money to get back? One hundred and twenty pounds. I can't save that much on P & T wages.'

She shook her head. 'I didn't know. It's a lot. Perhaps if you had a savings plan, a pound a week.' Although as she said this she knew it was an absurdly large amount of money for him to save. For a moment she considered offering to let him off some of his board money, but she had her children to think of, and although the rent made a difference, having lodgers cost money too. They had to be fed, and besides, she ironed their shirts, and changed their sheets once a week, pretending not to see semen stains on them, and kept the house warm.

'A quid a week. Rose,' he was saying, 'that would take two and a half years. I can't wait that long. It's like New Zealand is a prison. I've been talking to some jokers. They reckon there's good casual labouring jobs up in Auckland, good pay.'

'But you can't go until October. Your time doesn't finish till then.'

'I can't hold my horses until then. I *need* to go home. I don't have any choice, Rose, don't you get that? Please say you get it, because it does my head in.' His hands were clenching and unclenching.

In the morning he was gone. An envelope with a week's board inside sat on her mantelpiece. Peter looked drawn and sad. After a week or more had passed she received a letter with a forwarding address for mail C/- Mr P. Donovan, 105 Wellesley Street, Auckland. For when the immigration authorities came looking for him.

94

Chapter 9

At the Station Hotel, the jury gather for their second night. Ken McKenzie is becoming accustomed to this comfortable existence. All the same, he is pleased to be free of the close proximity of his fellow jurors. They have sat all day, shoulders and thighs pressing against each other, watching the parade of the judiciary, as far removed from his own life as they are from those of the accused and the witnesses. The sky outside is a tender addled blue, so that he senses the wind has dropped. He wants to go out in the fresh air and walk to the wharves and watch the ferries and hear the gulls cry. Instead, they must stay in this fancy Art Nouveau palace, with its arched ceilings and decorated bar, pontificating about the evidence they have heard during the day. He thinks it hasn't gone well for Albert Black.

As he stands, beer in hand, Jack Cuttance edges over to him. 'What do you reckon about the girl's evidence?'

'I don't know what to make of it,' Ken says slowly. 'My old man used to say there are two sides to every story.'

'Hot little number. I reckon her undercut's dripping.' Jack gives his butcher's laugh at his own joke. Ken can hear him in his shop when he is exchanging gossip with customers he knows well, men picking up orders for their wives, young men buying chops and sausages for barbecues on the beach.

'She said she didn't sleep with him, not all the way.' Ken is suddenly defensive towards the girl, even though he had thought her too glib, too ready in her evidence. The story that came out had tripped off her tongue too easily for his liking. 'I reckon she set her cap at young Albert and then changed her mind when she got a better offer.'

'If you call Johnny McBride a better offer. I saw his picture. He looked as if he was missing a couple of teeth.'

It had been in the papers at the time of the death, the story of it taking three days to verify the identity of the man killed at Ye Olde Barn cafe, a seaman going by the name of Johnny McBride. That, as it turned out, was the name of a character in a novel called *The Long Wait* by Mickey Spillane. Instead, he was revealed as Alan Jacques. When he died he'd been wearing a bright yellow and red pullover under a sports jacket, narrow trousers and emerald-green socks. A farmer had come from the south to identify him. Not much more than a boy, a child migrant who had been in the country just two years, shipped out to New Zealand with two younger sisters: old to be sent on the scheme, and old enough to be sent on his military training the day he turned eighteen. In the year before he was conscripted, he had worked on the farmer's land. A bitter little story, Ken thinks. 'Sounds like he lived in fantasy land,' he says, for want of anything else.

'So who really did start the fight?' Cuttance wonders.

Smooth James Taylor sidles over, gin and tonic in hand. 'Now lads, what'll you be having?'

'I'm fine, sir. Thank you,' Ken says.

'Pretty cut and dried, wouldn't you say? That girl's a smart youngster. Mind you, if she were my girl I'd give her a good spanking, hopping out of the window like that.'

Ken looks out of the hotel window, choosing his words. 'Well, sir, if she lied to her mother, she could lie to the judge.'

Taylor looks him up and down. 'I see. Bush lawyer are you, Mr McKenzie?' He holds out his hand for Jack Cuttance's glass.

Night has closed in around Mount Eden prison. From the outside it is lit in Gothic relief by searchlights fanning the perimeter. Horace Haywood, the superintendent, sits in his office, whisky bottle at his elbow. He pushes it towards Des Ball.

'You reckon it went badly for Black today?'

Des fills his tumbler. This is how these nights begin, Horace in his cups, looking for solace and company. The hanging of Eric Allwood has affected him, the way all the hangings do. Mount Eden is the only prison in the country where people are hanged these days, strung up on gallows in a corner of the yard, dropped off a makeshift scaffolding into oblivion. Des was present at Allwood's death, a warder considered to cope well with these occasions. The hangings are not condoned by all. The managers in the justice system are against them. They have been urging prison reform. Rehabilitate, they are saying, send men out better than they came in. But Sid Holland's government has said let them hang. His strong-armed Minister of Justice, the silver-haired Jack Marshall, has supported him all the way.

'It wasn't what I expected when I took this job,' Haywood says. It's not the first time he has said this to Des. His rise through the ranks of the prison system has been exceptional. For seventeen years he managed a prison quarry in the south. All of a sudden he was plucked from obscurity and given promotion, and as soon as one promotion was conferred another one followed. Now here he was, superintendent of the country's best-known prison. And barely had his new position registered than the death penalty, dormant for years, was reintroduced.

It is part of his work to prepare the condemned men for the gallows. To him falls the task of transferring the prisoner from his cell to a holding one in the east wing basement. It is he who pinions the prisoner's arms and he who fits the hood on arrival at the scaffold gate. It is he, Horace Haywood, who must position the noose tightly around the neck of the condemned; he who must signal to the hangman when it is time for the lever to be released. None of this rests easily with him. Once he had believed in God. For all those years when he had worked close to prisoners in the quarry he had believed — although perhaps he wouldn't have put it in so many words (but his wife may well have done) — that the light of God shone in every man, that nobody was beyond redemption. Now he is not sure that God is all that interested in what happens to men in prison.

'Doesn't it bother you?' he asks again of Des. 'The hangings. Doesn't it turn your stomach?'

Each time, Des says no, it is the way of the law, something that has to be done.

'I don't want to see another one die,' Haywood says. 'It's politics, you know. It's the government that wants them put to death.'

Des hesitates. 'The Prime Minister believes in taking a strong line.'

'The Prime Minister, oh yes. Him and Mazengarb and slippery Jack, great mates, the lot of them. Gentleman Jack, they call Marshall. Some gentleman. Major John Marshall — you'd have thought he'd seen enough killing on the battlefields to be sick of it. But no, he wants more. I suppose that's why Sid Holland made him the Attorney-General.'

'I don't know what to think, sir. I just do my job.'

'Your job? Yes, I suppose so. You do a good job, Ball. I like young Black. Decent manners, a quiet bloke, he doesn't give us any trouble. I've had some long talks with him.'

This is another thing about Haywood: he is a man who will sit in the cell with a man. It is unusual, but then Haywood is. So is his wife Ettie. An energetic prancing woman, some might call flighty, the way she dances about like a flitting bird. She organises a band within the prison and brings small gifts to the men, puts her arms around them when they cry. Des thinks they are the children she and Horace never had, and it bothers him. They are too close to the men. He has been in the service for twenty years himself; it doesn't occur to him to like a criminal. At least it's something he hasn't thought about. He believes he likes Horace Haywood nonetheless. In the beginning it had suited him that he could provide consolation for this odd, soft-hearted man. It gave him a role in a prison that put him above other guards. But time has passed, and he finds himself drawn to Haywood, sensing something indefinable about his nature that he might draw upon for himself, but it is always just out of reach. At least they can drink together. It's against the rules, but a bottle of whisky is permissible in the jail when there is a hanging — an excuse that Haywood stretches.

'Paddy's got a bit of lip when it suits him,' Des says. 'A bit of a temper.'

'He doesn't show it to me. He talks of his mother and little brother. Not so much of his father. I gather he was away at the war. Paddy's been through the Blitz. He remembers it.'

'It doesn't give him a licence to kill.'

'And what about us? Eh?' Horace drums his fingers on the desk. 'What of the priest and all the people who have to witness it? I still see Freddie Foster, fighting for his life on the scaffold.'

Foster had killed someone in a milk bar, a girl he was in love with whom he'd intended to frighten with a gun, only it went off. Or that's what he said, but the jury didn't believe him. There had been uproar over that one, pleas for clemency, an unholy row in the newspapers, and his mother coming all the way out from England to plead for his life with Jack Marshall. Not that it made a blind bit of difference. Haywood runs his hand over his head and shudders. When Foster was led up the gallows he went berserk. The hangman poked his fingers in his eyes to keep him still. 'Allwood made it too easy for us. He died brave.'

'He knew he was in for it, sir. He was a murderer.'

'Well, I can't say I cared for the man. He did a lot of talk about how he was going to create trouble, but in the end he didn't. I don't know, it's almost easier when there's a bit of a fuss. It felt like leading a lamb to slaughter. Have you ever watched sheep being led to the kill on the freezing works? No? There is a Judas sheep that leads the way. It's a big pet wether that trots ahead and the other sheep blindly follow to the place where the trapdoor opens and they fall through it to the killing floor. And then the Judas sheep trots away to the side of the pen where it gets a little treat.' He bangs his glass down. 'You know that Black has been seeing the priest?'

'Of course.'

'You know why?'

'He spreads his charms, that lad.'

'Doesn't it tell you that he's a man of conscience? He wants to do right by the girl.'

'He hasn't talked to me about a girl. Black's life has been full of girls. You have only to look on the witness stand.'

'This one is different. I can tell.'

'Perhaps it's time to turn in,' Des says. Drink is making Haywood maudlin. Sooner or later Des must take himself home and face poor battered Marge. The thought of Marge fills him with uncontrollable rage, a desire to punish her for frailty and her illness, and her persistent uncomplaining loyalty. Somehow he must get in his car and weave his way through the back streets of Auckland and sleep off nightmares. At least the children will be in bed. He doesn't see his children often. That's Marge, keeping them out of his way. Well, who can blame her? But he does.

Haywood turns a bleary face in his direction, filling his glass to the brim. 'You go off. Give our love to Marge. Very fine woman. You and me both, wonderful wives.'

'Sir,' Des says, 'Miss Zilich will be cross-examined tomorrow. Perhaps her story won't hold.'

Haywood's face lights up momentarily. 'Hope then?'

'You should go home, sir.'

Haywood raises his glass. 'Sleep here, I think.' His head slides to one side.

A boarding house of sorts, or so it was described. Paddy arrived in Auckland after an overnight train journey through the central heart of the country late in January. He had slept little. The train stopped often at sidings and small towns lit by dim lanterns over station platforms, staying a few minutes, then seemingly picking itself up with a long mournful blast of its whistle, hurtling further on into the night. Twice there were stops long enough for the passengers to alight and join a crush of people at a counter where they bought food. He remembers buying a pie and a cup of tea in a thick white cup at one stop, a rock cake and more tea somewhere else. He sat upright in a second-class seat, and in the shadowy darkness of summer he glimpsed canyons of bush and, it seemed to him, desolation. His heart felt as if it would explode with grief. He had left behind the only people in the country who cared about him, the woman who had looked after him as if she were his mother, his friend who had emigrated with him, children who had welcomed his presence, the wee cutie who had danced on his feet.

Peter had been awake when he left. He was lying under the covers of the bed, smoking a cigarette. Paddy didn't care for the way Peter smoked in bed, it made his head fuzzy and his eyes ache, but sharing a room was a small price to pay for living in that house.

'Paddy, my old mucker, don't go,' Peter said, as Paddy stuffed his duds into his suitcase.

'I have to, mate. I've got to get home to Ireland. It's all right for you.' He wasn't sure why he said this, but as he sat on the train bearing him away from his life in Naenae, he thought it was because he got letters from home and Peter didn't. Putting together the pieces of Peter's life, it seemed he had been without parents for a long time, although Peter never said what had happened to them. There were places he couldn't go in his friend's life. At some point he had had education. He had a future mapped out, and the difference between them was that Peter's would happen in New Zealand. He would get a good job and marry and have children. They would speak with a different accent from their father's. They would grow up to give him grandchildren who might have only the vaguest idea of where Liverpool was, and Peter would be content with that. Paddy didn't see his life like that at all. It belonged in the crowded streets of Belfast with the Black Mountain in the distance and the River Lagan streaming between its banks, and he and his family crossing Boyne Bridge on the day of the Orange Parade. Perhaps he would get a job at the shipbuilding yards now that he was nineteen, going on twenty. *Titanic* was built in those shipyards, the biggest, grandest ship in the world. Only it had sunk on its maiden voyage. This was how his life felt right now: a grand dream that had no substance at all, a journey into a lost place.

The tip of Peter's cigarette had glowed as Paddy turned out the light and walked out. He imagined the child Evelyn getting up in the morning, looking for him at breakfast and, later in the day, waiting for him to be dropped off at the gate by the P & T truck, the dawning realisation that he wouldn't be back. Not ever, although Evelyn wasn't to know he planned to leave the country as soon as he could.

The long day stretched ahead of him with nothing to do except lug his suitcase around, or sit on a park bench watching pigeons fight over food scraps. In the afternoon he went to the Waterloo Hotel, across the road from the railway station, only to be told by the barman that they didn't serve minors and to take himself off. An unseasonal wind had risen, or perhaps that was the way it always was in Wellington, summer and winter, wind rising on street corners and whirling fish and chip papers around your legs. He would be pleased to be gone. There was nothing for it but to sit the day out at the cavernous railway station. In the late afternoon he glimpsed the Hutt Valley unit preparing to leave. For a moment he considered jumping on it and going back to Naenae; it took all his resolve to remain where he was. He dozed, woke in starts, until it was seven thirty and the Northern Express was snorting and heaving smoke at platform eight, and he was borne away at last.

Towards morning, as the train slid through Auckland's suburbs, a man older than him woke after what appeared to be a good night's sleep, shook his watch and leaned over to ask Paddy for the time. They got talking after that. The man was from Auckland, a school teacher who had spent the summer in Wellington and was now going back for the beginning of the school year.

'No good asking you where to find work,' Paddy said.

'Oh, there's always something going. Meat works, digging ditches, depends on how tough you are.' The new friend had worked over long holidays when he was a student; he knew what was on offer.

'I've got to find somewhere to stay first.'

'Yeah, I can fix you up with that. My aunty's got a boarding house.' He wrote down an address and a telephone number on a small pad he'd pulled from his pocket. 'Give her a bell when you get to the station.'

He'd taken a taxi from the station, not knowing how far he would have to lug his suitcase. The early-morning air felt soft and warmer than in the south. The car passed up a long main street that the driver told him was Queen Street. There were shops and cafes, not open yet for business but full of possibility. Before the car turned left, he saw an avenue flanked by grand old oak trees. They travelled past a department store with mannequins stylishly attired in the windows, a small hotel called the Albion, a splendid church that looked like ones back in Belfast, climbed a ridge, and there, within walking distance of the main street, the house he was looking for. It was a rambling place, steps leading up to a rickety veranda that ran along the front and both sides of the house.

Paddy guessed the teacher had been having him on about the landlady being his aunt. The woman, who introduced herself as Gladys Wallace, Mrs Gladys Wallace if he didn't mind, claimed never to have heard of him. She was a thin older woman with blonde hair, and even this early in the morning she wore a bright slash of lipstick.

'You could be just the person I'm looking for,' she said. 'Have a look around.'

Mystified, he followed her into the house, which seemed oddly empty for a boarding establishment. The front room, above the street, was furnished with a plain table and an upright chair, and three easy chairs with curved wooden arms, the seats upholstered a long time ago with brick-red moquette. This room opened to a cubicle that held two single beds. A radio stood on the shelf above. Four more bedrooms flanked a passageway with blue flocked wallpaper, the doors heavily varnished. One of the rooms was locked. Albert took it to be Gladys's. The lavatory was outside, like at home, approached through a side door along one of the verandas, back down more steps and along a path.

'So what do you think?'

'Very nice,' he said.

'Good. You look respectable. I need a caretaker. I have to leave here, you see, for the time being. I've got a friend. He's asked me to go and stay across the harbour and help look after his sick old mum for a while.' She winked at Paddy then. 'That's why there's nobody here, I let them all go, a bunch of scruffs, not someone I could leave in charge. I'd rather have somebody in the house, mind you, than leave it standing empty. I'd knock a quid off your rent if you kept an eye on the place for a bit. What do you say, lad?'

The deal sounded like perfection. A whole house to himself. His spirits rose. Gladys would return from time to time, just to make sure all was well. 'No boarders, mind you,' she said. 'The neighbours will be keeping an eye out for me, so no funny tricks. The last person I left in charge thought they could make a bit extra on the side. I'll know if you get up to any malarkey. You know what I mean? Of course you do, you're an Irish boy, aren't you?' Paddy wondered if the teacher on the night train from Wellington had been her last caretaker.

When the formalities were over, and the landlady had gone (for she wanted to be off that day), Paddy lay down on one of the beds off the front room without pulling up the covers. He turned on the radio, tuning in to 1ZB, the music station, listening for a while until he fell asleep. It was evening when he woke. Although it was summer he was cold now. He walked through the empty house, marvelling that all of this, for the moment, was his kingdom. He couldn't think what his mother would have made of it.

In the narrow kitchen with its wooden bench he found a pantry but no sign of food. He locked the door of his newfound home, pocketed the key and set off to find one of the cafes he had seen in the morning. He might have turned left into Queen Street, but further up, on his right, he saw a crowd of young people moving purposefully, as if they knew where they were going, and he followed them. Shortly, he entered Ye Olde Barn cafe for the first time. The place was jammed full, young people dressed to kill, girls in their matador pants, Teddy boys wearing long, draped jackets, Edwardian and groomed, guys with bodgie-length hair which Paddy, too, had started to grow, a wave drooping over his forehead. He ordered steak and chips with two eggs sunny side up. A girl winked at him.

Johnny McBride was not there that night. He was still to come.

Chapter 10

There is a queue waiting for admission to the court in the morning. An air of excitement rustles through the crowd. The horns of passing cars are tooted, as if the drivers want to add to the carnival atmosphere. Middle-aged women in dark coats over twin-sets and pearls set off with white gloves and sensible hats, men holding onto their trilbies against the breeze: all huddle together, in wait for the doors to open. Overhead, the oak trees cast their dappled green spring light. Young people swarm, wearing their Technicolor clothes.

Rita Zilich, ushered in by a side door, is still dressed in her fitting black suit when she resumes her place on the witness stand. Oliver Buchanan appears relaxed, even warm, as he begins his cross-examination, a small smile hovering at the corner of his mouth as if he and Rita were about to have an intimate conversation that excludes the rest of the court. He balances his foot in a casual gesture on the rail of the stand. He begins by leading Rita through the same events that the prosecutor took her through the previous day. On the subject of her leaving home on the night of the party, he lingers for a time.

'So could you just tell us again, Miss Zilich, about your decision to go to this gathering. You'd been invited by my client, and his invitation was so irresistible that you decided to go, even though you knew your parents would disapprove? You must have found him very attractive.'

'He was just a casual acquaintance, he wasn't a special friend. There's a crowd that goes to the Olde Barn cafe. That same crowd has parties together. They drink a bit of liquor when they get together. When Paddy invited me to the party it was just like I was one of the crowd. My girlfriend Stella was going.'

'All the same, you went home, your parents saw you, and they went to bed believing that that was what you had done too?'

'Yes.'

'You left through the window?'

'Yes.'

'So, Miss Zilich, as I understand it, you arrived at the party and you and your girlfriend went outside to the lavatory somewhere near midnight. And there, Johnny McBride came upon the two of you. That right? You're nodding, we can agree about this. So what happened next?'

'Well, first he kissed Stella. Then she went inside, and Johnny kissed me.'

'So you sent Stella inside?'

'She's quite young. Just fifteen. I didn't think it was appropriate.'

'Oh, I see. But you, at the ripe old age of sixteen, thought it was all right to kiss this man. Perhaps you decided that this was your mark for the night, not Paddy?'

'It wasn't like that.'

'So what happened next?'

'Well, Paddy came out and asked us what we were doing. I was standing against the wall and Johnny was standing beside me — well, actually he was facing me. We said we were just talking. Paddy said we'd better go inside, meaning both of us.'

'Didn't he say "The neighbours will be complaining about the noise and will report it to my landlady"?'

'He never mentioned his landlady.'

'So did you do as he asked, or did you stay there with Paddy and Johnny?'

'I stood there a couple of minutes, then I walked away to the back steps. I stopped there. Paddy and Johnny had started fighting, I could hear them. I looked back. They were fighting at the end of the path by the fence.'

Buchanan pauses for a moment, his hand on his chin. Rita's expression is uncertain.

'Hmm. I take it that because you were walking away you never saw who struck the first blow?'

'That's right,' Rita says. 'I never saw who started it. I went to the front room and got all the boys to come out and stop the fight. When it was broken up, somebody suggested Paddy and Johnny shake hands. I don't know whether Paddy was willing.'

'And what about Johnny?'

'Johnny wanted to continue the fighting. He said to Paddy, "I'll come back tomorrow and finish this fight." They stopped then. Then we all went back into the front room and the party continued. At that stage Paddy went and lay on the bed; it's off to the side of the front room.'

'So he didn't seem very well?'

'I'd say he wasn't too happy. Well, he had got hit in the eye. It was all red and swollen.'

'I see. He'd taken a real hiding then?'

'I guess so.'

'You guess so. I want you to think hard and try not to guess. Do you remember what you or the others had used that evening to open bottles of beer with?'

'No.'

'Did you see some of the boys using a knife with a bottle-opener on it?'

'I didn't notice what they opened the bottles with. I only had one glass of beer that evening. But then some more fighting broke out and Paddy got up and he was in the fighting too. Johnny was standing by the fireplace, talking to some of the girls. I didn't see him holding a bottle of beer. There were bottles of beer all over the place, I suppose there were some near Johnny, but if you're asking me, I didn't see Johnny McBride throw a bottle of beer across the room towards Paddy. It was a long evening, Mr Buchanan.' The girl's lip trembles. 'I'm tired,' she says, 'just tired of all this.'

'It's a compelling narrative, Miss Zilich. A carefully crafted one, if I may say so.'

'Are you calling me a liar?'

'I'm not calling you anything, Miss Zilich, except your name. But we still have some ground to cover.' Buchanan's smile leaves his face as he calls for a recess. The witness needs some time to compose herself, he suggests to the judge.

In the holding cell, Buchanan talks to Paddy. He wants him to focus his recall. He believes he has the witness on the run. They have gone over Paddy's story several times, but Buchanan needs to be sure. He could have kept going with the girl and she would have cracked and gained the jury's sympathy. He doesn't want to be seen as a bully. His next line of questioning is vital. 'Think very carefully about Johnny McBride,' he says, 'and what happened next. I need to keep ahead of this young lady.'

Paddy shakes his head. He has told the story so often there are times he no longer knows for certain what happened himself. He is often confused these days. Buchanan looks frustrated.

'I'm doing my best,' Paddy says.

After the recess Oliver Buchanan leans forward, raking the witness's face with a long, quizzical expression. 'Miss Zilich,' he begins, 'who asked you to the party on the night of the twenty-fifth of July?'

'I'm not sure. Well, perhaps it was Ray Hastie.'

'Oh, not Paddy now? I see, so it was Mr Hastie. Well, let's just go back to the party when everyone was fighting. It started to break up, is that correct? I take it that nod means yes. Was Johnny McBride mixed up in the fighting then?'

Rita stretches her hands with their scarlet nails in front of her in a gesture of anxiety. 'Yes, I think so.'

'And you went outside to the front of the house where people were starting to leave? You stood outside and watched this fighting going on? Is that correct?'

'Yes.'

'Did you see Johnny McBride kick Paddy in the stomach?'

'Yes.'

'And in amongst this someone had a bottle in their hand. In your statement, you said you assumed it were Paddy.'

'Yes.'

'But you weren't sure that it was Paddy who had a bottle in his hand? You assumed it.'

'Somebody did.'

'You think it was Paddy because Johnny had kicked him?'

'Yes.'

'But Johnny may have kicked Paddy for some entirely different reason, couldn't he?'

The girl touches the tip of her tongue, like someone removing a fleck of tobacco from their mouth. 'He could have.'

Buchanan casts eyes towards the ceiling. 'Miss Zilich, what did Paddy do when he got a kick in the stomach?'

'He doubled up. He just bent over. Mack Thompson was there with his car, and I was going to get in it. When I got in the car, Paddy was leaning by the gate. Johnny and my girlfriend Stella got in the car. So when I got in the car, Paddy straightened up and came over and asked me to get out. I got out.'

'Of your own free will?'

'Not exactly. Paddy and Pooch Quintal came and pulled me out. Actually, I wanted to go home.'

'But you're telling me that Paddy was doubled up against the gate. He can't have been doubled up from a kick in the testicles and pulling you out of the car at the same time.'

'I didn't know he's got kicked in the goolies, not then. Well, perhaps it was Pooch, I'm not sure.'

'Did you ask anyone to help you? . . . Miss Zilich?' Buchanan's dark eyebrows brood above his eyes.

'Well — no.'

'Isn't what really happened, that Pooch Quintal took your hand and helped you out, and you followed him back inside the house?'

'What I'm trying to tell you is that I wasn't very willing.'

'But still you went inside, without resisting or asking anyone to help you. Anyone left inside?'

'Some of my girlfriends were there picking up their coats.'

'And still you didn't decide to go off home with any of them. The Quintal boys left then, is that right?'

'Yes.'

'And Paddy asked you to stay with him and you agreed?'

'He asked me to stay the night. I said I wanted to go home, but then he started looking around for the first-aid kit. After that he asked me to give him a mirror. He looked at himself and he threw the mirror on the floor and it broke.'

'Did he appear to you to be a bit drunk at the time?'

'No, not really, he didn't act as if he was drunk. His shirt and trousers had been ripped in the fight. He seemed pretty sick, and he was upset. Pretty upset with Johnny McBride. He said he'd kill Johnny.'

'Did you think he was just joking?'

'I told him he was. Anyway, I said to Paddy that if he killed Johnny he'd only get hung and it wouldn't be worthwhile.'

'So then Paddy lay on the bed and asked you again if you would stay the night. Yes? And did you not say, "I can't stay the whole night"?'

'Well, yes. I lay on the bed beside him. Eventually I said I wanted to go home and he lent me some money. Then he walked me part of the way to the taxi stand at the Civic and left me to go home. I don't know what time that was.'

'Miss Zilich, between the time that you lay on the bed and you decided to go home, can you tell us what happened?'

'There wasn't any hanky panky, if that's what you mean. I mean, there was no intercourse. He did try it. But after a bit he said he wasn't all that horny.'

Buchanan lets out a sigh. He digs under his gown and takes his handkerchief from his breast pocket, wiping his face as if he wished to rub something away, something he didn't want to see. 'You may stand down now, Miss Zilich. I have no further questions.'

As he listens to her from the dock, Paddy sees the story in slow motion, as if it were a film played frame by frame. From Belfast to Naenae to Auckland. From his mother and father and little Danny boy to Rose and Peter and the children to a boarding house where people came and went, even though they weren't supposed to. When it came down to it, he couldn't say no to the men he met at Ye Olde Barn cafe. There were men off the ships with nowhere to go when they were in port; drifters like himself, or as he had become; lads who had run away from homes somewhere in the provinces. They got over it and went home after a day or two when they ran out of money or their parents tracked them down.

Johnny McBride had stayed at the house in Wellesley Street.

In these unfolding frames, Paddy sees again his first meeting with Johnny at the cafe, when the newcomer tries to cut in on a girl he was seeing then. Her name was Raewyn. He wasn't sure why he and Raewyn were going steady. She said she would let him go all the way when they were engaged but not before. One weekend she took him home to meet her parents, the father careworn and older than he expected, the mother a bustling woman who worked mornings at Smith & Caughey's, the department store on the corner where his street joins up with Queen Street. The dinner was good, roast beef with all the trimmings and steamed pudding to follow; the house was comfortable, as if the family had money. 'You'll look after our Raewyn, won't you?' the mother said, as if much had been decided that wasn't at all.

Still, there was a certain allure in a good girl. Raewyn was small and fair with a high laugh; she worked for the transport department, a government job, filing forms, so he deemed her clever, a bit of a trophy. In a letter to his mother, he wrote: 'Mother, I'm going out with a nice girl, her family are very welcoming to me, her name is Raewyn. She would like us to get engaged but I'm not ready for that, being only nineteen and all. I don't plan to marry until I'm at least twenty-five with a bit of money in the bank.' It was baloney, pure and simple, but he understood what Raewyn was about as far as he was concerned, a girl he could introduce to his mother if he had to, and also a girl who was there to get him out of scrapes when he got in too deep with some other girl, an excuse not to see them again. For there were other girls, a whole gala of girls like petals falling from flowers, and some of them he made love to in the creaking old house where he stayed. If Raewyn knew, she didn't let on. He thought perhaps she didn't (he wouldn't know, standing here in the dock, because Raewyn has been in the past for some time). There were times when he felt sad for her, a try-hard girl.

It hadn't been difficult to find friends at Ye Olde Barn cafe. There was no *where did you come from?* and *who are you?* or any of that routine, although Raewyn's parents wanted to know all of that. There was just a crowd of people who took it for granted you were one of them. It wasn't like Elbe's in the Hutt. He had stood at the door of Elbe's and looked in one night, and a girl had come out and offered herself to him. He thought she was about thirteen, and he had turned and walked away in disgust. He wasn't going to get hooked up with carnies. Once Rose had asked him if he went to Elbe's and he'd said no, and she'd looked at him disbelieving. It hurt, that she would think that. Instead he had caught the train into Wellington and wandered through the empty streets. He had come to a brothel in Vivian Street, its dull red light spilling across the windswept street. It was a moment of deep loneliness. When he thinks back, he sees it as one of the moments that had turned him towards Auckland. Finding a girl, going to a dance, it was all too complicated when he lived in the Hutt.

Music spilled through Ye Olde Barn cafe and out over the street. Often people jived beside a cubicle, lost in a world of their own. The girls were older here, more sophisticated, although how to define this he wasn't sure. Some girl would give him the eye, and next thing they'd be off to a dance together, in that frenzy of movement

115

he loved, the body pounding, feet whirling, and he'd be intoxicated with it all and, as often as not, she would end up at 105 Wellesley Street, and he'd be inside her and joyful. The next night it might be another girl. One night it was a girl called Mamie, who worked in a bookshop; another time Sue, who worked in a chemist's shop selling make-up and worried about her boss finding out what she got up to. Him, he had no worries.

And then, one day, there was a girl called Bessie, a student teacher and a farmer's daughter from the Waikato, near Hamilton. Suddenly he was in love. Just like that. They met, if meeting her is the right way to describe how they encountered each other, when he was working on a building site near the ferry terminal. That was where she was heading. On an impulse, he walked off the job and followed her onto the ferry leaving for Devonport. He couldn't explain why he did this, it was just a compulsion to be near her.

'Hullo Mr Stalker,' she said, when he sat down beside her. There was something about her that rendered him silent as they sat watching the sea churning in a wake behind the ferry. 'Where are you going?' she asked.

'The same place as you, by the look of it. I didn't mean to follow you. Sorry. I'll go back when the boat turns round.'

'I'm Bessie Marsh,' she said, in quite a formal manner, ignoring his apology. 'I'm going to see my grandmother.' Her complexion was pale and milky, almost devoid of make-up, her light-brown hair curling around the edges of the head scarf tied beneath her chin. The perfect oval of her face made him think of Grace Kelly, and it occurred to him that she had no idea of how pretty she was.

'I'm Albert Black,' he answered, suddenly wanting to be inside his own skin.

'My gran's place is like home these days. I live in a hostel. I miss everything from the farm.'

116

'Yeah, I miss home too. I miss my mam.'

'You're Irish,' she said. 'Come with me and meet my gran, she's Irish too.' Only, when they got to the grandmother's house, she wasn't there. Bessie found them some lunch in the pantry, a round of bread and cheese, and a beer from the fridge for them to share. The kitchen was painted a pretty shade of yellow, like daffodils, and there were pictures on the walls of all the rooms. 'Gran won't mind,' she said. 'There's always something to eat if I come over. She expects me to help myself.' He supposed the two of them, he and Bessie Marsh, must have made some small talk as they ate their lunch, but he doesn't remember it later on. He did sing to her, the old skipping song that came and went through his head.

> *My aunt Jane, she took me in,*
> *She gave me tea out of her wee tin.*
> *Half a bap with sugar on the top,*
> *Three black lumps out of her wee*
> *shop.*

Bessie laughed and clapped her hands. 'You're like my brothers,' she said, 'they like to sing.' And then, somehow, they were in a bedroom that had dolls on a shelf, and Paddy, who for the moment had returned to being Albert, guessed that Bessie had been staying here in this house on and off all her life.

'I shouldn't be doing this,' she said, when they were lying in a tangle of limbs on the bed. 'I don't do this as a rule.' He thinks he might be her first, he can't be sure, but she'd wanted him — he hadn't taken anything she didn't want to give — with an intensity that took him aback, made their encounter astonishing to him. As he studied her, her skin seemed translucent; she had a mole on her left thigh. She was touching his face with her fingertips, as if absorbing his features. Somewhere in the house a clock chimed. She sat up, pulling her knickers from around one ankle. 'My gran might come home,' she said, panic-stricken. 'I shouldn't have, her house and all.' There was a small trace of blood on the counterpane that she was frantically rubbing.

'Are we going to wait for her?' Paddy asked. He was sure this must be love; there was something delicate and different about Bessie, as fresh as the breeze on the water they had passed over. He felt dazed and almost unbearably happy.

'I will,' she said. 'You should go.' Pleading with him now. He understood she was suddenly ashamed that she had defiled the house of the grandmother she loved, and that if her grandmother came home she would know and there would be all sorts of consequences. But he didn't think she was ashamed of being with him.

As he buckled his belt he glanced above him. He hadn't noticed this particular picture before. It was the Sacred Heart of Christ, the crucifixion of Jesus, depicting a crown of thorns and the wound of the spear. Beneath it hung a small wooden cross.

'You're a Catholic?'

'Aren't you?'

'I'm a Protestant. Northern Ireland.' As if that explained everything. Did it matter? he wondered. He had never thought to ask a girl her religion before, or not since he left Belfast, where it was spelled out in black and white whether you asked or not. He closed his eyes. Would she have made love with him if she had known? But he thought he knew the answer. There had been no stopping to think. None of it mattered to him. He'd been in Clodagh's house in Belfast; he knew more Catholics than he could shake a stick at. But he saw it mattered to her, as if the sin were worse, more mortal, for their difference. 'When will I see you again?'

'I don't know,' she said, flustered and uncertain.

He told her where he lived, and how she could find him most evenings at the cafe. She was hurrying him now. When he reached the wharf back in the city he realised he hadn't got a phone number for her, or an address for the hostel where she lived.

He didn't see her again for a long time, and it occurred to him that she wasn't a girl who would come looking for him at a boarding house or hang out round the cafe. After a month or so he stopped looking for her, as if she had been a vision of some kind. There was still Raewyn, holding out for her engagement ring, and the other girls.

Some days he worked and his pockets were full of money; other days he was counting out the cash to make it last for another night on the town. As the man on the train had told him, it wasn't hard to find work in Auckland; there was often seagulling to be had on the wharves or concrete to pour on a construction site, or trucks to stack with furniture for removal firms. He tried his hand at being a waiter, but spilled coffee over a customer on his first day at work and wasn't invited back. The yacht club gave him some cleaning that he liked because it was close to the sea and less gruelling than hanging on the end of a shovel. That was what his father did, and look where it got him. One afternoon a boatie's wife came back after lunch to pick up a jacket she had forgotten, one of those sleekly tanned women whose skin looked as if it'd been polished. She wore gold sandals and hooped earrings. When he asked if he could help, she took a quick look about the room and motioned to the washroom. Her skirt was round her thighs as quick as a fish jumping. Why do you think I came back, she said as he ploughed in. She moaned like an old sow. Would he be working here again? she asked. He smelled tobacco and gin on her breath. After she'd left, he found five pounds in his pocket. A wave of disgust washed over him. But a fiver was money and he didn't work for a week, just hanging out at the cafe, or playing a game of pool and drinking beer with his new friends. There were mornings he woke hungover, and when the nausea passed he would remember why he came to Auckland, what he was supposed to be saving for, but his pockets would be empty and it would start all over again, good resolutions and no willpower when it came to shouting a round.

He stopped for a beer, one evening, at the Albert Hotel down Queen Street and ran into two of his mates, Ray and Mack, and they said, *C'mon, the drinks are on us*. The Albert, just like his name, as if he owned it. Later, when he turned up at the cafe, Raewyn was sitting in a cubicle, a coffee in front of her, talking to a man. Albert will think of him as a man; when he stood up he was half a head taller than Paddy, with wide shoulders and a swagger.

'Raewyn,' Paddy said, 'sorry I'm late.'

'This broad's already taken,' the man said in a strange phony American accent.

'No, I'm not,' Raewyn said quickly. 'We were just having a chat. Johnny's been telling me about life at sea. Johnny, this is Paddy, my boyfriend.'

'Boyfriend, now — my, my, if that just don't sound like serious talk. Paddy, I'd shake your hand, but you know I'm sure a bit offended that the little lady didn't tell me she was already on reservation and you're here to take her away.' He flexed a fist in the air.

'Take it easy, mate,' Paddy said.

Raewyn was looking fluttery and nervous. She said, 'Paddy, Mum'll have dinner ready, and I really need to go. Unless you want to come with me? I'm sure she'd set another place.'

'Best not.' The beer he'd drunk at the Albert lay thick on his tongue. 'Another time.'

'Well, any time you're looking for a real gent, just come looking for me, Johnny McBride,' the man said.

Raewyn looked perplexed for a moment. 'That's the name of a Mickey Spillane character. He's in *The Long Wait*.'

'Now fancy a nice little lady like you knowing that.'

'We used to exchange those books at school. We got over them.'

He shrugged, accepting he had been put in his place. 'I'm just another Johnny,' he said, 'him and me, brothers under the skin.'

After Raewyn had left, Johnny said, 'You don't happen to know any boarding houses round here, do you? I'm in port for a few days.'

'If you've got the cash, sure, I can put you up,' Paddy said. He guessed Raewyn had already told Johnny he was in charge of a boarding house. All the same, he knew it was a mistake as soon as the words were out of his mouth. He'd kept his word to Gladys and never charged anyone before.

The next time he saw Raewyn she told him about the book, how the central character (she didn't say hero) was a man who had lost his memory and his identity, and how he dealt with adversity by creating chaos, chain-smoking butts, getting drunk and beating people up. It is odd, she remarked, the way the man talks. Is Johnny McBride his real name? Paddy didn't really care. He hoped he wouldn't see him again.

This was also the night Paddy told Raewyn they were finished. At first she was tearful, but then she said with a sniff, 'My mother said I could do better than you.'

Rita Zilich is making her way to the gallery to sit with her friends. Now she has given her evidence she can be part of the audience. As she steps from the witness stand, Paddy tries to remember why he had asked her to stay that night. Wounded pride, perhaps, but not over her. He had never really wanted Rita. Did Johnny McBride want her either, or was she just an excuse for him to pick a fight? Rita is walking away, into her own story. On that night in July, when they had fumbled and groped on the bed, and his groin ached with unresolved pain, she told him a little of herself. Soon, although she hasn't come to these conclusions yet, she will stop being a widgie; she will marry someone she may not yet have met in a white wedding dress and have children. Paddy's own name will fade into some private part of her life that her children will never know. He sees it all.

Bessie had come back to him; she came looking for him. Nobody had heard of Albert Black, she said, when she asked around. She had gone to the door of 105 Wellesley Street and the man who opened it said there was no Albert here. But she had seen him from the window of a bus as he walked down the street. She knew she hadn't imagined him. She knocked on the door again, and there he was.

'Teach me to dance,' she said that night. 'I've never been any good at dancing.'

He turned on the radio, found music and began with a slow waltz, holding her close. She was his girl then.

Chapter 11

In the beginning Paddy got along well enough with Johnny McBride after he turned up at the boarding house, though he had his reservations. It was not the first time he had allowed someone to stay over. There was a young Englishman called Henry whom he particularly liked. Henry seemed to have a bit of a chip on his shoulder, but when Paddy got to know him he thought he understood his problem better. Henry was a child migrant, he said, meaning that he'd been sent off to New Zealand without any choice in the matter. He was just a kid and was despatched straight to a farm, treated like a slave and lived in a shed at the bottom of the farmer's vegetable garden. He got hidings if he didn't milk the cows fast enough. God knows he'd never seen a bloody cow until he reached New Zealand. Henry stayed a couple of times, a seaman now on a coastal scow, a Teddy boy when he was in port, his clothes so sharp he could walk in a fashion parade, Paddy thought. 'I don't know why I was sent out here,' Henry said. 'After my parents got divorced they stuck me in a foster home.

But I liked it there, it wasn't too bad. Next thing I know, my father signed papers saying I was to be put on a ship and sent out here. I don't really know who I am and nobody wants to tell me.'

'I know about those we'ans,' Paddy told him. 'There were some on the same ship as me coming out here, miserable-looking little buggers. I felt kind of sorry for them. I was having a great time.'

'I never asked to be transported. You've got no idea the things that happened to us kids. Mind you, we didn't know what was in store for us on the voyage out. Some of the farms we landed up on, this country ought to be ashamed of itself. Your choice to emigrate, not mine.'

'Yeah, I guess so. I figure you're right about that.'

Henry was ironing his trousers, intent with perfecting a razor seam, while they had this conversation. 'You don't sound so sure.'

'Sure I'm sure,' Paddy had said easily. It was best to believe in this, to tell himself it was true. It was meant to be a great adventure, and there was not really a lot to complain about, especially now he had a real girlfriend. He might get used to living in New Zealand and not in Ireland. Although, dreaming ahead, perhaps she would like to go and live in Ireland. Well, chance would be a fine thing, but he couldn't help but imagine showing her the old town, taking her on the train to the countryside. Grand that would be, yes it would. For now, he had a roof over his head, enough to eat, as many girls as will listen to his chat-up line, though his mother would say they're a bunch of hussies. Not that he was chatting up any more girls now there was Bessie. He'd told her she was his girl, the only one. It was all very new, this feeling of being in love, and he had to remind himself now and then to keep his eyes to himself. He wished Bessie would stay with him some nights, but she wasn't free to come and go, he understood that. The hostel where she lived was called Rocklands Hall, a big old mansion set among trees out at Epsom. He once called for her there and felt as if he should be looking for the servants' entrance, it was so grand. The chatter and laughter of girls filled the stairwell. Before Bessie left with him, he had to meet the matron. She eyed him with cool appraisal: only very special girls stay at Rocklands, her look seemed to imply. That was a night when there was nobody but him staying at 105 Wellesley Street. Later Bessie lay on his bed, her body like a pale flung star. 'I wish I had somewhere better to take you,' he said.

Still, 105 was where he lived and he liked to have company in the big empty boarding house, not to have to listen to the creaking boards in the night and wonder whether there was an intruder and whether he would have to bang someone over the head, or get clobbered himself. Henry was a decent bloke, wild like all of them and fired up when he was on the piss, but he was up first most mornings with a fry-up for breakfast. When he went back to sea, the house felt ghostly again, night shadows dancing on the window panes as cars passed, the hooting of their horns leaving trailing echoes in the dark. July was cold, and rain settled over the city so that some nights he couldn't hear himself think for the sound of it pounding on the iron roof. On Sunday mornings the bells of St Matthew's woke him, reminding him he had promised his mother he would go to church when he came to New Zealand but never once has he done that. Sunday in Auckland turned his stomach: so pious, the pubs shut, Queen Street so quiet you could shoot a gun straight down the middle and nobody would come running.

And yet, when Johnny McBride turned up on the doorstep with his suitcase, Paddy wished straight away he hadn't told him he could come. There was something he couldn't fathom about McBride. He was big, perhaps six two in his socks, his shirt bulging with muscles, but he wasn't given to standing to his full height, rather in a slouch with his head dropped between his shoulders. Like Henry, he said he was between ships, coastal vessels for the time being, but soon he'd be on something bigger, one of the ships going to England. And he was buggered if he'd be coming back.

'Are you one of those migrant we'ans?' Paddy asked. Johnny had this strange hybrid accent, part American, part cockney.

'Never you mind where I come from,' Johnny said. 'Where I come from, that's my business, you know. I don't ask you questions and you don't ask me. We straight on that?' His face set in a scowl.

'Sure, dead on.'

'I'm no kid, all right? I'm twenty-four years old and nobody tells me what the fuck to do.'

Paddy felt himself flinch. 'My landlady's going to be back here very soon. You can't stay too long because I'm not supposed to take in boarders.' This was true, for Gladys had phoned the day before to say that her friend's mother was recovering well and that, at the end of the month, she would be back and she hoped all would be in order.

Johnny backed off for a while after that. Paddy thought Johnny needed him more than he needed Johnny. He decided not to charge him anything after all, so then he wouldn't be beholden to him for the money. One morning when Paddy was in the kitchen, he heard Johnny singing to himself in a harsh, boyish voice. He stood still and listened. It was a song he'd heard often on the boat coming out, but never quite like this, with such an edge of despair:

> Maybe it's because I'm a
> Londoner
> That I love London so
> Maybe it's because I'm a
> Londoner
> That I think of her wherever I go.

Paddy walked out to the front room, raising his voice to join in, but Johnny stopped short as soon as he appeared.

'You know nothing,' Johnny said. 'Shut up.'

For a few days more, the lodger slid around the house, keeping himself to himself, sleeping late. He got up earlier one morning and cooked breakfast, sausages and bacon, with a good side of toast he'd made on the wire grill. 'You see, I'm not just a pretty face,' he said, presenting the meal with a flourish, a tea towel laid on the table as a place mat.

Paddy thought that actually there was nothing particularly good-looking about Johnny, his nose bent as if someone had punched him, his slicked hair thin for a person of his age, as if he would bald early. One of his front teeth was missing, and Paddy wondered what it must be like for a girl to kiss a man with a hole in his gob. Johnny had had a girl to stay over the night before, but she'd gone by the time they sat down to eat.

'Mate, you're going to have to push off,' Paddy said.

'You telling me to leave?'

'I'll get thrown out if the landlady catches you here.'

Johnny swept the plates off the table with his arm and stood up, leaning over Paddy as they smashed. 'And what about me, punk? Where am I supposed to sleep?'

'I told you it was just until you got yourself sorted. You've done nothing about it, have you?'

Johnny stood, wiping his nose. 'I've got a cold,' he said, his voice sullen. 'Do you expect me to sleep under a bridge in my condition?'

Paddy was about to say that he might think about staying with the girl he was so friendly with, but he shut his mouth. He'd heard Johnny's guttural shouts of enjoyment in the night. Plus, Johnny seemed to be spreading his germs as well as his charms. Paddy could feel a cold coming on. His throat was sore and his head ached.

Johnny's face was full of menace. 'Another night then. Just one more, okay?'

Later, in the afternoon, Paddy walked into the living room and found Johnny cutting his toenails with a knife. 'That's bloody disgusting, you manky git,' he said.

'You going to fetch me a manicure set, *dar*ling?' Johnny said, spitting the insult in the air. He crooked his little finger above the knife.

Paddy sat down opposite him. 'This isn't getting us anywhere,' he said. 'That's a damn big knife.'

'I always carry a knife, don't you?'

'I carried one for a bit in Belfast, yes. My da carried one too. But Belfast is different. I reckon the cops catch you carrying a knife here, you're in trouble.' The cops. The words fell from his tongue; he was beginning to sound like a New Zealander. Or an American gangster, like the way McBride talked.

'You need a knife in a fight.'

'I don't like to fight. I only did that in school.'

'Well, I fight, nothing yellow about me. I carry a knife and I use my feet. When you get a person on the ground you keep him there. I've done a bit of prize fighting, bare-knuckle stuff, and earned a decent purse or two. Yeah, I'm not a good man to cross, kiddo. Matter of fact, I like a bit of a rumble. I've never lost a fight yet. See, I don't like people, I reckon most people are better off dead. If they get in my way that's where they'll be.'

'Yeah, well maybe we should go and have a pint,' Paddy said, hoping to break the impasse. Johnny was scaring him now, working himself up with spittle in the corner of his mouth. He could see the devil was in Johnny.

'I was in the army,' Johnny said, as if he hadn't heard him. 'The military cops put me in the slammer when I fought, but they never got the better of me.'

128

'When were you in the army?' Paddy asked. It was something that preyed on his mind. Rose told him before he left Naenae that if immigration caught up with him he'd be punished for breaking his bond and sent off to the army on his birthday, when he came twenty, the date just passed the week before — a fact he thought best to keep to himself.

'Oh, years ago,' Johnny said, offhand now. 'Well, we might as well have that drink you were talking about.'

They finished up drinking at the Albert and both of them were drunk when they turned up at Ye Olde Barn that evening. Paddy looked for Bessie, because some evenings she studied in the library and once or twice she had come along to the cafe to meet him, but it wasn't a place she liked. The first time she'd come she'd been wearing a dress she'd made herself, pink cotton embroidered with daisies, with her cardigan over it. He saw girls looking sideways and raising their finely plucked eyebrows at each other. She wasn't one of them. If Bessie had her way, they would go down the road to Somervell's milk bar because she liked creaming sodas made with sarsaparilla, or that's what she said. He thought it was because she didn't like the girls at the cafe.

'Don't you mind that a fella killed his girl in here?' he asked her the first time they went to Somervell's. It was where Frederick Foster, the Englishman, had shot his girlfriend. The story was all over the newspapers, and it was just weeks after he and Bessie had got back together that the man had been hanged.

'He said it was an accident.' Still she shivered. 'His poor mother, she came out here to try and save him. It shouldn't be.' He thought then that she had a tender heart.

Paddy yearned to bring Bessie to Wellesley Street again, but while Johnny McBride was there he wouldn't do that, the place squalid and smelling of rancid fat, and Johnny's toenail clippings on the floor, wet cigarette butts in the ashtrays. It was like nobody ever taught him how to live a decent sort of life. But Paddy wasn't going to clean up after him. Nor was he having Bessie slumming it.

The flu hit him next. Paddy stayed in bed, dosing himself on aspirin. He heard Johnny come and go but he didn't have the energy to argue with him or the strength to confront him. The fever made him dream. His mother appeared beside him, holding a cool compress; he waited for it to descend on his forehead, but when he woke there was nobody there. He slept again and dreamt he was walking through late-autumn leaves in Antrim with a cold wind whipping his face, and, later again the same night, he was on a holiday one spring, the only holiday they ever took as a family, with his mam and his da and little Daniel at Ballycastle, looking towards the streaming headland, his feet surrounded by wild flowers. Daniel held his hand and looked up at him, his freckled face full of trust that his brother Albert would never leave him.

He woke again, sweat streaming off him, and got up to walk through the house to the lavatory out the back. It was quiet and the air dead still, and he thought Johnny McBride had gone, but when he looked through the open door of the room the other man had been occupying he saw his suitcase was still in the middle of the room, his skivvies strewn around. He opened the outside door, and the scent of flowers that had assailed him in his dreams rose up to meet him. A daphne bush stood in a patch of earth beside the house, the fragrance overwhelming. It reminded him of Rose's garden.

The fever left him. He felt cool and cleansed, though his legs still wobbled beneath him. After that, he slept again for several hours, this time without dreaming. In the morning, he decided he was well enough to look for work again. He picked up three days of cleaning at the yacht club, making sure not to make eye contact with any of the women. He didn't see the woman he'd poked in the washroom. When he was paid, he told himself he would really save this time and put money aside towards the trip home. Perhaps he would go and see his parents and Daniel and all, and come back. Bessie would wait for him. It confused him to think about this; he was in a muddle and he knew he needed more time to recover from the flu. Something had to change, but right now he couldn't see what to do. Before he met Bessie he'd been wondering if he would be better off back in Naenae living with Rose. But now he thought there was no turning back, and besides the law would catch up with him, as Rose had predicted. Things could only get better if he resolved the problem of Johnny McBride. It was a place to start.

That evening Gladys Wallace, the landlady, phoned again. She would return at the end of the week, on Thursday to be exact, at around three o'clock. She hoped she would find everything spick and span. Her neighbours, who she talked to pretty well every week, had told her that although things seemed quiet at her address they had seen a few people coming and going. 'You know what I said, Paddy, no sub-letting.' He wondered if this was a veiled hint that she knew more than she was letting on.

'You've got to get out. Don't you have a ship to go to?' he said to Johnny.

Johnny said that right now he wasn't going anywhere. 'Look,' he said, trying an affable tone for a change, 'the landlady's not going to stay here, is she?'

'How would I know?'

'Nah, she'll go back to her bloke and you'll have the place to yourself again. Why don't I just clear out while she's here, and then come back?'

'Friggin' no.' Paddy felt his temper boiling. He swore at Johnny then, shouting, 'Fuck away off. I mean it, I'll call the fucking cops on you.'

Johnny's lip curled. 'You won't call the cops on me. You've got too much to hide.'

'Get out, gob-shite, get — take your stuff and shove off.'

'Go blow,' Johnny said, standing with his fists in the air as if he were going to throw punches. Then, quite suddenly, he dropped his fists and walked out. His suitcase stayed in the bedroom.

Paddy thought he would be back, and was afraid. Johnny McBride, the other Johnny McBride, who lived in pulp fiction, wanted to kill people who stood in his way.

In the night his spine tingled with terror.

Chapter 12

Rose and Peter and the children knew the date of Paddy's birthday and sent presents, carefully addressed to Mr P. Donovan. The children had chosen after-shave lotion, and Ned, the older boy, wrote in an accompanying note: 'Peter says you're old enough to shave now, ha ha.' Peter's gift was a new razor, a sleek steel one with a handle that fitted perfectly in his hand. They must have had a conversation about his whiskers, he thought. Because his beard was so dark his chin always had a bluish tinge by evening. If he was going out he would shave twice a day. Rose sent a wooden box that contained jars of homemade marmalade, a pullover she had knitted, and a book called *East of Eden* which was the latest novel by her favourite writer, John Steinbeck. 'It's a big book, Paddy,' she wrote, 'and you might not have time to read it straight away but here's hoping that someday you will find it as enjoyable as I did. It's about good and evil, and country places, like out here in Naenae with the market gardens all around, and it starts with a character who is a young Irish immigrant, just like you.'

That wasn't what his father would have said. He imagined his sharp reprimand, reminding Rose that his son was an Ulsterman. The pullover was made from soft green and brown flecked wool with a knobbly texture. When he was sick he put it on for extra warmth and thought again that he shouldn't have left them. He shouldn't have left anywhere.

His mother's parcel arrived after the birthday, and he had wondered if she had forgotten, but it was forwarded on from Rose's address so she must have posted it months earlier on a very slow boat. The mail was a problem for him. He hadn't had the nerve to tell his mother that he went under a different name here in Auckland. Just send it to the Post Office, Mam, with the name Albert, c/- of Mr Donovan, he had written to her. Mr Donovan and he lived at the same address. The parcel contained a white shirt, not one he would have chosen, a little stiff-collared and formal for the life he led now. He thought that it was something she couldn't afford.

She wrote: 'To think that I have a son out of his teens now, a man of twenty years. I will never forget the first moment I saw your bonny wee face, I could have sworn you smiled at me the moment you were born. What it is for a mother to fall in love with her child. Or a father, for that matter, and it is a pleasure I hope someday you will have. Of course next year will be your true coming of age, the big twenty-first. I don't suppose we will see you for that grand occasion, but your da and I are saving for something special when it comes round. We have in mind a good watch. Well my dear son, I expect you will celebrate this milestone of two decades of life with all the friends you are making in New Zealand. Be sure and have a happy day and all.'

It was this letter from his mother that got him thinking. Now that Mrs Wallace was coming back, it might be time for him to move on. Or that is what he could tell Johnny McBride, if he turned up.

Johnny's suitcase was still in the room and clothes strewn around, his possessions a dead giveaway, even if Paddy packed up the stuff himself and hid them in a wardrobe. She would be bound to find them. In the front room Johnny's toenail clippings lay on the carpet, in the kitchen ants ran over uneaten food and scummy dishes from the boarder's last meal. In the toilet, out at the back of the house, there was a dried spill of vomit. Paddy began a ferocious round of cleaning. He was moving out, that was his story. Perhaps he would leave anyway, he was yet to decide. If he could find a smaller, nicer place that would be more suitable for Bessie to visit, he might see more of her. It might really be goodbye to 105 Wellesley Street.

In the meantime, he could celebrate his recent birthday and have friends around, and Bessie might come if he asked her in advance. As soon as the idea took hold of him, it seemed like a festival of treats. There would be music and they would dance.

He sat down and wrote to his mother: 'Thanks a bundle for the shirt Mam, I'll look real sharp in that. I'm doing very well here, fortunate to have had a great place to live these last few months, although I'm thinking of moving on soon. Mr Donovan will probably shift with me, he and I will set up somewhere together. I've got lots of friends and plenty of work to be had. Well, who knows whether I will get back to the old Dart any time soon. That is what British people here call the home country. Some people just speak of home, which I do in my heart, and others call it "the mother country", although the citizens of New Zealand seem very independent in their spirit and for how long will us immigrants think of ourselves as separate from them is hard to say. Anyway, now that I'm twenty I'm starting to think about settling down in this country, looking towards a steady way of life. I've met a really nice girl but perhaps I will tell you more about her another time, this is a different girl from the last one I told you about, I really like her. Your always loving son.' He failed to mention that he had just nine pounds left over from his last job.

It took him a while to get through to Bessie. The matron allowed calls only at certain times. He wondered if Bessie had been avoiding him, but there were exams coming up and the last time they had spoken she said she was studying hard. This was a disappointment, for he imagined they might have gone to the zoo over the weekend, now that the weather had fined up, but she had been adamant that she could not see him then.

'Can you ask for a night out?' he said, when they finally spoke. 'Stay at your grannie's? They wouldn't mind that, would they? Sure c'mon, girl.'

After a silence, she said, 'I need to see you, Paddy.'

'You'll stay the night?'

'They don't give us leave except at the weekend, you know that.'

'Not even with Grannie?' He drew circles with his finger round the telephone while he spoke. He could see her perfect face that made him think of Grace Kelly. She was, he supposed, too good for him, he had figured this from the beginning.

'I don't think so, no.'

'But you'll come to the party? Bessie, it's my birthday and all. Well, it was, but you know, I had the flu and that.'

'I didn't know it was your birthday.'

'I was twenty last week. You don't need to buy me a present. Well, ha ha, I don't expect you would anyway, just bring yourself, that would be a fine present. How about I come and meet you at around eight o'clock at Ye Olde Barn?'

And she said yes, yes she would see him there, but she doubted she could get a late pass, as it was a weeknight, and perhaps she would just have some coffee after they'd had a chat, they would have to see how things went. He found this conversation mysterious, but then Bessie had been that from the start. But she was going to come, and as a last part of his preparations he tidied out the side room where he slept and made it up with clean sheets, smoothing the bed cover, plumping the pillows.

On Tuesday afternoon he found Rainton Hastie, or Ray as they called him, and Ted Quintal, and Henry, the Englishman who had stayed with him at Wellesley Street, drinking in the Albert. There was Jeff Larsen, who hung out with them from time to time. He'd come from Rotorua, a town he left to get away from playing rugby, which his father wanted him to keep playing after he left school. Well, that wasn't for him. Paddy liked him, a bloke with a laugh or two up his sleeve. He was a freckle-faced man, twenty-two or thereabouts, trailing a couple of convictions for burglary. He'd been in Borstal but he'd steer clear of that in future, he could tell you that. It was a mug's game. He could give hot tips on the races. And there was Lloyd Sinclair, whom they called Cookie and looked just a wee fella, a bit young to hang out with; he was another child immigrant, and Henry was keeping an eye on him. Paddy had hardly got the word out that he was having a party than Ray was organising it, as if it were his own gig. Ray was one of the flamboyant blokes, a permanent partygoer if you believed half of what he said. He was wearing a floral shirt under a blue jacket, and white shoes with heels. 'We'll get Pooch on the guitar. We can hire a steel guitar at the Maori Community Centre. We'll buy some beer.' Pooch was Ted's brother.

'A bottle of gin for the girls,' Paddy said. Afterwards, he thought it should have been Pimm's; that's what girls drank: not so alcoholic. His mother liked a gin and tonic on the odd occasion she let her hair down, not that she'd have admitted it if you asked her. He'd seen his da bring home a bottle on her birthday and she'd had a quarter of a tumbler, and then, when she thought he

137

and Daniel weren't looking, she'd whisper to his da that perhaps another one might not go astray. It was gin he bought anyway, and Ray bought two dozen beer. Ray said they ought to go along to Ye Olde Barn and find some girls. As they were preparing to leave, Johnny McBride walked in. He saw Paddy and turned his back. He was accompanied by a youth so baby-faced it seemed impossible that he would be served at the bar, but he was.

'He's not invited,' Paddy said. If Johnny heard, he didn't let on. Paddy was overcome with sudden panic. 'We can't have too many people,' he said, 'we'll have to keep the noise down. The neighbours, they'll tell my landlady.'

'Too late, my old son,' Ray said, 'we've bought the booze. You're on.'

Henry followed them to the door. 'I'm supposed to be putting out to sea tonight. I won't be coming to the party,' he said.

'Not to worry, some other time.'

Henry said, 'Paddy, you want to be careful of that guy.' He nodded towards Johnny, who was hunched at the bar with his head down.

'Is he your mate? I wouldn't have thought it,' Paddy said. It came out mean, which was not what he intended.

'Go easy,' Henry said. 'He's a crazy mixed-up kid.'

'What do you know that I don't?'

Henry shrugged. 'Perhaps he's not as bad as you think.'

'He's a piece of shite, a skitter if ever there was one.'

'If you say so, Paddy. I'm just saying, mind how you go. Johnny doesn't always mean trouble but he makes it anyway; it's how he is.' Henry turned away, sharp in his waistcoat and long pale-grey coat, his skinny tie, his shiny shoes. He didn't seem to care that New Zealanders looked at him sideways in the street. Paddy had been with him one day when a man with a red boozy complexion had stuck his face in front of him, saying, 'Don't you think you're looking for trouble when you dress up like a queer?'

He recalled the calm way Henry had answered. 'I wasn't trying to attract attention,' he'd said. 'I just like these clothes. They're the same colour as yours, just a different cut.' The man had backed off. Paddy remembered that Henry had been a companionable, kindly guy while he stayed at the house. Some chill of apprehension passed through him, a feeling that he might not see Henry again, and it made him shiver, like somebody had walked over his grave. It was not like him to have premonitions: those were for the old people back home. He held out his hand. 'Henry?' The other man turned back to him and they shook. 'No hard feelings?'

'Go well, Paddy,' Henry said.

Will he see Henry again? Much later, when Paddy is in prison, he will wonder whether they did actually see each other again. But surely that wouldn't have been possible, for Henry was going to sea that night? Henry was about to become part of a blur of shadows that would overtake him very soon. It must be, he will come to tell himself, that Henry is a presence.

For now, Ray was ordering a taxi to take the beer to the boarding house. He and Paddy and Ted piled in for the short ride up Queen Street and over the Wellesley Street ridge. Ray put down a dozen of the beer inside the house, looking around with a critical eye. 'You haven't done much to liven the place up, have you?' he said.

'It's not mine.' Paddy thought he'd explained all of that to Ray.

'Well, you know, if it was me I'd put in some black wallpaper and nice white carpets and plant a few pretty girls all dressed in pink around the place, kind of accessories, if you know what I mean. Some nice mirrors round the walls so we could see the girls dancing double time.'

'I'm not planning to stay much longer.' Already he was certain about this. He'd made up his mind.

'Hey, it's time we rounded up a few people. You can't have a party without guests,' Ray said.

Paddy said then that it was too early, the party wouldn't start until after eight, but Ray was off and out the door, Ted following. Paddy felt a new wave of anxiety. If he didn't follow them, there was no telling how many people would turn up.

It's a party, it's a party, a party. The words flicked around Ye Olde Barn cafe. He saw Rita Zilich, dressed in a tight red sweater tucked into a skirt so slim he could see every curve of her buttocks. He had seen her before and thought, in the past, that he might sleep with her if she were interested. That was before he was taken. Rita ran the tip of her tongue around the arch of her top lip.

'Paddy,' she said, 'why it's you. On your own, are you?'

A tune had just finished on the jukebox. He made his way over to it. He wanted sex: for a minute or so he wanted Rita, here, there or anywhere. He slipped a sixpence in the slot and selected 'Danny Boy'. Slim Whitman was singing and the song was all the rage, a hit-parade favourite. Funny how the old songs came back. Rita was at his shoulder. 'Well, Paddy? Ray's asked me to your party. I'll be there a bit later.'

'I'm meeting my girl,' he said. 'I'm meeting Bessie.'

'Pity,' she said. 'Any time you're free.'

'I'll keep it in mind,' he said.

Chapter 13

Paddy did not, as Rita had told Oliver Buchanan at his trial, go home after he left her at the taxi stand. How would Rita know where he went? Instead, he began walking blindly towards Epsom. The trams were stilled, silence blanketing the streets of Auckland. He needed to find Bessie. No, that was not right, he was deceiving himself. He knew where she was and that he wouldn't be able to see her, but it seemed that if he could be close to where she was, where she lay sleeping, or perhaps was wide awake like he was, he could connect with the spirit of her, make her understand what had happened that evening. The piercing cold of the July night entered his bones, but still he kept walking, mile after mile towards Epsom and the grand old house where he knew Bessie was.

He wanted to explain to her that after he had drunk a beer, or perhaps two or three, he didn't remember now, he looked at the time and saw with a start that eight o'clock had been and gone. He had left the party and gone running up the rise, down the hill, down past the old low Albion with its pressed tin ceiling, past the church, and the mannequins in Smith & Caughey's, to meet Bessie at Ye Olde Barn cafe. The place was full, every cubicle taken. It took him a few minutes to spot her, sitting alone on a stool, an untouched coffee at her elbow, as if she had just bought something she didn't want in order to keep her place at the counter. She was staring into space, seemingly oblivious of everyone around her. When he walked up and tapped her on the shoulder, she jumped, her eyes possum lamplights. 'I thought you weren't coming,' she said. 'Well, I was beginning to wonder. Can we find somewhere to talk?'

'We can talk later,' he said. 'When everyone's gone. Everybody's up at the party now.'

'Can't they have the party without you?'

'Not really.' He was suddenly uneasy, aware that he was in charge of the house. The place was filling when he slipped out, there were more people than he expected, like word had got round all over town. The girls had tied a piece of string across the room, attached to the two chairs. The competition was to see how low they could go as they danced beneath it, knees bent, faces turned upwards. They were shrill with laughter as they bent and doubled. He knew he had to get back.

'Paddy, you know I can't stay,' Bessie was saying. 'I'll get thrown out of the hostel if I'm not back in time.' Her voice held a pleading note that grated with him. It was not what he expected from her, not like the girl he had met on the ferry.

'Just for a little while. C'mon.'

She'd climbed down off the stool, followed him reluctantly out of the cafe. She didn't look like someone dressed for a party. Under her coat she wore a pleated tartan skirt and a green woollen jersey. At that particular moment Rita appeared, her hooped earrings glittering in the streetlights, her lips painted in a glossy red curve. She had changed her blouse for a bright-blue satin one.

'Made it,' she said, hooking her arm through Paddy's. 'Thank goodness my parents go to bed early. So who's this then?' she said, looking Bessie over as if she hadn't seen her before.

'This is my girlfriend, Bessie,' he said, and untangled his arm from Rita's.

Bessie stepped up her pace and began walking ahead of them.

'So are you in the dogbox or something?' Rita said, and laughed.

'Bessie, wait,' he said. She wheeled around, looking at him and Rita. 'It's not what you think.'

Rita flicked him a glance and spoke to Bessie. 'Hey,' she said, 'it's okay. Ray Hastie was the one who asked me to the party. I had to go and check in at home. We just bumped into each other, Paddy and me.'

Bessie appeared to relax. The two girls drifted ahead of him, beginning to chat. He thought then that it would be all right, the two of them would get on. Rita was telling Bessie about her job, and how fast she was at shorthand, and how her boss had told her she'd get a pay rise. That was a relief, because she was fifteen when she started work at the beginning of the year and you don't get taxed until you're sixteen. But now she had had her birthday and her four pounds a week had gone down six shillings. Bessie was nodding her head. Four pounds a week sounded like good money to her, she said. At training college that was nearly what she got paid a month. Mind you, she had her board and nice meals. Rita clicked her tongue and said something like, what a pity, they should be paying brainy girls more, chattering away until before they all knew it they were back at the boarding house.

Bessie stopped at the bottom of the stairs, letting Rita go ahead.

'We can talk out here,' she said.

'I need to make sure everything's okay,' he said. Music was wafting down the street; someone was singing 'Twilight Time'. He joined in, mounting the stairs, with Bessie trailing behind him *each day . . . just to be with you* and held out his hand to her. He recalled later that she had looked very pale, almost ashen-faced.

Rita threw off her coat and straight away Ray Hastie began to dance with her, the pair of them shimmying together, thighs touching and parting. Paddy couldn't help watching her. In fact, the whole room stopped to watch and applaud. That was the moment he looked across the room and saw Johnny McBride leaning against the mantelpiece.

He walked across. 'You weren't invited here,' he said.

'I'm your lodger, remember,' Johnny said, and laughed, showing the gap in his teeth. 'This is my mate Stan,' he said, indicating the baby-faced boy who had been in the pub with him.

Rita spun round, saw them and disengaged herself from the dance. 'Do you want to dance, Paddy?' she said, and flicked her provocative little tongue over her top lip again.

'Not now,' he said. Bessie stood transfixed in the doorway. She hadn't taken off her coat.

'Bessie won't mind, will you, doll?' Rita said. 'Oops, I think she does.' So that he knew that under all the friendly talk Rita had been setting Bessie up for humiliation. She turned to Johnny. 'You'll dance with me, won't you?'

Bessie stared coldly into the room and turned to go. Paddy followed her to the door. 'Bessie,' he said, 'I told you, it's not how it looks. C'mon, just relax, have a good time.'

'You're all drunk,' she said.

'I am so not. I haven't had a drink all day, I swear. Well, perhaps a couple, but I'm not pissed. Do I look pissed?'

Bessie kept on walking down the stairs. 'I'm going to catch the tram,' she said.

He found himself walking alongside of her, trying to keep up with her angry footsteps. He was beginning to feel furious too. 'So what did you want to talk to me about? Eh? Don't give me that silent treatment, I won't have it.'

'Oh, you won't have it, won't you? You don't own me, Paddy,' she said, still looking straight ahead. He saw that she was crying, and he thought there was defiance in her expression, the way she clamped her mouth shut in a tight line as if she looked down on him and all of his friends. They were supposed to have been her friends too.

'What's the matter? Have you got your pinny pain?' he said, racking his brain for why she should be in such a mood.

'My what? Oh, you don't know anything.'

They had arrived at the stop and right on time the red Epsom tram rattled up, tram number 101, he remembered that, it was the same number back to front and upside down.

'Tell me,' he shouted. 'Bessie, what don't I know?'

She turned her cold face towards him. 'You make me sick,' she said as she climbed on the step.

He couldn't believe she was saying this. While she could still hear him, he called, 'Bessie, listen. I'll be at Ye Olde Barn tomorrow night. Seven o'clock. Meet me. Please.' She paused, just long enough for him to know that she had heard him, before she was swallowed up into the tram's bright interior, moving away from him.

He kicked a rubbish bin as he passed, overtaken with fury. Perhaps, after all, he hated her. She had made a fool of him, turning up in her school-marm clothes, standing there at the party not speaking to anyone, walking out on him. A part of him wanted to go after her, jump in a taxi and follow her tram to its stop. But there was the party. The house. There was Johnny McBride to be taken care of. And there was the girl and he wanted her.

The music had reached a crescendo, the girls stamping their feet, belting out 'Comin' round the Mountain':

We'll kill the old red rooster
  when she comes, when she comes
We will kill the big red rooster
  when she comes, when she comes
We'll kill the big red rooster,
  we will kill the big red rooster
We'll kill the big red rooster
  when she comes, when she comes
Oh yes we'll kill the big red
  rooster when she comes.

The girl Stella, who was Rita's friend, was running her fingers along the forearm of the young lad who wasn't supposed to be there, tossing her red curls and sticking out her breasts. Johnny was nowhere to be seen. Nor was Rita. Paddy wanted to tell her he was free for the night. All he wanted now was to be beside a girl, feel the soft slide of her skin beside his, her hair beneath his hand, and he didn't much care whose it was.

He put his hands in the air, signalling for them to keep the noise down. As it subsided a little, he heard a voice from outside. He knew the voice. Then it went quiet.

Outside, on the veranda leading to the back-yard toilet, Johnny stood kissing Rita.

'Rita, come inside,' Paddy said.

Johnny dropped his arms from around the girl's waist, moved towards him, smashed his fist into his face. His brain felt detached from his skull. He raised his fists to hit back. Johnny said, 'I'd watch it, you yellow Irish bastard, there's no fight in you. I'll kick you till your sides cave in.'

Rita had run screaming into the front room. The Quintal boys, Pooch and Ted, two others, Jeff and Mack, now appeared round the side of the house, grabbing his arms and those of Johnny McBride.

When they were all back inside, the party was subdued, the atmosphere turned morose: you could feel the way everything had turned flat. Paddy lay down on the bed in the cubicle next to the front room, his head beating like a drum. He called the boy, Stan, over. 'Bring me that knife,' he said. They had been flipping tops off bottles with a kitchen knife.

The boy stood, looking petrified. 'Nah, mate, you don't need a knife.'

'I need to open a bottle of beer. Get me it, mate, I need a drink.'

'Cool down, Paddy,' Jeff Larsen said.

There were red lights dancing in front of his eyes. 'I said get me the goddamn knife.' He found himself lunging off the bed, taking Stan down with him, and then there was more fighting, all over the room, bottles smashing, chairs overturned. Girls started hurrying towards the passage where their coats were hanging; Ray began to pack up the guitar. Paddy rushed through the house, grabbed Johnny's suitcase and ran back, throwing it at him. 'Take your stuff . . . Don't come back.'

Rita picked up her coat and started to leave in Johnny's wake.

Paddy drew in great gulps of air, rushing down the stairs after her, a glass in his hand. Or was it a bottle, he couldn't remember. Or had Johnny taken a bottle with him when he left? All of those moments so filled with confusion. Mack Thompson was revving the motor of his car and people were getting in. By the time he reached the street, Rita had climbed into the back seat beside Johnny.

'Get out,' Paddy said to her. 'Get out of the car. You're with me tonight.'

Johnny climbed out of the car then, fists and feet flying again, kicking him off balance, swinging his foot high, catching him in his groin, making his balls explode. Ted came down from the veranda

147

and held him up while Pooch went over to the car, his hand held out to the girl. Johnny stood over Paddy, scowling at Ted and Pooch as they supported him against the fence.

'I'll be back to finish this off tomorrow,' he said, before turning on his heel and returning to the car. When it moved off, Paddy saw that Rita was standing on the pavement.

Inside, she said nothing. Ray had finished packing up the steel guitar to take back to the Community Centre. The last partygoers left, some calling goodnight, most of them just slinking off into the shadows of Wellesley Street. He put his arm around Rita. The effort of standing was too much, so he lay down on the bed. The girl sat down beside him, unbuttoning the tight satin blouse, the bright white orbs of her breasts exposed.

'Not now,' he muttered. 'Soon.' Rita stood up again, starting to pick up beer bottles and put them in a carton, her blouse still carelessly undone. He found himself unmoved. The knife lay on the floor, one he had carried from his days in the Post and Telegraph for slashing pine trees and now used for peeling potatoes. Rita placed it in the carton with the bottles.

'Never mind that,' he said, 'get me a mirror.'

She looked around distractedly, took down the one that hung over the mantelpiece; it was heavy and she held it stiffly before her as she handed it to him. When he saw his face with his swollen eye, he swore and dropped the mirror; it shattered into a thousand pieces. 'I'll kill him. I'll fucken kill McBride,' he said.

'You want to watch it,' the girl said, 'he might kill you first.'

'Stay with me, Rita,' he said. 'Stay the night.'

'I can't stay the whole night,' she said.

Not that it would have made any difference, his dick a limp rag of beaten meat. What he said next would come back to haunt him: *I'm not that horny tonight*. He thought he had shamed himself, and her, and all of them. Most of all, he had shamed the girl he might have loved, taking her there when she was tired and she had wanted him to herself. He had let Rita make a fool of her. Well, that's what he thought, for what else could he have done that made her so cold and distant towards him? She must know that she was his girl, not Rita, that it was her he wanted. Surely.

None of these were things he would tell to a jury.

He stood outside Rocklands Hall, breathing in the scent of magnolia, the slim tree branches trembling above him in the darkness. The blank windows gave nothing away about the occupants. The time before, when he had been to call for her, he had glimpsed the magnificent staircase, the elegant chandelier that hung in the entrance hall. Long ago it had been a grand country residence. A fine rain began to fall and he shuddered in the cold. He had walked so quickly, so heedlessly through the night he hadn't noticed it before. The walk had for the moment made him oblivious of the pain he still felt in his groin, as if something were numbed there. After standing for ten minutes or perhaps longer, for time seemed meaningless now, he turned and began to walk back to town. The pain had returned, his chest full of phlegm so that his breathing came in ragged gasps as he stumbled one foot after another. The distance he had travelled in an hour or so earlier in the night now stretched before him like a far journey. The streetlights were dulled braziers in the misty rain, but he could barely remember the way he'd come.

As he lurched on, everything that had become vile and pointless in his life assailed him. He could not blame Bessie, nor Rita, and for the moment he wouldn't blame himself. In all of heaven's way, there was nothing more pitiful than the unforgiven. This was something his mother had once said to him. He could never forgive Johnny McBride for the events of the night. His mind was clouded with things that must and must not happen again. He must somehow see Bessie; he had to believe that she would come to him in the evening to follow, and that she would do the forgiving. He must contrive never to see Johnny McBride again. His hate was so fierce it carried him on further than he thought he could go, but with his hatred there was fear. He saw again the knife that McBride had shown him at the boarding house. At last he collapsed onto a bench at a tram stop. The rain had stopped but he was drenched through. Dawn was breaking, the clouds parting, sullen bonfires of light falling between them. The first tram of the day trundled towards him and stopped. He boarded it and rode back into the city. There was a stirring in the streets, a beggar uncurling himself from a shop doorway, the smell of bread from a bakery; a girl took her high-heeled shoes off outside the Albion Hotel and gave him a weary, disinterested glance, business done for the night. He handed her half a crown and walked on.

He approached the house, and his fear re-ignited. In his haste to leave, he hadn't locked the door. Johnny might have returned. Very softly, he slid the latch open. When he was inside and saw that the front room was empty, he placed his back against the wall and sidled along towards the passage like a man in an Alfred Hitchcock picture. Each room was empty. There was nobody breathing in the house except him. He stripped off his wet clothes and slipped naked between the sheets and slept. Again, his mother came to him in a dream. She was trying to tell him something but he couldn't hear what it was. Something about buildings being on fire, flames lighting up St Anne's Cathedral. It is the Blitz all over again, and somehow he has lost sight of her as bomb after bomb shrieks through the air. He has been so terrified he can't move, and when he looks up he sees that she has gone on ahead and he is supposed to be following. A man beside him drags him down to the ground and another bomb comes. A woman on fire runs past him and he thinks it is his mother.

He is hiding behind a wall as the bomb explodes. Bricks fall and loose mortar showers him. The smell of burning is everywhere, like paper held over a gas flame, like petrol, like meat. He doesn't know how long he stays there. Then she is running back to him. Albert, she is crying, Albert, I thought I'd lost you. Oh God, dear God, how could I lose my son, Lord forgive me. It was the Easter Tuesday Raid and she was behaving as if he were the risen Christ. Perhaps none of that is exactly how it happened. He had an idea his mother had put him in a closet, and the shelter had come later. Never mind, he had heard the stories; everyone told stories of what they had seen in the shelters. There was fire; he knows he saw fire.

When he woke, several hours had passed. He could hear rain on the tin roof as the red dawn had predicted. It was another Tuesday and any day now the landlady would come. He reached up and turned the radio on, and felt himself slowly coming to life, although he felt so ill all he wanted to do was lie in bed.

He must clean the house, he must clean himself, his body, his clothes, the inside of his head if that were possible. He looked in the jar where he kept his money. There was fifteen shillings and eightpence, all the money he had in the world. The whole idea of a party had been nonsense. Tomorrow he'd have to find work again. Perhaps that was what his mother was telling him, that he must work hard and save one hundred and twenty pounds to take him home to Ireland, where she would care for him and keep him safe from harm.

Before he did anything else, he must speak to the girl. He rang the number at Rocklands Hall, and asked to leave a message for Bessie Marsh. There was a long pause. He gathered that the phone had been put down, and in the distance the voice of the woman who answered the phone called to someone. The brisk voice of the matron came on.

'Who's calling, please?'

'Albert Black,' he answered, and already he knew that something was wrong. 'I want to speak to Bessie Marsh.'

'Miss Marsh doesn't live here anymore.'

'You must be mistaken,' he said. 'Bessie lived here last night, I saw her off on the Epsom tram.'

'Miss Marsh left the residence this morning.'

'No,' he shouted. 'You're lying. She wasn't late.'

'Mr Black, I've nothing more to say to you.'

'Where has she gone then?'

The phone clicked and the line went dead.

He felt himself trembling as he replaced the receiver. Some dull chime echoed in his head, but he couldn't make sense of it. Whatever had happened he must trust that Bessie would meet him tonight at the cafe. If she didn't come, he would go to her grandmother's house the next day. She would be there, or her grandmother, whom he had still to meet, would know where she was.

When he had finished cleaning the house, he dressed in a fresh blue linen shirt, his good brown jacket and dark trousers. His eye was swollen larger than the night before and the colour of grape hyacinths, but at least he felt respectable. In Queen Street he would get his hair cut, tired as he was of licking it back into a duck's tail with grease. He would be a regular bloke again. At the door, he hesitated. The night before he had watched Rita throw the kitchen knife in the carton where she'd collected the beer bottles. The carton stood near the front door, ready for him to put out for collection. Somewhere, nearby, Johnny might be waiting to pounce, and the ache in his balls flared again. On impulse, he reached into the carton and the knife was still there, as he remembered. He took it out and put it in the inside pocket of his jacket.

After he had been to the barber, and seen his hair emerge

in a luxuriant dark crest, his hollow stomach reminded him that twenty-four hours had passed since he had eaten. At the Continental Cafe, in Victoria Street West, he stopped and ordered a meal of steak and chips. The food lay uneasily in his stomach. He still had hours to pass until the time when he hoped to meet Bessie. A shifty sea wind was blowing rain in his face. Opposite the cafe stood the Royal Hotel, a comfortable large establishment with a tidy bar, a place not frequented by the Ye Olde Barn crowd. It seemed as good a place as the next to pass some time. He could be on his own. He liked to drink alone. In the Royal he wouldn't have to go over the events of the night before. He figured that he was unlikely to encounter Johnny McBride.

He drank a beer, and ordered one for the barman. He needed to make it last, to keep some money for himself if he were to take Bessie out. Nor did he want to be drunk when he met her. His head throbbed and he felt his stomach churn. He ordered a second drink, hoping the fizz would make him belch. The barman was eyeing him up with an unfriendly look. 'Another one for yourself,' Paddy said, trying to buy favour. The second beer had dislodged the contents of his stomach. He made it just in time to the toilets where everything came up, a foul chunder, the sound of his vomiting loud enough to be heard next door in the bar.

When he emerged, the barman shook his head. 'That's enough for today,' he said. 'You're cut, man.'

The bar was filling with workers finishing their day before the pub shut at six. A crush was mounting all around him.

'I'm all right, it's just that I've been crook,' Paddy said. 'I've had my spew, I'll be fine.'

'I reckon you're too young to be drinking in this bar,' the barman said. 'Or any bar. I could call the cops.' It was the first time his age had been questioned since he'd gone to live in Auckland. In the

Albert, nobody really cared whether he went into the pub or not.

Out in the street, Paddy turned over the money that was left. One shilling in sixpenny pieces, and eight pence. And it wasn't all right. There was nothing for it but to make his way to Ye Olde Barn and wait it out for the next hour until Bessie arrived.

It was not until he sat down that he saw Johnny through the archway. Johnny walked past and he could swear their eyes locked. The two of them, staring each other out. If he ran, he thought Johnny would follow him. If he stayed, there was safety in numbers. The Quintal brothers were there, and Jeff Larsen, a whole crowd of them, and over on the other side a crowd of Teddy boys in their finery, but he didn't take all of them in. He was watching Johnny set himself in the last cubicle. The room was swirling with smoke. He walked to the jukebox and took out one of the sixpences, slipped it in the slot, choosing 'Danny Boy'. As he waited to hear Whitman's opening notes, Johnny walked towards the jukebox, his hand flicking forward and pressing the button that said 'Press to change program', overriding Paddy's choice on the Wurlitzer.

'Danny Boy. What sort of shit is that? Sissy yellow Irish junk.' The space in the cafe filled with the sound of 'Earth Angel', the singer imploring a woman, his earth angel, to be his, his *darling dear* . . . Johnny laughed.

'Go blow,' Paddy said.

Johnny overrode the song again, and his sixpence was lost.

'Come outside,' Johnny said.

Paddy walked back and sat down beside the Quintal brothers. Johnny had called him a dirty yellow Irish bastard, had smashed him in the face. Is it now, when did it happen? Yesterday or today? Is it now, is it then, is it happening this minute? His head spun, and the walls seemed to cave in around him, the steadily rising rhythm of the angel bouncing back and forth across the narrowing walls.

Johnny McBride still stood at the jukebox, hands on either side of it, head down, slouching his shoulders forward.

'My eye,' Paddy said, speaking to no one in particular as he touched his face.

Then suddenly everything seemed clearer and he knew what to do.

The air had a pure, singing quality that shut out the sounds around him, his head light.

Chapter 14

Oliver Buchanan sits with his elbows on his polished dining-room table, staring into space. Papers are strewn around; his brief lies open before him.

'So. Did it go any better today?' His wife stands hovering with table mats in her hand, waiting to lay the places.

'Yes, I think so.'

'You don't sound sure.' She is a taller woman than he had expected to marry, slim and dark, half Italian. They met in London when he was travelling as a young man. She was, at that time, studying at the Royal School of Music; this was before the war. Although she still plays the piano, she stopped yearning to perform in concerts when the war came, or perhaps she never did: it was her mother's idea that she be a famous pianist. She dreamed that her daughter would light up the world. Besides, they had small children at the outbreak of the war and Oliver said that there were safer places than London. Like New Zealand. It seems to Oliver that whatever she touches she makes beautiful and that she succeeds very well in lighting up his world. The room where he sits is gently illuminated, the walls hung with paintings from Italy, and also those bought in galleries in Auckland: Woollaston's blue landscapes of the West Coast, one of Frank Gross's moody inner cityscapes, a Frances Hodgkins that his wife loves of an artist sitting alone at a table. Outside, through the white French doors, lies the spring garden bursting with irises and cream-throated freesias. The house is filled with their scent.

'Are the boys in for dinner?' he asks, without moving to collect up his papers.

'They are.' She hesitates, her hand moving to the back of his neck and resting lightly there. 'What is it, Oliver?'

'I cross-examined the prosecution's star witness today. Rita. One of the girls with name suppression.'

'And?'

'She's just a kid. I gave her a hard time. I made her cry.'

His wife sits down. 'I see. But you need to get to the truth.'

'I'm not sure that I did.'

'She'd been keeping bad company, yes? Is this the girl who climbed out the window to go to the party?'

The trial is so sensational that her friends tried wheedling details from her at their morning-coffee gathering earlier in the day. Oliver always says he doesn't like to bring his work home with him, or not in the sense of burdening her with the details of what it entails. But the weight of this trial is making him withdraw from her and yet he needs her close to him.

'She'd have been better staying at home that night, that's for sure,' he says. 'Her parents' hearts will be broken. She's not stupid, she's smart and pretty and sixteen and believes that nothing will touch her, that she's right about everything.'

'Oliver, does it matter? This man, Albert Black, he stabbed a man in cold blood. Surely there's nothing more to be said?'

'It's what happened before he stabbed Jacques that interests me.'

'So one thing led to another, you think?'

'Something like that.' As he speaks, their sons burst into the room, fencing helmets and swords in their hands, flushed and laughing at some joke between them. One is twenty-two, the other nineteen. They are taller than both Oliver and his wife, tousle-headed dark young men with caterpillar eyebrows like his own. Both of them joined the university fencing club when they began their studies.

'Dinner in twenty minutes, boys,' their mother calls when they finish greeting each other. They always kiss her lightly on the cheek, both sides, the European way.

Oliver begins collecting up his papers, leaving the table clear. 'You see,' he says, 'you call them boys. Your children, bearing swords.'

She begins to put the place mats in order. 'Albert Black is a boy with a mother, is that what you're saying?'

'Yes.'

'So was Alan Jacques.'

'Who abandoned him long ago.'

'Poor boy,' she says. 'But there are sisters, aren't there?'

'So I believe.'

'A father?'

'He came back from the war and moved in with a bus conductress. There were a whole lot of children, so he put them all in a home. This boy and a couple of his sisters were shipped out here. I've heard that one of the ones back in England died just before Jacques was killed.'

'It's a terrible story,' she says. 'Did the girls go to their brother's funeral?'

'I don't think so. Things aren't working out well for them. Or so I'm told.' Their sons are distracting Oliver. The older one does a mock feint towards his brother with his sword, even though it is sheathed. '*En garde!*' he cries.

'That's enough!' Oliver finds himself shouting. 'Stop it this minute.'

His wife looks at him, startled. But she thinks she sees it all. 'Perhaps that, all of that, has something to do with this whole mess,' she says. 'The dead boy had troubles of his own.'

It had taken several days for the police to identify the dead man. Everyone who was interviewed, including the accused, had provided the name of Johnny McBride, although the newspapers respectfully called him John McBride, as if his mother would have known better than to call him Johnny. Laurie Corrington, the cook at Ye Olde Barn cafe, was one of those who assured the police that this was his name, and repeated his claim to pretty well every reporter in town. Laurie had been bending over the grill at the front of the cafe when what he described as 'the incident' took place. He knew Johnny, he said. He often came in for a feed. Nice chap, he said, always said hullo to him. Bit of a rough diamond, but no worse than the others. Said he was hoping to go to sea and work his passage to England.

'I turned round just at that moment when it happened. Johnny got up and sauntered over to the jukebox. I saw a man get up from one of the cubicles and stand behind Johnny. Yes, it was Paddy all right. Suddenly Johnny staggered and fell back. At first I thought Paddy had hit Johnny and I hopped along the counter to put a stop to things. We don't like violence in the cafe. Then I saw the blood. I had a white apron on. It was splattered with blood.'

Laurie had dashed to the door and run down the street, his blood-stained white apron flapping around his knees. He ran as far as Victoria Street, yelling for a policeman. There he found two constables. They had dashed with Laurie back to the cafe, one losing his helmet on the way, not stopping to pick it up.

The ambulance came. 'Mr McBride was still conscious at that time,' Laurie said. 'The knife was still sticking out of his neck where he'd been stabbed. The boys rolled him over from where he fell, but you know his pulse was very weak, you could tell that he was going. Poor devil,' he said, 'he'd just had to move out of his digs. He had a suitcase with him, everything he owned. Somebody said there'd been a fight over one of the girls, well, you never know, do you? Anyway, it was me that called the ambulance, yes sir, you do what you can.'

In the suitcases the police found information at odds with who Johnny McBride was supposed to be. Instead of identification for McBride, they found papers belonging to a person called Alan Jacques, just nineteen years of age, not twenty-four, a child migrant who had arrived two years earlier. He'd almost grown up when he left England, hardly a child, barely a man, but when his two sisters were shipped off to New Zealand he'd been sent along with them. In one of the suitcases the police found a number of banned books by the American crime writer, Mickey Spillane. One of them was called *The Long Wait*. The central character was called Johnny McBride.

After several days a farmer from the south was tracked down and called on to travel north and identify the dead youth. Yes, he said, when he saw him at the mortuary, that's him, Alan Jacques. The farmer told police he had employed the boy when he first came to New Zealand. He'd been gone about a year. The kid didn't much like being in the country, and complained about the work. 'Anyone would think he'd appreciate the country life and the opportunities here,' the farmer told reporters who had waited outside while he made the identification. 'I don't know, he kept saying he wanted to go home, didn't like milking cows.'

'What about the sisters?' he was asked.

'I had those girls at the farm the first summer to give them a bit of a holiday. The younger one was pretty useful at haymaking time. I reckon she'd be about thirteen then. The other one was older.'

'Was the boy violent when he was working on the farm?' a reporter asked.

'Not that I saw. Well, he used to read those books, you know the ones Mazengarb banned. Quite right, too; I should have taken them off him, we're a decent family. Don't ask me where he got them. He knocked around with a rough crowd in his days off, perhaps they gave them to him. I did hear he got into some scraps when he was in town.'

'Did you ever give him a hiding?' the reporter asked.

'That's enough of that. He did all right at my place, he had a bunk in the lean-to. I didn't take any lip from him. Anyway, he went into the army after he turned eighteen.'

Perhaps it was the army where he'd learned to fight, the farmer reflected. But how would he know; he hadn't offered to give him a job on the farm when he came out of the military, and he hadn't come looking for one. There were plenty more where he came from. All he knew was that the boy lying on the slab in there was Alan Jacques and he had nothing more to say.

It had been Oliver's duty to inform Albert Black of his victim's identity. (It was hard to know what to call him, or either of them. Paddy or Albert? Alan or Johnny? Formal or informal? He felt that he should keep his professional distance, but Paddy seemed to fit best.) He watched the stunned look on Paddy's face, the growing bewilderment. 'Why didn't he tell me?'

'What difference would it have made?' Oliver asked, trying to conceal a hint of sarcasm.

'Perhaps I could have been a friend to him. He wanted to go home, just like me.'

'It doesn't seem as if Johnny wanted friends,' Oliver said, softening a little.

'He was just a lad. Younger than me. I should have known.'

'Known better than to kill him? We could agree on that.'

Paddy put his head down almost to his knees and wept. 'I didn't mean to,' he said. 'I meant to frighten him. I thought — oh well, it doesn't matter.'

'You thought what?'

'I thought that I would scare him off, give him a bit of a nick, and maybe I'd serve time and get deported back home. Well, something like that, I wasn't thinking very clearly. I'm so sorry. Oh, the stupid little shite.'

Oliver asks his sons if they read Mickey Spillane's novels. They smile, shrug and tell him it's kids' stuff. The older one is doing a degree in English literature. At the moment he is reading the works of Thomas Hardy. Oliver recalls a phrase of Hardy's. Wasn't it he who said that *For every bad there is a worse*?

Oliver has read *The Long Wait* and is repelled. It startles him now that someone could identify so closely with the amnesiac anti-hero of Spillane's novel. He marks a paragraph in the book: *One was going to die. One was going to get both arms broken . . . one was going to get a beating that would leave the marks of the lash striped across the skin for all the years left to live.* Was it possible that, like the character at the book's centre, Alan Jacques had so lost his own sense of identity that he believed in the new one?

He stays up late re-reading the book with a mounting feeling of self-disgust. In spite of himself, he is compelled to read on. His family lie sleeping as he reads. When he finishes, he steps outside. It is a clear night in the beautiful garden. The stars sparkle with a sharp, edgy brilliance. Stars have always fascinated him, and now at close to midnight he sees the Milky Way trailing its pale radiance across the sky. In the northern hemisphere, summer will have moved into autumn. Oliver cannot imagine wanting to live anywhere else but here in Auckland. He has tried living abroad and it didn't suit him. But the young men in this tragedy — neither of them wanted to be where they were, and one has already died. His sympathy for Alan Jacques has been aroused, but he sees that it's possible that what Albert Black has been saying might well be true too: that he was terrified of Alan Jacques, the boy who called himself Johnny McBride.

If Black saw himself as an outsider, Jacques' feelings went further than that. The outcast. Someone was going to die and, as it so happened, it was him.

Horace Haywood knows he should be at home with his wife. Since they transferred north to Mount Eden prison, she has few friends. Instead, she comes to the prison and visits the inmates. She brings them treats, sweets and home baking, and sits talking to them when they are down, as if she were their mother. Their children, because he is in charge of them, the father figure. The circumstances are unusual, he knows that, and the surprised prisoners know it too. Sometimes, when one of the men is particularly unhappy, Ettie will put her arms around him and comfort him. She has tried this comforting approach with Albert Black, but he seems, in some respects, his own man. Black never discusses his crime with other prisoners, nor with the superintendent, and certainly not with the superintendent's wife. There are days when he sits in his cell and sings to himself, and this is disconcerting in itself. Although Black laughs and exchanges cigarettes with men in the exercise yard, Haywood sees him as standing aloof from what took place on the day Alan Jacques died, almost as if he didn't believe it happened. It troubles the superintendent. If the man is found guilty and sentenced to death, it will be his duty to supervise his welfare from the time sentence is passed until the execution takes place. And, after that, there is still the family with whom he must communicate and relay the final words, the last moments of a man's life.

Neither he nor Ettie enjoy a life beyond the prison walls. Once the killing of a man is done, it's so easy to encounter his friends and relatives who live in the city. This is unspoken between them, but both he and Ettie know. At least the family of Black, if he is found guilty, live far away where the superintendent won't have to see them. It is impossible for him to forget the mother of the Englishman, Frederick Foster, who has so recently been in New Zealand to plead for her son's life, and remained in the city after his death. Not that he blames her, she was a fighter; it angers him that Black is not fighting more, because he can't fight for him.

'How do you think the case is going?' he asks Des Ball, pushing the whisky bottle towards him. They will have one more, he thinks, and then he really will be away home. It won't do for him to stay here another night. That is how chaos and riots begin, the warders slacking on their duty, the men taking advantage.

'The girl was a bit at sixes and sevens on the stand,' Des says. 'Too early to tell what the jury's thinking.'

'Buchanan's going for manslaughter?'

'That's right.'

'On the grounds of provocation? That's stretching it a bit, isn't it? It was going on twenty-four hours since he got a hiding from Jacques. Was he still hankering after the girl?'

'Who knows? He didn't look at her when she was on the stand, just looked straight ahead.'

'It's as if he doesn't understand he could die too. What's with him, does he want to die? Doesn't he understand that death is forever? None of us are immortal.' Haywood's voice is angry. 'I've watched too many men swing since I've been here. You know, I worked in the Paparua prison quarry down south. I worked alongside the men for seventeen years. I never thought I'd be selected for a job like this. I thought the world was as rock solid as the stone in the quarry. I believed God took care of things. Do you believe in God, Ball?'

'Sort of. I was brought up a Catholic, sir.'

'I might have guessed. I watch the priest when we execute men in this prison. He's a good man, Father Downey, a good man. He makes the sign of the cross and I see how he's suffering. But I wonder if he really believes God is lifting up this poor sod we're just cutting down from the gallows, and putting him in some better place. Perhaps you can tell me, Ball? I hope it's just darkness when my time comes. Perhaps that's what Black wants too.'

After a while, broken only by the echoing shouts of men in their cells, Des says, slowly, 'Black doesn't want to die. I think he still hopes he'll be deported.'

'Sent back to Ireland? Well, I hope it stays fine for him.' Haywood stands, unsteady on his feet again. 'Got to go home,' he says. 'Have to go home to Ettie. Time for an early night.'

'The dinner in the oven. Yeah, I know, tell me about it.'

Haywood looks at his warder with sudden sharpness. 'You go home too, Des. Go home. Marge all right?'

'Not bad, sir.'

'Children all right?'

'So far as I know, sir. Don't see them so much. They're growing fast.'

'You're a fortunate man, Des, you know that? Fortunate.'

After the second day of Rita Zilich's testimony, the jury gathers again at the Station Hotel for drinks in the upstairs lounge bar. James Taylor has a knack for remembering what everyone drinks. Ken

165

McKenzie wants to escape to his room; he still hasn't accustomed himself to the closeness of the space he and the eleven other jurors occupy. The small room at the courthouse where they take recesses, drink tea, eat lunch together is claustrophobic. The window is a push-up one. The Classics lecturer, whose name is Arthur, has claimed its ledge for himself, perching on its sill, so that he sits slightly above them, and for the most part feigns indifference to the conversations around him, moodily smoking Camels while leaning his head on his fingertips with his free hand. At the hotel, he orders a whisky sour straight up, drinks it quickly, eyeing the door.

'What did we make of the evidence today?' Taylor says.

'Still say she's a lovely girl,' Jack Cuttance says. 'Smart too, if you ask me, but I wouldn't trust her.'

'Oh, I don't know,' Neville Johns says, puffing away on his pipe. 'A bear with a moderately sized brain, I'd say.'

Two or three of the men nod in agreement.

'A good typist if what she says is true,' the accountant offers. 'I'd probably hire her.'

'So what do you think, young Kenneth?'

Ken blushes, wishing he'd been passed over.

The lecturer says, with weary impatience, 'Mr McKenzie reddens. I'm sure he admires Miss Zilich for attributes beside her typing skills.'

Ken sits up straight. 'I think she's missing some things out of her evidence. That's what I think.'

'*Really?* What makes you say that?' Taylor leans forward, balancing his gin and tonic on one knee.

'I don't know exactly. It was just the way her eyes looked over to her friends when she was being cross-examined.'

'But surely she was just seeking reassurance? It's a huge thing for a young lass like that to take the stand,' Taylor says.

'I think she liked Paddy, Albert Black that is, and now she doesn't want her boyfriend to know. I don't think she told the truth about everything, the way it all happened. She made it sound like she was forced to stay with the defendant, but then she told him she couldn't stay the whole night with him. She had to get back home before her parents found out she was missing.'

Arthur, despite his languid appearance, has begun to pay attention. 'But he couldn't get it up, he had a limp penis. Wouldn't that be enough to make her want to go home?'

'No, I don't think it was like that,' Ken says. As he speaks, he finds himself wanting to piss, just like when he was in school and the teacher wouldn't stop asking him questions he couldn't answer. 'She said she couldn't stay the night *before* Paddy couldn't get an erection. She didn't know he couldn't.' He stops then, sure now he is going to piss himself.

Jack Cuttance, coming to his rescue, says, 'Poke her. She didn't know he couldn't poke her.'

Taylor is nodding, looking wise. 'We'll have to see what the next witnesses have to say. Well, they hung that chap Foster. It's a big decision.'

'Hanged,' the lecturer says. 'They hanged Frederick Foster. Pictures get hung, people get hanged.'

Taylor turns away in anger.

The lecturer has changed his mind about leaving. He goes to the bar and orders himself a second whisky sour. 'Perhaps you've got a point,' he mutters out of the side of his mouth as he passes Ken. 'Work in progress. Not that it changes much. I mean, what does it matter who she wanted to fuck? She's of age, she can fuck who she likes. Or, young Kenneth, are you a good moral boy at heart, a true blue conservative farm boy on the lookout for a virgin? Good luck with that. A knife in the back's still just that. A severed spinal cord and a whole lot of blood.'

'Black got beaten up.'

'Aha. So you really are sympathetic to the accused?'

'I might have done it myself. If I'd been him.' He didn't mean to say this, it just slips out.

Arthur looks at him in surprise, with a glimmer of dawning respect. 'Well. That's big talk. I wouldn't have thought it.'

'I know how to use a knife. As farm boys do. We learn how to slit an animal's throat when we have to. Sir.'

'The meaning of life is that it stops then?'

'I beg your pardon?'

'Ask Kafka's pardon. Oh, never mind. We're all animals. When we're dead, son, we're dead. I tend to agree with you. Albert Black shouldn't swing. Up to us really, isn't it?'

Chapter 15

The boy on the witness stand is nervous. The seventeen-year-old wasn't supposed to be in Auckland the day Alan Jacques died. Stan Cameron told his parents he was going to stay at a friend's house for a few nights, the same as he often did. He would stay for the weekend and for a few days afterwards. His family live at the top end of Tinakori Road in Wellington, opposite the Botanic Gardens, in a house overlooking the magnolia trees. He is a printing apprentice, working on the morning newspaper; the presses roll into the early hours of the morning. In winter it is a fair walk into town if he misses the bus, what with the wind whipping through the cavernous spaces of the trees in the park. By next summer he hopes to have saved enough money for a bicycle. Instead of the story he told his parents, when work finished and the paper boys were delivering the first edition, he caught a bus to Auckland. In his head, he told himself he could get away with taking a day off work. He would be there and back before anyone knew he had gone. It was just that he longed to see what Auckland looked like.

He had heard that it was a big place and that things happened there. Nothing happened in Wellington. Nothing. Not that he could find. He hadn't imagined that this secret excursion of his would land up on the front pages of the very newspaper he worked for. His employers had been generous, or perhaps his mother had been pitiable enough when she went to plead on his behalf for his job once he'd come home. Now he is back in Auckland and almost all of the players of those two nightmare days are present in the room. All except one, and he is dead.

In Auckland, Stan booked into a rooming house in Symonds Street. He paid ten shillings up front, and found himself sleeping on one side of a double bed with a man on the other. The idea that you might find yourself sharing a bed with another person in cheap digs had never occurred to him, and it made him nervous, finding himself in this situation. The other man appeared young, although he was tall with heavy shoulders. He wore unusual clothes. Stan put out the light before he took off his shirt and trousers and climbed carefully into bed, clinging to the edge.

The man said his name was Johnny McBride. 'It's all right,' he said. 'I fancy girls.'

They slept back to back. Johnny snored off and on, and the boy thought Johnny smelled of booze and sweat. Eventually, he fell into an uneasy sleep. At some time in the night he woke and was sure he heard his companion sob, although his breathing suggested he was still asleep.

'You need a feed,' Johnny said in the morning, as if it was established that they were friends. 'I know a place that's open all night, seven days a week.'

It was Sunday morning, Ye Olde Barn cafe almost empty, except for a couple of older men reading the *Sports Post*.

That was the beginning of a friendship that lasted two days.

They drank sly grog in a flat in Onehunga. The flat was the home of Ray Hastie, although he said his real name was Rainton; apparently everybody went by this name or that in Auckland. The walls of the flat were decorated with posters of girls wearing bikinis, and there was one daring picture that covered half a wall, creased where it had been folded, of a girl with big breasts and not a stitch on her. Her arse was arched towards the camera's gaze. Is that your girlfriend? he'd asked Ray, but Ray had just laughed and said you wouldn't catch him with just one girl, girls were more fun when they were in numbers. Someday he was going to have a house full of them, so that he could look at them all day long.

The boy had been hankering to try his luck at getting admitted to a pub, something he wouldn't dare in his hometown. The next day he went with Johnny to the Albert Hotel, where he was served without anyone raising so much as an eyebrow. As the day passed, he guessed he wouldn't be at work on Tuesday, or perhaps even Wednesday. Already he would have been missed. It would cost him a toll call to ring the newspaper office in Wellington and they would guess it wasn't true if he said he was sick.

In court, Gerald Timms, the lawyer, isn't interested in any of these details. Timms has gone through Stan's statement, marking the points he wants illuminated. It is a good statement, he told him beforehand.

His voice wobbles when he says he is Stanley Cameron of Wellington. His father is in the packed gallery of the courtroom, waiting to take him home, back south, as soon as he can get him out of the place. 'I know the accused,' he says. 'I knew him as Paddy. I'd known Johnny McBride for two days up to the time he was deceased. I knew Paddy a bit shorter than two days. On the morning of Monday the twenty-fifth of July, I was in the Albert Hotel. Later in the day Ray Hastie asked me to go to a party at 105 Wellesley Street.

171

I got there at about half past six and I stayed there till about quarter past eleven. There had been some trouble at the party, though I didn't see all of it. I went out for about twenty-five minutes.'

'Where did you go?' Timms interjects.

Stan Cameron is ashamed of his answer because his father will hear it. He knows already, of course, but admitting the lie in front of all these people seems as bad as anything he has to say. 'I knew there would be somebody on the night desk at my work. I went down to a phone box to try and make a toll call to say I wouldn't be in on Tuesday but I'd be sure to be back on Wednesday. I was going to say I was crook but I couldn't get through. When I got back to the party I saw that Paddy had been in a fight. He had abrasions round the eye and his shirt and trousers were ripped,' he said in a well-rehearsed voice. 'I also saw Johnny. There was no sign of injury or damage on him. Paddy asked me for something. He was lying on the bed and he called me over. He asked me for a knife.'

'He asked you for a knife?' Timms's voice is soft and insistent.

'He did. I did have one, it was the one my dad gave me for a Scout knife. It was a folding pocket knife. It had a bottle-opener attachment. I'd had it out earlier.'

'And what did you say?'

'I said no. I was afraid to lose it because my dad gave it to me. When I refused him he grabbed me by the coat and ripped it. There was a slight "altercation" but no blows, just a bit of a scuffle.'

'So he got in a temper? Flew off the handle, you might say?'

'Yes, something like that. Some of the men pulled us apart. I didn't stay long after that struggle. I wasn't very sober, so I can't remember exactly what I did. I did go back to the boarding house where I was staying, and Johnny turned up later and stayed there too. I don't think he slept too good, I'd say he thrashed around in the bed a bit, not like the first night. He was talking in his sleep as if he was mad with someone.'

Stan looks sideways at the gallery. He sees the girl, Stella, sitting with Rita Zilich. Stella had seen him and winked as he entered the courtroom. She is wearing a black wide-brimmed picture hat trimmed with a rose over her curly auburn hair. It is clearly distracting to those sitting behind her, but she is oblivious. He knows she has already given her evidence. The night of the party she had touched him in a suggestive manner. 'You're new around here,' she'd said. But then things had all gone amok.

'The next day was Tuesday, the twenty-sixth of July,' Stan continues. 'Johnny and I went to a snooker room in the town. I spent time with him on and off all through that day. There were a couple of other blokes with us, one was Jeff Larsen but he wasn't very friendly towards Johnny. I can't remember the name of the other one. We went backwards and forwards between the snooker room, and for some lunch at a cafe, and the Albert Hotel. Johnny bought some new clothes and went back to the boarding house where we were staying to get changed, then he came back to the Albert. After six o'clock closing we walked up the street and went for a meal at Ye Olde Barn cafe.

'Anyway, there were four of us who'd been drinking together sitting in a cubicle and a couple of people I didn't know. We ordered our meals and the accused walked in and sat down in the first cubicle, facing towards the rear of the cafe. I went down to Paddy's table to say hullo, to show there were no hard feelings on my part. There were some men I knew from the night before. I didn't sit down with them. I talked to Ted Quintal and offered them cigarettes, but Paddy said he didn't smoke. I thought he did, but he didn't seem interested in anything. I went back to my friends and told them I was going outside to the public lavatory, which they told me was

173

the next street up, on the corner. After I'd been there, I started back to the cafe but I found the door closed and a crowd gathered. I wasn't able to get back into the cafe. I saw nothing more of what had happened inside.'

Timms places his hands beneath the edge of his gown. 'So, from the time you went into the cafe with McBride, up until the time you left, what were his movements? If any?'

'While I was there he talked to people in the opposite cubicle and then returned to his seat. He stayed in his seat. I think. From the time he entered the cafe with me until I left, with the exception of talking to the people in the opposite cubicle, he remained in his seat.'

A parade of young men emerge from the Crown witness room where they have been cloistered, their swagger gone, their expressions tight. Rainton Hastie gives bland evidence about the night of the party. It is evidence that distances himself from trouble. He wasn't in the cafe on the night of the incident and it is easy to see how pleased he is about that.

Ted Quintal gives his normal occupation as that of a presser, but right now he is serving a sentence of imprisonment for car conversion. Pooch, whose real name is revealed as Claude, is in Borstal in Invercargill for the same crime. The brothers had gone for a joy ride, as they termed it, in a car they had 'borrowed' the day after Johnny McBride's death. The authorities have declined to send Pooch north for the trial, his evidence considered not significant enough to justify the arrangements needed to transport him to and fro between Invercargill and Auckland. So Ted is on his own. Pooch, Ted says, had been playing the guitar at the party. Johnny was in a strange mood. At some point he'd asked Pooch to play 'Maybe It's Because I'm a Londoner' and for a few minutes everyone had sung along, except Paddy, which was a shame because he was the only one in the room, apart from the girls, with a singing voice, one that soared above the rest, but he turned his back on them as if he wasn't listening. It is true, Ted says, that Johnny and Paddy were fighting and it ended with Johnny kicking Paddy in the testicles. But then, Paddy had tried to rush Johnny with a broken beer glass in his hand, so it is not surprising someone got hurt. He doesn't really know what it was about. Rita Zilich, he supposes. In the cafe, the next night, Paddy spoke to him, showing him his black eye. He'd said, 'It's a beaut.' Nothing else but that. Just Paddy saying it was a beaut. He doesn't remember Johnny McBride stopping to talk to them as he made his way to the jukebox.

Ted is inclined to give smart answers when Buchanan cross-examines him. When Buchanan asks him if Johnny was standing in front of the jukebox in order to select a record, he says, 'Yes, well, I don't think he'd just be bending over inspecting the mechanism.' He agrees that he saw Johnny fall.

'Did he fall flat on his back?' Buchanan asks.

Ted hesitates then. 'Actually,' he says, 'his seat hit the ground first. He did not then fall flat on the ground, his head hit the partition, and he didn't bounce down onto the floor then. He stayed where he was with his head twisted. A tall chap and another man picked him up. I saw blood coming out of his mouth and nose. And then I left. I got right out of it. I was anxious to be away.'

Lloyd Sinclair, known as Cookie, takes the stand. He is, he says, seventeen years old, an apprentice armature winder. He was born in Glasgow and he's been in the country for five years. He'd taken his girlfriend Miriam to the party at 105 Wellesley Street. He'd seen the fight between Paddy and Johnny, and heard Johnny say he'd be back the next day to continue the fight. Cookie describes the scene in the cafe the following night, the way Paddy had come in and sat down beside him, while Johnny went to talk to someone in another cubicle. 'Paddy's condition,' Cookie says, 'was not quite drunk, I'd say, but not quite as sober as he could have been. Well, he wasn't drunk. I saw Johnny McBride leaning over the jukebox. The next thing I saw was Black got up from beside me and took one or two steps towards Johnny, and then he put the knife through his neck.'

'What movement did his arm make?' Timms makes a theatrical gesture, imitating a stabbing gesture.

'He approached Johnny from behind, from the right, and the first I saw of the knife was as Paddy's hand came down towards Johnny's neck. After the knifing Johnny straightened up, turned to his right and collapsed on the floor on his back. I helped to move Johnny and saw the knife then. It was to the right centre of the neck and just about collar level. Paddy stepped back into the back section of the cafe, behind the archway. He said, "Go ahead and call the cops, I don't care." He walked out and Jeff Larsen went after him. I didn't see Johnny speak to Paddy at any time that evening in the cafe.'

All of these rivers of words, the same story told over and again, each with its own embroidery built into its narrative, as the men describe a shifting febrile world where their days and nights seem to merge, allegiances sliding swiftly from one point of view to another.

Oliver Buchanan lifts his head and breathes deeply as if preparing for a race, or perhaps simply to rise above the fetid air that seems to emanate from this parade of youths with their grimy fingernails and tobacco-stained hands. He turns to face Cookie Sinclair and his expression is severe.

'You finished work in the morning, then you went up to Albert Park with your girlfriend for the whole afternoon. After that you came down to Ye Olde Barn at five o'clock. Correct? Yes. But you can't remember if you had a meal before Paddy came in?'

'I can't remember definitely whether we did have one or not.'

'You can't remember whether you spoke to Paddy other than a greeting?'

176

'No.'

'You can't remember whether Paddy spoke to anyone else in the cubicle?'

'He spoke to Pooch. I don't think he spoke to anyone else.'

'But you're not sure of it?'

'No.'

'Can you remember what he said to Pooch?'

'Not now.'

Cookie had walked backwards and forwards around the cafe, talking first to one person then another, then wandered outside for a time, he thought seven or eight minutes. Like the other young men who have given evidence, he is sure, then not sure, of Johnny McBride's exact movements inside the cafe. Months have passed since the incident, as they all refer to it now, and it seems to Buchanan that alliances have been formed, stories hardened, that an impenetrable wall has arisen. It is as if they were afraid to acknowledge their friendship with the accused, lest it tarnish them and their own safety. He asks Cookie to describe what happened next.

'Well, Johnny fell backwards. He sort of stood up, straightened up, turned to his right side, and he spun as he fell and landed on his back.'

'Then, you said, it was you who turned him on his side?'

'I didn't say that.'

'Did you help turn him on his side?'

'We moved him. There was an assistant in the cafe, I don't know his real name, it might have been Laurie. Anyway, we moved him. We tried to sit him up.'

'It was then you saw the knife?'

'I saw it previous to that when he stabbed him.'

'When you put him down again, did you put him on his back or his side?'

'I didn't put him down.' Sweat gleams on the young man's forehead, collecting around his nostrils. Buchanan sees the acne on his face redden as if he had been put under a blow torch.

'Who put him down?' the lawyer asks.

'I don't know. I don't know, he must have been put down by someone because I didn't. I looked around, took my girlfriend outside, and when I came back Johnny was lying down. I don't know if he was lying on his back or his side.'

Buchanan thinks, he is afraid that he might be responsible for the death. And who is he to tell him that he is not? He is a boy who has literally had blood on his hands, trying to do the right thing, and now he is afraid. All of them, afraid. Cookie, Buchanan thinks, is asking himself, as perhaps he has every night since the killing, whether his actions caused the knife to plunge deeper into Johnny McBride's neck and sever his vertebrae, and whether, had he been left sitting, he might yet have been saved. 'Let's go back a little,' he says, more kindly. 'You didn't see Johnny coming down the passage towards the jukebox. Did you see anybody else during the time you were sitting there speaking to Paddy?'

'No.'

'Do you think it possible someone might have come to the cubicle and spoken to Paddy while you were there?'

'Possible but improbable.'

'Stan Cameron has given evidence today and said that he came from his cubicle and offered a cigarette to both Quintal and Paddy at your cubicle. Do you remember Cameron coming to your cubicle and offering cigarettes there?'

'No.'

'Did you see Cameron in the cafe that evening, before the fight?'

'If I did I don't recollect that.' Tears are rolling down the witness's face, his voice trembling. 'I say I don't *remember* him coming to my cubicle.'

'Oh. So just remind me, what were you doing while you were in the cubicle?'

'I was talking to Pooch. He was on the right side of me.'

'So that, talking to him, you'd be turned away from anyone who came to the end of the cubicle?'

'That's right. I was. Turned away, that is.'

'Thank you, Mr Sinclair,' Buchanan says. 'I have no further questions.'

After that, a pathologist is called. He had examined the body of the deceased at the time of the fatality. The single blow that severed Jacques' vertebrae had killed him. A very neat cut and, perhaps, something of an unlucky accident. The pathologist says he couldn't have made such a cut with any certainty himself.

A policeman, a detective sergeant called Bob Walton, takes the stand. He describes how he had been on duty at the Criminal Investigation Branch at the Auckland police station on the night of the twenty-sixth of July. Shortly after seven o'clock, the accused, Albert Black, was interviewed in the presence of himself and the Superintendent. Black was warned, as was the custom, Bob Walton told the court, that he was not obliged to say anything regarding what had happened that night, that anything he might say would be taken down and might be used in evidence. The accused had said, 'Is he dead?', meaning the victim. And he was told that it was understood so. He said, 'Are you sure he is dead?' And Mr Boston told him that he was.

Black had asked to see a solicitor then, and from the list shown him he had chosen, at random, Oliver Buchanan.

Chapter 16

'They're ganging up on Black,' Ken McKenzie says to nobody in particular, although all of them are huddled in the jury room, taking a tea break. There is strong tea from an urn, and gingernuts. 'His mates, or what used to be.'

'What makes you think that?' the accountant asks.

'I reckon they've talked to each other. They've got a story and they're all sticking to it,' Ken says, indicating the young men who have given evidence. He is thinking about Ohaka, the place where he comes from in the north, and his family of vigorous siblings who play rugby and drink more beer than they can hold. It occurs to him that, although he's probably never played a game of rugby, Albert Black is not so different from his brothers, a young man with good looks, an easy charm and a way with girls. 'He's different from them. He comes from another country. They're Kiwi blokes.'

'So what's wrong with that?' Wayne, the gasfitter, asks. 'The sooner Black's called to the stand the better. You'll see him for what he is, a crock of Irish shit.' It is as clear as the nose on their faces, he elaborates, that the defendant is a guilty man. They can reach a verdict and all get on with it.

'Nothing wrong with being a bit different,' James Taylor says, appearing thoughtful and reflective.

His friend Neville Johns, the company director, tamps tobacco in his pipe. He has a full lower lip with a small dent in it where the pipe habitually sits when he is not in the courtroom. Its odour makes Ken's head ache. 'He probably comes from a poor background,' Neville says. 'Not like young New Zealand men.'

'It's like the Yanks during the war,' Wayne says.

'But he's from the UK,' the night watchman says, speaking up for the first time.

'He's an Irishman. Taking our girls. It's all the same.'

'That's bullshit.' Jack Cuttance speaks up, his face suddenly flushed and angry.

'I beg your pardon?' Taylor's voice is shocked.

'Young Ken's right. If someone's not like you, you don't want to know. I see it in this room. There's you and your mates —' and here he gestures towards Taylor, and Johns, and Leonard the accountant — 'wanting to run the show. The bosses. Have a drink. Oh, Mr Cuttance, it's a beer for you, you working fellow who gets his hands dirty. Oh, over in the corner, is it, Mr Cuttance? You don't want to sit too near a butcher. I might stink of raw flesh. As for you lot,' he says, waving in the direction of the night watchman and men's wear salesman, and other of the Queen Street workers, 'you've got slack jobs. You don't know what it's like to make do with what you've got. What do you know about Albert Black? You've been listening to what a bunch of low-life kids have to say. Who's to know what really happened that night? You lot don't know nothing.'

'Temper,' says Frank, the woodwork teacher. 'Well, you're used to knives, Mr Cuttance. You're saying the knife just slipped into Alan Jacques' neck by accident?'

'I'll get you,' Jack says, his teacup rattling in his saucer.

'There you go,' Frank says, and smiles. 'You know, if I'd got my hands on them when they were at school, I'd have thrashed the daylights out of the little sods. I'd have straightened them out.'

It reminds Ken of the woodwork teacher who walloped him when he was at school. He sees the man's veins standing out on his forehead, his eyes popping as if they were about to burst. Old Crackers the Whacker, they called his teacher, and here he is, cooped up with a man just like that, and it frightens him. Somebody, the night watchman, he thinks, begins to shout at them all to shut up, and the volume of noise goes up in the cramped room so that it feels as if they are angry animals trapped in a cage. There is banging on the door; it is flung open by a court official. They must be silent or they will be stood down from the jury if they cannot contain themselves, they are told. Do they want to force the abandonment of the trial?

A silence descends, a shuffling of feet, Neville puffing on his pipe with heavy *pouf poufs*. Arthur, the lecturer, breaks it, saying, 'We're told Albert Black's going to take the stand. Why don't we leave tearing each other to pieces until the defence has had its say?' He puts his hand on Ken's shoulder as they file out.

And so there he is, the killer on the stand, his hands clenched by his sides, his handsome face, which has been set and stony throughout the unfolding evidence, giving little away as he speaks. His voice seems drained of emotion as he begins.

'I am the accused. I was born in Belfast, North of Ireland. I'm twenty on the sixteenth of July past. When I came to New Zealand, I was eighteen years old.' He describes how he'd been a caretaker at

105 Wellesley Street West, how he had lived there alone for a time, with the occasional person coming to stay.

'I met Johnny McBride approximately a month before my arrest. I first saw him at Ye Olde Barn,' he says. 'He was talking to a girl I knew at that time. He spoke to me then. I can't remember the exact words, but the effect of the conversation was that he had no place to sleep that night, so I asked him to come up to my place and spend a few nights till he got on his feet. He did that. We got on quite sociable at first. He stayed for about eleven days all told until I said he'd have to find another place to stay because the landlady was coming. I was worried about that because I had no authority to have anybody else in the house. I thought she might think he was paying me board money and I was sticking it in my pocket. He wasn't paying me board money. Whenever I told him to go he wasn't very pleased. He suggested he should go out and wait until the landlady went away, and then come back. I wouldn't have it, so he went. He left his possessions behind. It was a Thursday that he left, in the morning. That was the Thursday before the twenty-sixth of July that he left. I saw McBride on, I think, it was the Friday or Saturday in Queen Street. He saw me but didn't acknowledge me.'

It is a long statement that takes nearly an hour. He describes the party, the arrival of Rita and what he calls her come-hither looks at him. The jury hears how he had taken Bessie Marsh down the street to catch her tram.

But he doesn't tell them how his heart was breaking when he walked back to the party. Nor does he tell them how he wanted to feel a woman's skin beneath his touch, to slide his fingers over the soft silk of her body, and that Rita was willing. He does tell them about how he found her kissing Johnny McBride on the veranda, and how Johnny had come at him then.

'I told them if the landlady saw them, there would be a complaint to her. McBride said, "Go on, blow," — meaning "go away". I told them what I'd said before, that there might be complaints. The next thing he punched me in the eye. Rita disappeared into the house. When I got the punch I staggered backwards, then forwards; he kicked me in the stomach. I was winded and doubled up. Then he kicked me in the leg, causing me to lose my balance; he kicked me on the left leg, below the knee. I lost my balance and fell on the ground. Up to this stage, I had not landed a blow on him. When I was on the ground he was just aiming his foot back to have another kick and I jumped up, knocking my head against his chin. That only stopped him for a moment. Then we were punching each other round the body, and then two chaps from inside the house came out and separated us. I was doing very poorly in this fight. If it had gone on, I was in no position to defend myself. I wasn't feeling too well and McBride was using his feet. A couple of chaps from inside the house came out and separated us. We went inside to the kitchen. When we were in the kitchen McBride called me a dirty yellow Irish bastard. One of the crowd suggested we shake hands. I was for it. I would have shaken hands, but he refused. He said he'd come round the next day and finish the fight.'

As Ken listens to Albert Black recite the story of that evening, he sees it as it happens. Paddy, or Albert (because he can't get his head around the difference between the two, the man who is accused, and the boy in the fight who everyone in the room knows as Paddy anyway), is describing the scuffles inside the house, how he'd asked for a knife to open the beer and been refused, how McBride had got involved again and again, until Paddy had thrown him out. He closes his eyes when the fights are described, and when the accused comes to the part where he is kicked in the testicles his hands instinctively touch his groin. He opens his eyes, embarrassed, and sees other of the men reacting in the same quick, furtive way.

Their nuts, their crown jewels, they will say afterwards when they are debating the case, the agony of it, like they couldn't ever be put back together again.

Then there is the half-hearted evening that had drifted into morning with the girl Rita. Paddy wasn't that horny, she'd said, and Ken supposes the kick had left him incapable of sex. Ken has little experience of sex; mostly it has been with girls who work on Karangahape Road, and each time he's paid he has thought he will never do it again, that somehow he will find himself a real girlfriend. For the most part he just tugs away at himself. Paddy has mentioned his girlfriend, and he wonders what she makes of all this. He looks down the length of the courtroom and sees the pale girl who has sat with her hands in her lap, not looking to left or right, and never towards Rita and her friends. Ken wonders if there are things Paddy isn't telling the court. He thinks Paddy didn't much care about Rita, that she had simply been there on a whim for both of them. Didn't she see that? he wonders. Not that important, just troublesome. And now there is a life at stake.

Paddy reaches the point where he is about to leave the boarding house the next day and head for the city centre. 'Just before I left my room, I saw a knife. It was on the top of a carton of rubbish. I put it on the inside of my coat pocket. I did that because of what McBride had said the night before, about coming back the next day and finishing the fight. He'd told me he was twenty-four years old. I'm five feet eight and three-quarters tall, and he stood well above me. I thought my chances in a fight with him were nil. I thought that because he had much more experience than I did, plus he was pretty good at using his feet. I thought, also, that I had already tasted that the night before and it was as much as I could take. I took the knife and put it in my pocket. I intended, if he had me on again and got me on the ground, I was going to use it to protect myself. I've only done fighting when I was in school.' He stops there, takes a deep breath. 'I haven't got a taste for it. I was frightened.'

Ken shivers. It is exactly as if *he* had spoken these last words.

Paddy describes the drinks at the hotel, how the barman refused to serve him. He had gone into the hotel with fifteen shillings and eightpence. When he left he had one shilling and eightpence, and he'd shouted the barman twice, so it wasn't as if he had had that much to drink. He had gone on, he says, to the cafe to meet his girlfriend, with an hour to spare. 'I had my back turned to the rest of the people who were in the cubicle. I don't think I spoke to anybody. I ordered a cup of coffee from the waiter. I wanted to play a tune on the jukebox but Jacques came up and stopped me, and called me a dirty yellow bastard, speaking just kind of ordinary. He used to stand in a slouch with his shoulders hunched up. His head he used to keep drooped. He was standing that way on this occasion. When he called me a dirty yellow bastard I just said "Go blow." Then he said he was going to punch me in the eye and that was what he did, a short punch. I didn't do anything immediately. I was pretty dazed and my senses weren't working. He walked forward a little, he said, "Come outside" or something like that. I sat down again. He was standing slouched by the jukebox, waiting for me to go ahead. I took the knife out of my pocket as I rose from my seat. I took it out to defend myself when I got outside. I knew I didn't have much show against him once we were in the street. He was the kind of fella who'd kick you till your guts dropped out or your sides caved in. I wasn't intending to use the knife inside the cafe, I was just overcome, or something. Maybe it was fright or funk, I don't know what it was. All I remember is making a lunge at him. I just couldn't help myself. I couldn't help myself because I'd lost my head. When I made the lunge I didn't think anything would happen at the time. I didn't mean to hurt him so bad.'

Gerald Timms, the prosecutor, perches one foot, clad in its fine leather shoe, on the edge of the stand. 'Mr Black, tell us again what you did after the stabbing?'

'I walked outside. The only thing I can remember is being at a shop on the corner of Wellesley Street.'

'What were you doing there?'

'I just stopped to think.'

'What did you think when you were there?'

'I realised what I had done. I thought it best to go up to the police station.'

'How did you feel?'

'I felt very confused and upset.'

'Why would you feel that?'

'Well, I'd just stabbed a man. I was sorry I'd done it.'

'Did anyone come along and speak to you?'

'I was just turning the corner to go to the police station when Jeff Larsen came along. I've always got on well with Jeff. I thought he was kind to come after me. He said he'd seen what happened.'

'Did he say what that was?'

'Well, I took it he saw what I've just told you.'

'But your story is different from what the other witnesses told us.'

'I don't know why they said that. Jeff knew what happened.'

'Really? So what happened next?'

'Jeff said he would come to the police station with me.'

The events at the party are rehearsed again, the way Paddy had come upon Rita and Johnny embracing on the veranda, the fight that had taken place. It had become almost an incantation, Ken thinks, like a country and western song where the verses tell each chapter of the story but the chorus is a refrain that repeats itself over and again, always coming back to the same point.

'I suggest to you,' says Timms, 'that all of this happened because you were annoyed on account of Johnny cutting you out with this girl you had designs on.'

'That's not correct.'

'But you did have designs on her?'

'I was getting the look. But it wasn't that important. I wasn't annoyed at Johnny McBride paying her attention. I didn't care that much. A fight started, and I got belted and I was very annoyed about that.'

'Later that night, when everyone except Rita Zilich had gone home, you were lying on the bed and muttering to yourself. You were thinking about Johnny McBride?'

'Yes.'

'Thinking about this black eye you had?'

'Thinking about everything in general connected with him.'

'You were muttering that you were going to kill Johnny McBride?'

'Yes, I did say that. I didn't mean it. I just wanted to sort him out.'

'And Rita asked you how you were going to kill him?'

'No, that's not true.'

'But you heard her give evidence to that effect? You're nodding, I take it that means yes? And she said you said you were going to strangle or knife him?'

'Incorrect. I never said anything about strangling or knifing Johnny McBride. She's lying when she says I did.'

'Can you suggest why she's lying?'

'Perhaps she was very fond of McBride and was playing both ends against the middle.'

'But it's a very serious thing to say about you, isn't it?'

'Yes, I heard her swear I said it.'

'And you say she's lying?'

'Yes.'

'What were you going to do when your girlfriend arrived at the cafe?'

'Go to the pictures maybe, or to a dance.'

'Really? Mr Black, you only had one and eightpence in your pocket. That wouldn't have taken you very far. I don't think you were there with the intention of meeting her.'

'Objection, your Honour,' Buchanan says.

'Objection sustained,' the judge responds.

'I was waiting for her,' Paddy says. 'I was waiting.' His face crumples.

Buchanan rises to his feet. 'Your Honour, I'd like to clarify a matter with the defendant.' The judge looks at his watch. 'Briefly.'

Turning to Paddy, Buchanan says, 'Throw your mind back to the time when McBride passed you in the cafe on his way out. You knew he was going onto the street? Were you afraid he'd attack you on Queen Street?'

'Yes.'

'When he saw you following him out, he turned to go to the door?'

'He headed for the door.'

'Do you say he went ahead of you towards the street door?'

'Yes, that's as I remember it. So he was in front and I was behind him.'

'And that is where you were when you struck him with the knife?'

'Yes.'

'Is that what you want us to understand, that you struck him as a measure of protecting yourself against an assault you were afraid of?'

'Yes.'

'Against the assault you thought he was going to commit on you when you both got to the street? You struck him as protection from that?'

'That's correct.'

'And that was the thought in your mind at that time?'

'Yes.' Paddy's voice sinks to a whisper. He leans forward, supporting himself against the ornate railing before him. 'My mind was a blur,' he says. 'I'm confused about it all.'

The judge adjourns until the next day when the closing addresses will be made. The hour of judgment is close.

This is the last night the jury will meet at the Station Hotel. Tomorrow it will likely be over. If they have come to a verdict, they will go their separate ways. The men loosen their ties. Second and third drinks are being downed. A torpor has infiltrated their conversation as if, in spite of their differences, they have come to a point where they have each other's measure, almost a camaraderie. Only Arthur and Marcus and Ken are keeping to themselves. Ken still feels tongue-tied in the presence of his fellow jurors and, although he and Arthur have exchanged sympathetic words, it still seems to Ken that the lecturer thinks he is above it all, and presumably above him. He can't fathom Marcus who, at the beginning of the trial, had been full of smiles but now appears sunk in a brooding inner silence, almost as if he is afraid of something. The Queen Street men remain clustered, people who speak each other's language, exchanging gossip about family and friends, but tonight even they are becoming expansive. The night watchman had known both the accused and the deceased by sight. James Taylor asks him whether he had not felt compelled to declare this recognition when he was called, but he shrugs it off. The bodgies and widgies are simply part of the life on the street. On reflection, all twelve of them are part of what goes on in the city, aren't they? There would be no jury at all if they were to exclude one or another amongst them.

'One of those two is telling lies,' Neville Johns says. 'The girl or the boy.'

'Both of them, probably,' the woodwork teacher says. 'God, I remember a couple of kids that used to fuck like rattlesnakes in the playground in the lunch break. They were like a couple of prize fighters, the way the other kids cheered them on. They'd look at you as if butter wouldn't melt in their mouths if you spoke to them about it.'

'It'll be the girl, I expect,' Wayne, the gasfitter, says. 'A tart if you ask me. What was she doing out when her parents thought she was at home in her bed?'

'Not that he could get it up,' the gasfitter says. 'Pathetic.'

'That's what Mr Mazengarb was talking about in his report,' the accountant says. 'All those bad girls egging boys on. Disgraceful.'

'I don't think it was about the girl,' Ken says, clearing his throat. It still feels like an intrusion when he speaks in this gathering, but at least he has found the nerve to say something when it seems sufficiently important.

'So what do you think it was, Mr Wise Guy?' It's Frank the woodwork teacher again.

'He was frightened, like he said. I think he was scared and he didn't have anyone to tell.'

'You're soft,' Frank says. 'He killed a man; he deserves to be punished.'

Arthur appears suddenly to unwind himself. 'You're talking about life and death,' he says. His interruption silences the group, almost as if a stranger had entered the room. 'Are you so sure of

191

yourselves that you can honestly decide what he deserves? Are you all so far above reproach that you have the right to make this decision? I'm not sure that I am.'

Johns tamps his pipe, a twitch at the corner of his mouth. 'Perhaps we should be lenient. Myself, I'm inclining towards it. He's but a boy.' He turns his groomed hands over in his lap, as if considering what they would be like if they had blood on them. 'There might be a case for manslaughter.'

There is a benign murmur around the room: not exactly agreement, but an expression of some common feeling that things have gone far enough, that there is still time to draw back from the killing of the boy. It feels as though a lightness has fallen over them, that, while one or two of them remain intransigent, one by one they are shedding themselves of the responsibility for a second death.

This is the moment when the barman, who has been absent for a few minutes, walks into the room, a pile of the *Auckland Star* tucked under his arm. He hands out the newspapers to each of the jury members. The headline shouts its message: GRAND JURY JUDGE SAYS BLACK IS 'NOT ONE OF OURS'. And there it is, a report on the findings of the Grand Jury that had had Albert Black committed to trial by jury, presided over by the same Mr Justice Finlay in whose presence the trial is now being conducted. In his opinion:

> *The offender is not one of ours, except by*
> *adoption and apparently comes from the*
> *type that we could well be spared in our*
> *country. He belongs to a peculiar sect,*
> *if you could call it that, or a peculiar*
> *association of individuals whose outlook*
> *on life differs from the normal. It is*

unfortunate that we got this undesirable
from his homeland. It is a case of an
apparently deliberate stabbing in a
restaurant in Upper Queen Street, and
there seems to be no opening of either
provocation or self-defence, or any of the
defences usually presented in a case of
this kind.

The judge had said that. Even before the trial began.

It is there in black and white.

The morning newspaper, delivered to their bedrooms the next day, carries the same story.

Chapter 17

Des Ball lays out two steak and kidney pies on plates, and a bottle of tomato sauce, on Horace Haywood's desk. 'I got them from the kitchen, cook's special,' he says. 'You better eat something, sir.'

Haywood has already drunk a third of the bottle of Scotch in front of him.

'Ever occurred to you, Ball, how handy it is to have the kitchen right next door to the gallows? Not so far to take the condemned man's last meal?' The kitchen in Mount Eden jail is a vast space filled with gas burners and vats from which food is ladled.

'He hasn't been condemned yet.'

'But it's there, the writing on the wall, eh?' Haywood bangs his fist on the newspaper lying alongside the pies.

'Sir, perhaps the judge has a point. Do we need his kind in the country?'

'You want to see him go down? Don't you, eh?'

Des scratches the back of his head. 'Funny, it's hard not to like him. But neither can I see past the knife in the back. I reckon this jury's a weird lot, they look all over the place. They could go for manslaughter.'

'If the judge gives them that option. He's already laid down the law, even before he heard the evidence. He says there was no provocation. You've seen the newspaper.'

'You never know, perhaps he's heard enough to change his mind,' Des says, trying to calm the other man down. 'Sir, Mrs Haywood's been asking for you, she wants you to go home.'

Busy, childless Ettie Haywood, who loves the prisoners so much, sitting all alone at home, practising her bouffant hair-do and shortening her skirts. She has rung the prison three times tonight. Haywood won't pick up the phone, so she has rung what the warders grandly called the reception desk, the place where men are admitted through the stone archways, then measured and weighed, as their world begins to shrink smaller and smaller, until they can't see themselves or who they are anymore, just shadows of themselves. Ettie's heart will be breaking. She will know that Horace is on the bottle. She will know that the outlook for Albert Black is bleak. Once, she had patted his hand awkwardly and told him she knew all would be well for a boy like him. Now she won't be so sure.

'Does Black know?' Haywood asks.

'We haven't delivered newspapers. Room service is a bit slow round here.'

'Strange how word gets around this place. Take a drink, man.' Haywood pushes the bottle towards Des.

'One,' Des says. The last time he staggered home from one of these sessions, Marge had locked the door on him and he'd had to get a ladder from his garage so he could break the window and undo the catch to enter his own house. Never mind that Marge shouted so loudly he could have sworn the neighbours heard.

A light had come on across the road, a curtain lifted, but nobody came.

Ken McKenzie lies awake in the Station Hotel, his eyes as dry as rusks. His life has been without ambition up until now. He is twenty-seven: time is rushing past him and nothing more important than his own survival has been the height of his achievement. It occurs to him that so far his life has depended on the decisions of others: his father, his siblings, his uncle and aunt, the man he works for at the electrical workshop. At school he did what he was told because keeping out of trouble was the surest way not to display his weaknesses, his uncertain bladder, his lack of cleverness, or so it was said, although he passed his matriculation exams when nobody expected it. A bit of a fluke, jolly good luck, it was said at the time.

And, when it came to his future, it was his family who decided he should leave the farm, be cast out, as it were. It was his uncle who decided on the work he did. Although he likes his aunt and uncle, quiet people whose children have already left home, and who tolerate him so long as he doesn't disturb them while they read the evening paper or listen to the news on the radio, he wonders how long it will be before they tell him that it is time for him to have a grown-up life of his own. And then — what he will do next is a mystery he has yet to explore. Perhaps his relatives will tell him, but will it be something he wants to do? Tonight, something has stirred in him. His uncle expects him to phone each evening to let him know if he is doing all right and also, Ken guesses, hoping that he will drop some gem of information about the course of the trial that he and his aunt can polish before passing it on to the neighbours. Wink, wink, nudge, nudge, a little tap on the side of the nose.

But tonight Ken hasn't phoned. His uncle won't be able to

resist telling him what to do, even though he knows, just as Ken has learned over the past three days, that it is illegal to influence a juror. Still, his uncle might whisper down the phone a little aside, like *Go get him, boy*. Because Ken knows what his uncle would do were he in this situation. He doesn't need to be told. The sky, as seen from the window of the lounge bar, had shimmered with spring light that made him think of the sky up north, and then, as night gathered, a layer of cirrostratus cloud had descended over the city, indicating a front. Lights had popped up in the dusk, and he thought that he liked the city well enough to stay, but not as he was, that he needed to change, and he must decide for himself what to do next.

In the meantime, there is the small matter of a man's life to be decided. A boy who has lived on the margins. Like him — not that you would think so if you were to look at them side by side. But when it comes to Albert Black, he knows. The judge has spelled it out. Not wanted here.

There is a quiet tap at the door, almost indiscernible, so that for a moment he thinks he is mistaken, and then it comes again. He climbs out of bed and opens the door a crack. Jack Cuttance stands there, a dressing gown over his flannel pyjamas. He slides into the room quickly as Ken closes the door behind him.

'A bad business,' he says, taking a packet of cigarettes out of his pyjama pocket and lighting up a Capstan. He draws down a lungful of smoke and pours it back through his nose. 'Mind if I sit down?'

'They won't let him off, will they?'

'Guilty as sin, that's what they'll say. Maybe he is. The girl says he was planning it.'

'And he says he wasn't.'

'But who to believe? They expect me to go with them, Taylor and his mates. They reckon I don't have the brains to think for myself. I can tell it in their eyes. You know, sometimes I look in the eyes of an animal before I kill it. And there's an instant where I swear it knows. You heard an animal scream when it's killed?'

'Yes,' Ken says, 'I came off a farm.'

'Yeah, I remember you saying that. You've been on Black's side since the beginning. Why is that, I wonder?'

Ken hesitates before answering. 'So far as we know, Black's only made one mistake. In the criminal sense. Don't we all make mistakes?'

'So tell me about yours.'

'Oh, I don't know. Nothing criminal.' Only, from where he is sitting now, his whole life looks like a mistake, a dereliction of duty to the self. 'Perhaps that's my problem. I've never taken a chance on anything.'

Before he can elaborate there is another soft knock at the door. It is off the snib and Arthur pushes it open.

'Close it,' Ken says.

They look at each other, three unlikely conspirators, sitting in a row along the bed, like blackbirds on a telephone wire, Ken thinks. Arthur wears pyjamas made from silken material and light leather loafers instead of slippers.

Arthur says, 'There are just the three of us. The rest will find him guilty.'

'And you don't think we should?' Jack says, testing the water. He and Arthur have barely exchanged a dozen words over the course of the trial. 'I mean, what's your point of view? If you don't mind me asking?'

Arthur suddenly sinks his head into his hands, his elbows on his knees. 'I can't tell you,' he says, his voice hoarse with emotion, 'how I've searched my conscience these last few days. My life, my vocation has been the study of classical literature. I've been looking for answers, listened in my head to the words of the philosophers, as if they would guide me in everything I did.'

'So what have they told you?' Jack asks, his tone quizzical, almost amused.

'Nothing I want to hear. Black killed Jacques, we know that. But if we find him guilty, we as good as put the noose around his neck. If we find him not guilty, we're denying his actions too.'

'Well,' says Ken, 'if we can't agree, they'll have to have another trial.'

'True, no majority verdicts here. We abdicate responsibility and hand it on to someone else, is that what you're saying?'

'I think we should try to persuade the others to see our point of view,' Ken says.

Jack makes a grunting noise. 'Frank? Wayne? I don't think so.'

'When Socrates was put to death,' Arthur says, as if talking to himself, 'it was believed he would achieve spiritual immortality, that he would live on in an afterlife. But I cannot believe that.'

'Well, perhaps this Socrates fella wasn't horsing round with some girl behind his sheila's back,' Jack says. 'I mean, he might have got a better deal.'

Arthur says, more firmly, as if he is pulling himself together, 'I cannot believe we've earned the right to decide who should live and who should die. I don't believe in the death sentence. And here I am, being tested by an Irish youth of no particular consequence to stand up and be counted. There are powerful men on this jury, believe me. When this is over, the word will be out: watch this fellow or that fellow, he's not up to much. They'll sit at dinner tables where chancellors and professors dine, and they will say a dismissive word that will carry on and over to where it's meant to be heard.'

'You mean,' says Jack Cuttance, 'that you're afraid for your job if you go against them?'

'Perhaps. Yes, it could happen, I've seen the way things go in this town.'

'I doubt they'll shop for their meat elsewhere if I stand up to them. I do a very good line in smallgoods.'

'It's easy to joke,' Arthur says. 'I'll stick by my principles.' He is taking quick shallow breaths as he speaks.

'We should get some sleep,' Ken says, surprising himself, making a decision to turn the men out.

When they are gone, it is two o'clock. He lies down and drifts back again into a shallow, uneasy slumber.

Oliver Buchanan walks through his house, his feet bare, so that he won't disturb his sleeping family. He looks at his wife, a slant of moonlight falling through a parted curtain across her still face. Her skin is like porcelain, her dark hair fanned across the pillow. Stopping at the doorways of each of his sons' rooms, he half wishes one of them will wake, so that he might suggest a cup of hot Milo, a piece of toast smothered in Marmite, comfort food they liked when they were children. Neither of them stirs. Perhaps it is as well, for he is the one who needs comfort and it's not something he can ask of them. He has no wish to burden them with the sorrow of his day, the certainty of calamity in store. Instead, he looks at each sleeping youth and their beauty, a reflection of their mother's, which astonishes him over and again. They remind him of Michelangelo's studies of youth. His children. Their faces in repose. The whole world ahead of them. How much about their lives does he really know? he wonders. A man thinks he knows his children, but does he really? Young men are expected to be warriors, to be pioneers and soldiers, so brave of heart. He asks only that they are good men. Perhaps not even that: simply that they survive in the world unscathed, without doing harm to others. Once, he would have wished them to follow the law, as he has done, but now he hopes they will not. The law, as it stands at this moment, seems cruel and unjust, a carapace for power and revenge, designed by men who have been to war and can't let the past go; must hunt down enemies for the rest of their lives.

This is the first trial Buchanan has participated in where the death penalty is a likely outcome — all the more so since the delivery of the newspapers. He isn't an unduly religious man but he was brought up in the faith of his mother, a devout Anglican. She asked that at her funeral he read the words of the twenty-third psalm, which she loved so much, and the words flood back to him now, even though his mother has been dead ten years or more: *Surely goodness and mercy shall follow me all the days of my life and I will dwell in the house of the Lord forever*. Will goodness and mercy prevail? He fears the worst. The boy in the dock is a good-looking fellow. Not tall — a point the accused had made himself — a lean fellow but a good chest on him, a keen look in his green deep-set eyes. A mother's son too. Like all the young men who have gone to the gallows this year. He corrects himself. All the men who have ever gone to them. And thinking about his own sons, who live in the fine, careless rapture of youth and privilege, he sees how their very existence could collapse with one false step, how easily things can go wrong.

He returns to the table where his papers lie scattered. There is something missing but he can't find the piece. Something about Larsen and his testimony.

Paddy knows what the newspapers have reported. Earlier in the day, Ettie Haywood told Edward Horton, the prisoner serving life for the murder of Kitty Cranston. It was the brutality of that murder that led to the reinstatement of the death penalty in 1950. Horton likes reminding his fellow inmates that he escaped the gallows because the penalty wasn't retrospective. 'You're dead fly, aren't you?' Paddy said, the first time Horton told him this. Horton looked at him, bewildered. 'You're a bit cunning,' Paddy said. 'Never mind. Sure it's the Irish in me and proud of it.'

Now Horton is in the bowling team that has monthly outings to play on greens beyond the prison walls. There are twelve lifers in the team, and Ettie Haywood makes a point of chatting to them all as they prepare for the trips. She likes to keep them informed of what is going on in the world, it helps them to keep in touch with reality, she says. In fact, she often brings a newspaper with her so that she can read them the headlines. When she saw Horton that day, she had the paper in her basket. He had asked for it: 'Just a quick skim, Mrs Haywood', was how he put it. And when, unthinkingly, she put it in his hands, his face lit up with an unpleasant glee.

'They're after you,' Horton told Paddy when they met in the exercise yard shortly before lock-up.

Paddy thinks he mightn't sleep, but sleep and tobacco are the only drugs available, and sleep is the one he likes the better. It falls on him in deep draughts of unconsciousness when he allows his mind to go blank, to find what he calls the black hole inside his head. When he sleeps he dreams again of Ireland, always Ireland. He is out in the countryside, beyond the city confines. He is on holiday in Ballycastle with his mother and father and wee Daniel. The heather is blooming on Knocklayde Mountain and rustling in drifts all around them; they are at the very tip of Ireland and the sea stretches in front of them. Look, there's Scotland that you can see from here, his mother cries, as they wade through the undergrowth.

Dragonflies are dancing above them. They are singing, all of them together, the patterns of song that run through their lives:

> The big ship sails on the
> ally-ally-oh
> The ally-ally-oh, the ally-ally-oh
> Oh, the big ship sails on the
> ally-ally-oh.

Just as he will sail away. He is leaving them. He is going far. In his dream he is moving towards the pale face of the girl he could love. He is awake and it is darkness again.

The night is not yet over for Buchanan. Jeff Larsen has given evidence that echoes that of other witnesses, varying only in that he had followed Black from the cafe after the stabbing and walked him to the police station, where he left him. Well, he was a mate, he's said in his evidence, he thought someone should see him right. He hadn't seen what happened in the cafe. That's what he said.

Buchanan goes back over a newspaper file and comes to a clipping. There had been more trouble at Ye Olde Barn cafe on the Saturday night following the death of Alan Jacques which involved, as the paper put it, Teddy boys, bodgies and widgies. Jeff Larsen had been there when someone let him know that sugar was being put in the petrol tank of his car. Larsen had rushed to the scene. Some sugar lumps were already in the filler pipe and another ten sitting on the boot of the car. Larsen said he had no idea why anyone would want to sabotage the engine of his vehicle.

If it were a warning, Larsen had taken it. The next day he disappeared. The police had gone looking for him, for, as it happened, Larsen was on probation. He'd lain low until the police found him just before the trial and bound him over to give evidence. He was hardly the prosecution's most willing witness. Buchanan rubbed his eyes as the night grew thin, needing to sleep. Larsen's evidence was the same as that of the other witnesses, and Black didn't seem to know what his friend had seen. There were blind alleys at every corner. If they had ever liked Albert Black, it seemed that none of them did now.

And here was another thing. A fifteen-year-old girl was found further down Queen Street the same night, selling herself. When the police stopped her in the middle of a blow job, she said she was raising money for Johnny McBride's funeral.

Everyone, it seemed, was suddenly McBride's best friend.

Chapter 18

The hour is upon them.

Gerald Timms rises to make his closing speech for the prosecution, summarising evidence that he suggests is proof of what he describes as the premeditated murder of Johnny McBride by Albert Black. As the two men approached the jukebox in Ye Olde Barn cafe, nobody saw McBride strike the accused on that evening of the twenty-sixth of July 1955, he tells the jury. The defence of provocation should be put aside. No such thing happened.

'Look,' he says, 'there was a quarrel over the affections of the young lady who has given evidence at this trial. A brave young woman. It takes courage to come to this court and recount the events of the night before a murder. Imagine, there she was, torn from her friends, finding herself alone with a raging, angry man planning to kill his rival.

'It's plain from her account,' he says, nearing the end of his remarks, 'that the accused was so incensed with the deceased man paying attention to the witness that he killed him at the first available opportunity. A cold-blooded murder, committed by a man this country could do without.'

Timms nods to the judge as he makes this comment, as if offering endorsement of what had been put before the Grand Jury, an opinion that has now travelled the length of the country. 'This,' he concludes, 'is simply the case of a violent young man who brooded over an affront to his self-conceit.'

The courtroom is hushed. Rita Zilich, dressed again in her black suit, her beret slouched over her right ear, tilts her head, chin up, as she squeezes closer to the young man beside her.

Pearson, Black's senior counsel, begins his closing address. Albert looks straight ahead as the lawyer walks to face the jury bench, some four feet away from the jurors, his feet planted a little apart to give him balance. Buchanan finds himself holding his breath. He has prepared a brief for Pearson, who is busy on other legal matters besides this case, and wishes that he could deliver the address, but it is not the place of junior counsel. He is not sure that Pearson is as passionate about this case as he is. Although Black had chosen to be represented by him, the system has selected Pearson to deliver justice on his behalf.

'Gentlemen of the jury,' Pearson begins, 'the charge against the prisoner is one of murder, and the punishment for murder is death. That simple statement is sufficient to remind us of the awful solemnity of the occasion that brings you and me face to face.

'Albert Black is a twenty-year-old youth who has never faced a criminal charge in his life until the events of the twenty-sixth of July this year.'

He pauses to let this register. It is a good start. The members of the jury shift uneasily in their seats.

The lawyer asks them to inquire of themselves whether they really believe, in all sincerity, that the motive for the actions of the accused was rivalry over the affections of Rita Zilich. He puts his hand on his chin, as if searching for the answer to a puzzle. 'That is learned counsel's argument. But, you know, if you stop and think about it, that doesn't make sense. The witness suggested that she was forced against her will to spend the night with the accused, and that, on this night, he made death threats against McBride. But the accused says this isn't true, apart from a vague remark about wanting to kill McBride. Remember, this was after McBride had severely beaten and wounded him. It's a remark that many of us might make in the heat of the moment, given the circumstances. He denies that he discussed any method of killing McBride. It's one word against another, isn't it? On the issue of whether Miss Zilich was forced to stay with Black on the night in question, this, too, is one word against another. Whose evidence to believe? Miss Zilich wasn't exactly truthful with her parents on the night in question. Can you rely on her evidence?'

In the gallery there is uncomfortable rustling. An older woman stifles a cry, her hand over her mouth. She looks across the room towards Rita, her cheeks channelling tears. Rita turns, startled, and sees her mother.

'Let's look at this matter in more detail,' Pearson says. 'She tells us she was forced from the car by Black's associates. But then, removed from the car, she walks back into the house, without asking for help from any bystanders, and there she has stayed with Black until everyone leaves. As she enters the house, her girlfriends are still collecting their coats. She doesn't ask any of them to rescue her. Presumably she says goodnight to them. The accused lies down on the bed while she picks up a few glasses here and there. It's quite a domestic little scene. When Black asks for a mirror, she gets one down off the wall. It's heavy, an effort for her really. Now remember, there is nobody else in the house and

Black is lying down. She doesn't have to do this. Black takes one look at himself and his bruised face and drops the mirror, although she says he throws it. When he asks her to spend the night with him, she tells him she can't stay the whole night, which of course we understand because she needs to be back at home when her parents wake up. Finally, she lies down on the bed where there is a failed attempt to have sexual intercourse.'

Paddy's face shows a flicker of emotion; his head droops for an instant.

'None of this occurs because the witness has been forced to stay. Clearly she was not. When she makes the decision to go home, Black lends her ten shillings and walks her to a taxi stand.

'Of course, if you are looking at all of this from a moral perspective, you may find it reprehensible that Black already had a girlfriend whom he was attempting to betray. But moral failings are not evidence of murder. However much you may have heard about and read of moral disintegration amongst the young in this country, you cannot draw on the perspective of Mr Mazengarb and his colleagues to determine the guilt or innocence of Albert Black. I venture the opinion that monogamy is a habit instilled in us by society, not one that all of us are born to; young people may decide to mate without great discrimination before they settle on a partner for life. Black had tried his luck with the witness, and you might say he had won, in the sense that she had chosen him, rather than McBride. So why on earth would the accused decide to go to Ye Olde Barn cafe the following day and kill the man she had spurned in his favour? This doesn't make a lot of sense to me, nor should it to you.'

Pearson pauses so long that the audience might wonder if he will continue. Buchanan is watching the men in the jury, trying to see what is going on behind their eyes. Some of them have lowered their glances.

Pearson resumes, almost weary in his tone, as if what he is about to say hardly needed explaining. 'Albert Black says he was afraid of Johnny McBride. Well, that's reasonable, surely? You may have some sympathy for the deceased, McBride, or to give him his true name, Alan Jacques, and it may not be entirely misplaced. After all, he's dead. And, as it turns out, he was younger than the accused, though he didn't look it, and claimed to be much older. He arrived in New Zealand as a child migrant, something he didn't choose. Nor did he want to stay in this country. Like many young people who were and continue to be subjected to forced migration, he simply wanted to go home. But make no mistake, Jacques was a streetwise, bitter young man who had had military training and an aptitude for violence that he employed when things didn't go his way. He read not just for entertainment but in order to find justification for his own violence. His hero was a cult figure, the central character in a fiction called *The Long Wait* by the writer Mickey Spillane. He adopted the name of this character as a fictional representation of himself, the unhappy youth who was in fact Alan Jacques. He discovered, too, new ways to hurt and humiliate his victims. Jacques, or McBride, as you will, accepted hospitality from Albert Black when he found himself without shelter. But the accused could only shelter him for so long, and when it came time for him to leave, the deceased refused and turned on him. This is what the fight was about, not the girl. Jacques beat Black until he couldn't stand up, kicked him on the ground, would have kicked him in the head had he not been prevented, and he kicked him in the testicles. Albert Black, the accused, tells us he doesn't have a taste for fighting and has not fought since schoolyard scraps in faraway Belfast. He had good reason to be afraid of Johnny McBride.

'So, fearing for his life, he slips a knife, an ordinary kitchen knife that he uses for peeling potatoes, into his jacket pocket. That is not a sensible decision, but one driven by his fear. Members of the jury, we expect somehow that young men will be as wise as we are when we are old. Sadly, that is not always the case.'

Buchanan feels himself relaxing. These are his words and Pearson is delivering them with eloquence.

'You have heard from various young men who were present in Ye Olde Barn cafe on the night Alan Jacques died. Black says that the deceased came into the cafe, punched him in the face and invited him outside. These witnesses have a common story that is at odds with his version. They say they did not see this action. They saw nothing. Their heads were turned away. They were talking to their girlfriends, or they had gone outside to the lavatory. They had been drinking that day, all of them. Who is to know who saw what and who is telling the truth, the witnesses or the accused? And what are you to make of the evidence of Jeff Larsen, the man who got up and went after Albert Black and walked with him to the police station? As it happens, this young man tried to evade appearing in this court. The police had to go and bring him here in order for him to give any evidence at all. Sometime after the arrest of Black, Larsen's car was interfered with. Is it possible that his version of events was closer to Black's story, that he saw something they didn't or weren't prepared to acknowledge? You might like to consider the possibility that Larsen was intimidated by his see-nothing friends.

'Members of the jury, this is life and death.' Pearson rocks back slightly on his heels.

Some of the men sitting before him return his gaze, or else stare at their fingernails, rub stubble on their chins or glance sideways at the gallery, as if to wish themselves away from probing eyes. Some are beginning to look unwell, even feverish.

'You have before you this mortal boy, one who has made a

mistake, unintended, but a mistake nonetheless, with terrible consequences. Death is forever,' Pearson says, 'as Albert Black now understands better than most of us. All around you, in this courtroom, you are surrounded by the beauty and vitality of youth, as well as its vanities and arrogance. The young occupy an uncertain universe. Mistakes can be made in the heat of the moment by the vulnerable young. Who amongst us has not had the thoughtless moment that cannot be recovered? Yet none of us have had to pay with our lives. In the clear, long light of all the days that lie ahead of these young people, most of their mistakes can be overcome and forgiven. As we grow older, we put behind us the belief that we are immortal; we gain a greater sense of wisdom and understanding of consequences. Our passions turn to questions of truth and justice as well as the passions of the flesh. As people who pray for forgiveness for yourselves, you have now the opportunity to forgive another. May you be guided by goodness and mercy.'

Words, good words, flying out and around the courtroom, whispering their way into the ears of their audience. Words that would make you weep if you were a good-hearted man or woman, as some of those present do, while others turn their faces away.

Buchanan looks at the jury. Some of the men have quivering faces. He knows already the ones they can count on. There is one surprise among them. But there are not enough. There are simply not enough.

Chapter 19

'Well, Black,' the judge says, as his summing-up comes to an end, 'you have had a long, anxious and careful trial. There is only one sentence that can be pronounced. You are either guilty of murder or not. It is up to the jury, twelve good men and true, to decide on your innocence or guilt.'

Of course, Ken McKenzie thinks, they have been deliberating all along. At the Station Hotel, minds had been made up before the closing addresses. These words have wrung his heart, but not those of his fellow jurors, or not many of them. And whatever good words Black's counsel has had — some of the hard and fast among his fellow jurors might have been momentarily swayed — the judge has put short work to that. He has effectively ruled out manslaughter, saying that it is applicable only if provocation can be proven and, given the time that had elapsed since the fight at 105 Wellesley Street, they should be cautious about such a verdict.

Once they are inside the jury room and the doors close, James Taylor says, 'This shouldn't be difficult, gentlemen. Let's start with a show of hands to see who thinks Albert Black is guilty.'

'It's irrefutable,' says the accountant.

Heads nod around the table. Hands are raised, eight in all.

Ken, Jack Cuttance the butcher, Arthur the lecturer, and Marcus from men's wear, who has hardly spoken at all except to the night watchman and the grocer in the intervals between their duties, keep their hands in their laps. Ken sees that Marcus's face is set in a frightened grimace as if he can't believe he is doing this.

'How can he not be guilty?' Wayne the gasfitter asks. 'A knife in the back of the neck is murder.'

'But it was a fluke,' Ken says, recalling the words of the pathologist. He is endeavouring to sound calm, hoping they might still listen to reason. 'Remember, he said even he couldn't have hit the exact spot the first time, even if he'd tried.'

Neville Johns speaks then. 'The judge clearly believes he's guilty. You can make all the fancy excuses you like, a good New Zealand man wouldn't do a thing like that.'

So it is there again, Ken thinks, the prejudice against the outsider that the judge expressed to the Grand Jury. It is alive and well in the room; it has been there all along.

'Irish. One of those Mickey Doolans,' Wayne says.

'He's an Ulsterman,' Arthur remarks quietly, 'a Protestant lad. Not that it should matter what his religion is.'

'He speaks like a bog-trotter.'

So they range, backwards and forwards, reliving the moments of the trial that have struck them the most. The girl is pretty and well spoken, don't they think? An impressionable girl who'd done a silly thing, going to that party, but she was brave all right, and you could see she has a bit of spirit.

'Larsen wasn't brave,' Ken says. 'I read that bit in the paper about Larsen being bound over to give evidence, just a little item.' It's something that's been buzzing around in his head like a blowfly in a bottle. 'They found him and brought him back. Like Mr Pearson said, he must have been scared of giving evidence. The others wanted to shut him up. Why would they do that?'

'Mr McKenzie,' Taylor says, any friendliness of the past days evaporating like cold mist in the hot room, 'that did not form part of the evidence. They didn't recall Larsen to the stand. It's too late to speculate.'

'I tell you, it was in the paper, they put sugar in his petrol.'

'That leads us nowhere.'

'But it does, don't you see that? Those witnesses, they want to be on the right side of the law. I reckon they've all got things to hide.'

'It's a little late to play Sherlock Holmes.' Taylor's voice is cold.

'Don't you care if there's a miscarriage of justice?' Ken's voice is anguished. 'This is a man's life.'

'Gentlemen, we need to move along,' Taylor says. He speaks as if Ken is a recalcitrant child. 'I believe most of us are of like minds. Sir,' he says, turning to Marcus, 'I'm surprised that you don't share our views.' He nods to the other men from Queen Street. 'Your friends seem sure enough.'

'They think it's not worth arguing over.'

'Is that true?' Taylor says.

There are shrugs and silence. Marcus casts his eyes downwards, his fingers knotting and unknotting.

'You don't seem very sure about this.' Taylor looks around at the man's friends.

'We all have our secrets,' the night watchman says.

'You mean he's a faggot, and you're not,' Johns says, with quiet menace.

'I'm not,' Marcus says in a high, terrified voice.

214

'You know what happens to faggots if the law gets hold of them, don't you?' the banker says. 'Perhaps you fancy Black.'

Marcus raises his hands in a gesture of submission. Ken closes his eyes. There is a thick smell of men's bodies around him, sweat, tobacco, an ugly tension that has descended. He supposes he has known that Marcus is a queer man, perhaps everyone has. It is not something he had dwelt on during the course of the trial. But he sees that Marcus's friends knew and have been afraid for him all along.

'Guilty,' Marcus says in a whisper.

'That makes nine of us in agreement. Come on, my friends, what's the worst that can happen to Black? Yes, he can be put to death, but I expect there will be a plea for leniency. He's young, he'll probably get shipped off back to Ireland after he's served a long term in prison.'

'You don't know that,' Arthur says. 'You've invented a scenario that suits you, so you can go home and sleep easy and not think about it again. If you find him guilty, the judge is bound to pass the death sentence once the verdict is delivered. All the rest is speculation on your part. Suppose you're wrong and Black is put to death, will you still be so sure of yourself? Some of us beg to differ with you.'

'It's true, Black did stick it to Johnny McBride,' Jack Cuttance says, as if he is beginning to waver. 'The trouble is the death penalty. I do it to animals and that's hard enough. It's worse to think of it done to a man.'

Johns tamps his pipe, his lower lip stuck out. 'Was that your lady wife you were talking to the other night, Mr Cuttance?'

Jack stares at him, a vein in his throat suddenly beginning to throb. 'You listened to my conversation?'

'I waited long enough to use the phone. I was standing right next to the booth and you didn't seem to notice. Very affectionate,

I thought, quite erotic in fact, all the things you're planning to do to your lady.'

The only sound in the room is Johns puffing on his re-ignited pipe. The smoke curls higher, drifting around their heads. Ken notices spittle running down the side of the banker's mouth when he draws on the pipe, and the sight of it makes him feel sick.

'I'll have to go with guilty then,' Jack Cuttance says. He doesn't look at Arthur or Ken. His face is drained of colour. 'I've my kids to think about.'

'Good man, well then, we're just about there,' Taylor says.

Ken finds himself shouting. 'You didn't listen. You didn't *hear* anything except what you wanted to hear. You're a bunch of narrow-minded bigots.' And then it happens, the worst possible thing. His piss runs down the side of the chair; its smell, like citronella oil, mingles with the whole grubby atmosphere. '*Not* guilty,' he says, his misery plain for all to see.

'Not guilty,' Arthur says. But somehow, his and Ken's words are lost, as if they simply don't exist in the room.

Ken says, 'Arthur, you can stop them.' The faces he sees are implacable, their distaste and indifference clear, except in Cuttance who covers his face with his hands. Marcus is leaned so far over the table it's impossible to see his expression. 'So I'm a farm boy who's pissed his pants. I piss you off because I disagree with you. It doesn't mean you shouldn't do the right thing.'

Arthur puts his hand on his arm. 'It's no fault of yours. We can sit here for hours or days. Their minds are made up.'

'You've changed your mind too. What is it? Your important job too?' He can stand up for himself and hold his ground. But first he will have to change his pants. Perhaps he will be found unfit in his absence. It's all over, he knows.

Arthur hesitates and sighs. 'Funnily enough, it might improve my standing, being the rogue juror, the man of principle. But it's not going to change anything here. Ken, they were always going to find this man guilty. At best we can cause a hung jury, and the next jury might see it differently. Or not. I can't deny that Black killed Jacques. Was he provoked? I think so. Was he defending himself? The witnesses say not. I believe it was manslaughter, but the judge isn't having that. The best one can hope for is leniency.'

Rita Zilich and her friends fall silent from their ceaseless twittering chatter as the jury is ushered into the courtroom for the last time. Only an hour and forty minutes has passed since they left. Another four minutes pass while they take their seats. The hushed quiet is broken momentarily by a crowd of girls who have rushed to the courthouse in their lunch break, two taxiloads of them. They smell of perfume and fish and chips, and hastily eaten egg sandwiches, the surreptitious sucking of Irish moss jubes. In the dock, Albert Black holds onto the railing in front of him, fingering it as if he were trying to read Braille.

The judge asks James Taylor if the jury finds the defendant guilty or not guilty of murder.

'Guilty, your Honour.'

Paddy sways forward so that Des Ball, standing on one side of him, and a court attendant on the other, have to step up and take his arms to support him.

'Have you anything you wish to say?' the judge asks.

After a few moments while he composes himself, Paddy says in a calm, flat voice, 'Nothing to say, sir.'

Mr Justice Finlay, his long patrician face grim, lifts the black cap, which is not a black cap at all but a square of black fabric, and places it on the top of his wig. There is a moment when he fumbles it, arranging it so that one point falls towards his face. 'You have heard the verdict of the jury,' he says. 'The sentence of this court, therefore, is that you will be taken from here to the place from whence you came and there be kept in close confinement until the date yet to be confirmed of your execution, and upon that day you be taken to the place of execution and there hanged by the neck until you are dead. And may God have mercy upon your soul.'

In the silence, the palpable perfumed silence of the courtroom, Paddy turns and stumbles to the trapdoor leading to the cell below. At the back of the court the pale girl who has sat throughout the trial, her eyes following every movement of the unfolding events, begins to sob, her cries becoming louder, until an attendant ushers her away.

The sun is brilliant in the sky as the jury enters the light, leaving the court behind them. They have been excused jury service for seven years. Most of them hope they will never be back, or so they say, as they walk out beneath the pale green of the spring trees. Some shake hands before they disperse, promising to see each other before long. Ken turns to leave, his sodden trousers cold against his leg. Arthur holds out his hand to him and Ken takes it.

'I'm sorry,' Ken says. 'If it weren't for me.'

'No, not you. I gave you my word. When it came to the point I could see no hope at all. I kept telling myself Black might be spared. There's sure to be an appeal, a bit of hue and cry. You should get along home, put it behind you.'

'You listened to me. That's something, I suppose.' Ken's voice is cool.

'I'm as sorry as you.'

'Are you? I've never met an educated man before. I didn't know what to expect.'

'I'm no different from you. I had opportunities, that's all,'

Arthur says. He has taken a small notepad and a pencil from the breast pocket of his jacket. His shoes glint in the sunlight as he scribbles down a phone number.

Ken has begun to shiver in his trousers, despite the warmth of the sun on their backs. 'Opportunities aren't for everyone.'

'You could still make some. Carpe diem, Kenneth, my friend. It means seize the day.'

'You think better of me than I deserve,' Ken says. He is mocking the man now, though Arthur is oblivious to his undertone.

'The university calendar for next year should be out any day.' Arthur hands Ken the piece of paper. 'Ring me if you think I can help.' He turns on his heel, walking away towards the university. In a peculiar way, Ken wants to laugh. It occurs to him that he is no better and no worse than the lecturer. As he heads towards the bus stop, he tears the piece of paper into little pieces and dumps them in a bin.

In the van with its darkened windows, Albert and Des sit in silence. Des doesn't know it yet, but when he gets home his wife and children will be gone. He will understand soon enough that Marge has taken as much as she can and she isn't going to take it anymore. It will surprise him to learn that she knows when trouble is coming, that she can read the signs from the stories in the newspapers and put two and two together. He will wish with all his soul that he had trusted her more with the grief that lies in his heart, the things he has seen. When the vehicle stops at intersections, trams clattering past make the only sounds. School is coming out for the day and children's high voices can be heard. The van moves on, back towards the prison. Then, in the gloom, Albert begins to sing, his voice tentative at first, but rising and filling the van:

Wallflower, wallflower, growing
up so high
All the little children are all
going to die
Except for Albert Black — he's
the only one
He can dance, he can sing
He can dance, he can do the swing
Fie for shame! Fie for shame!
Turn your back to the wall again.

'Shut up, Black,' Des shouts. 'Shut the fuck up or I'll smash you.'

Paddy stops just long enough to say, 'Have you always been a cold crackers, Mr Ball? Have you never lived? You'd best make the most of it, you never know when your time will come.'

Later, in the long night that lies ahead of him, Des will think that the Irish boy has the second sight.

And Paddy's voice carries on, relentless in the dark, as the gates open to let the van through and they are back at the prison again.

Fie for shame! Fie for shame!
Turn your back to the wall again.

Rita's mother looks at her daughter as if she doesn't altogether recognise her. She has sat up late, waiting for her. It is close to morning.

'Rita,' she whispers, 'what have you done?'

'I didn't mean for this to happen.'

'Did you lie to that court?'

'I don't know, Mum. It's the way I remember it.'

'You're soiled goods.'

'I know. I'll make it up to you, I'll stay home. Let you find me a nice boy.'

'If your father and I can. And what of the boy who is to die?'

Rita is wordless, her eyes suddenly full of tears. 'He was a nice enough boy, Mum. Not a bad boy.'

'May God forgive you, Rita,' her mother says.

Chapter 20

And it is Sunday morning and her husband wants her to lie in the bed with him.

'It's the drink talking,' Kathleen says. 'Sure and you came in late last night.' The sheet, raw against her cheek, needs washing, but each wash day that comes around the mist has descended, bowling in from the Black Mountain, and she will decide to leave them for another time.

He pulls her against him, and deep in his chest she hears the rattle of his sob. 'What's a man to do?' he says. 'For a while I forgot.' His hand runs up the length of her thigh and there was a time when she would have welcomed it, the two of them making boys together.

'I can't forget,' she says, 'not for a moment. I haven't slept the past week.'

'Kathleen, I know that,' he says, and she feels the agonised clench of his fingers beneath her ribcage before he releases her.

'There's Daniel's breakfast to be got.' She is easing herself out of the bed, holding the wall for support. A narrow room in the thin house, two up, two down, and cheek by jowl with all the others in Gay Street that runs off Sandy Row.

'You're going to do it then?' he says, his voice quiet now.

'Get his breakfast, yes of course. You don't want the boy to go hungry.'

'The other thing? That you talked about. The idea that you had the other night?'

Kathleen turns to face her husband as she draws on her petticoat, takes a print dress from its hanger and slips it over her head, before choosing her best cardigan, a mauve one knitted in blackberry stitch. Oh yes, and it reminds her of the times when she and the boy took a bucket and walked in the fields beyond the city belt, finding blackberries wild on the bramble, the luscious squelch of the juice running down their chins, the way the kid scrambled laughing amongst the vines as if he didn't feel the thorns because he wanted to please her. Showing off a bit, she supposed at the time, but what did it matter, happy as a thimbleful of sunshine. That was him, her little Albert, with the blue cotton hat that she'd sewn herself pulled over his hair, black and glossy like the ripe berries, his skin the colour of milk, and now he is a grown man on the other side of the world, gone off to make his fortune. Some fortune.

'Boil me a mug of water and I'll take to the whiskers,' says Bert.

'You're coming with me then?'

'Aye. Get the boy ready.' He sees the expression on her face. 'He'll have to get used to it, it's been in the newspaper. It was spoken of in the hotel last night.'

'How?' she asks. 'In what manner did they speak of it?' She hasn't shown her face in the street these past few days. The disgrace scorches her cheeks.

'They shook my hand. They said they were way sorry about it all.'

'But what did they say about young Albert?'

'A good lad, that's what they said. Your boy wouldn't stop a snail on its morning walk. We know that, that's what they said.'

'We will have to tell Daniel, then. And him only ten. His brother, the murderer.'

'You don't believe that.'

'That's what they believe in New Zealand. The judge has put on the black hat. To hang him by the neck until he's dead.'

'I'll see to that,' he says, 'while you're putting out the breakfast. I'll speak to Daniel.'

And, for a moment, it doesn't seem so terrible, now that she and her husband are together on this. There is hope in the air, and when she glimpses the light outside she sees that it is a blue morning, a torrent of sunlight flooding across the houses below Boyne Bridge.

Kathleen takes out the fat pad of paper she has been hiding in the lower drawer of the tallboy. The pages are flimsy, etched with faint blue lines. The pad has cost her a whole shilling, the price of a steak. It is a big hope that it might be filled with names but it's worth a try. Anything is worth it, and the three of them, she, her husband and Daniel, the small boy born late to them, all that remain of their family, are off to St George's where they will stand at the door after morning service and hold out this pad of paper to the members of the congregation as they file past, full of the blood of Christ, and ask for their mercy, ask them to sign the petition she has written out, imploring the faraway Government of New Zealand that the life of her son might be spared. She imagines the names, soaring across the pages: there are forty lines to a page and fifty sheets of paper. God willing, she will need more pads, and they will starve rather than go without all the paper that might be needed.

She dons her hat, a blue felt with a pheasant feather tucked in the ribbon, and pulls on her coat, for autumn is on them now, the sly sun now slinking between the clouds, but it has no warmth. Her husband is dressed in his white shirt and good suit that has seen better days, but what would he wear but that, for church, and on the days of the Orange Parade. She braces her shoulders as they step out along Sandy Row, tilts her chin up, eyes ahead. Clodagh calls out, 'Good morning to you, Kathleen, good morning, Bert, and how is the wee man today?'

Kathleen stiffens, but it is Daniel her neighbour is asking after. He has been home from school the past week with a cold while she is away at work in Jennymount Mill, where every weekday she smooths out the beautiful flax cloth cascading out of the big machine, its surface texture riffled like cream half churned. She is ashamed to have thought the worst of her neighbour, who keeps an eye on the boy so that Kathleen doesn't miss a day's work. There are plenty more lining up for the jobs, and the industry is going out the way of the tide. Clodagh has stiffened with age in the years they have lived in Sandy Row, her joints thick with rheumatism, the feet so swollen and crusty, the skin so split, she wears slippers all day.

'He is very much recovered thank you, Clodagh. And yourself?'

Clodagh folds her hands over her large waist. 'I'd like to be getting along to my own church today, but I can't make it. Will you say one for me, Kathleen?'

And before she can stop herself, Kathleen's face is streaming with tears. Bert takes her arm as if to move her along.

'It's all right, let her have her cry,' Clodagh says, nodding her head. 'We've heard about your troubles. We know about the young one that went over the sea. He was a good lad. I remember wee Albert, he'd go a message for me without asking for a penny.'

There is no time like the present, and Kathleen opens her purse, pulling out the pad and the pencil. Across the first page she has written the words: *A petition to the Government of New Zealand to have mercy on our son Albert Black and not to send him to the gallows.*

'Would you be willing to put your name here, Clodagh?' she asks.

And in a minute, there it is, the first name, Clodagh McGuire, Sandy Row, Belfast.

But there is more, for Clodagh puts her hand in the pocket of her vast apron. 'I'd been watching out for you, Kathleen,' she says, and takes out a coin that she presses into the palm of Kathleen's hand. 'It's the lucky coin that Uncle Niall brought back from the Somme. It was a new penny when he first got it, with a glow like firelight dancing on its face, he told me, he knew it had to be a lucky one. May it keep you safe.'

Kathleen stares at the polished penny, and it still has that deep, dark glow upon it, as Clodagh says, its date 1916, the same year as the Battle of the Somme. It bears the words *King Edward, King of England and Defender of the Faith.* 1916. That battle when two thousand and more men from the 36th Ulster Division walked into the blinding death of enemy gunfire, and another five thousand wounded and the men who came back never the same. Thousands of houses in the Shankill where the women waited with dread for the postman's knock and the pale buff-coloured envelope bearing the news. Whole families of boys gone at once. And yet they were proud, proud to be Protestant Ulstermen, wearing their Orange sashes on the Twelfth.

'Thank you,' Kathleen whispers, the words stuck in her throat. For it was not just the Orange men who had fallen but men from the Falls as well. Brothers in arms. Perhaps things will be all right after all.

Her husband is beckoning her, impatient now. Young Daniel hurries on ahead, jumping puddles as if he hadn't a care in the world. Kathleen thinks to herself that whatever his father said to him hasn't sunk in. He is still a child and already the memory of his brother is blurring. They hurry along towards the town, past the terraced houses, the barbers' shops, the grocers', the haberdashery with a mannequin posed in the window, chaste in a loose dress that drops beneath the knee, the hardware shops, the pubs. Many pubs, closed for Sunday, just the proprietors sweeping the fronts where the cigarette butts landed, and a rising smell of spew on account of patrons who hadn't held their beer, and then they cross Boyne Bridge. But the penny which Kathleen still clasps reminds her of the Twelfth, and the last time young Albert was there for the Parade.

She hears again the skirl of bagpipes, the flutes and the drums, sees the arches erected over the streets, hung with orange bunting and flags of the Empire. Perhaps it was this that had driven him away, she thinks. On the day of that last Parade he seemed to have lost some of the Ulster spirit, as if he wanted to break away, be his own self. Could he be right, that the difference between the two faiths is not as important as they have been taught all those years?

Faith or not, they have arrived at the door of St George's Church. It isn't her own St Anne's, but because of the war and the restoration (and here she pauses to shudder; even now, all these years later, the memory of the Blitz scalds her brain), it is a church that comforts her, with its sandstone exterior and Corinthian portico, and inside it the tiny jewel-like stained-glass windows and ancient paintings. The walk along High Street always makes her think of the River Farset that flows under the pavement, the water completely shrouded on its journey towards the junction with the River Lagan. She has never seen this river, it was covered over long before she was born, but just the idea of it there in the dark beneath her feet makes her imagine things that lie below the surface, things that people know and don't know about each other. She will see now what her own people have to say about the plight that has befallen her family.

At the door they are met by a vestryman she knows slightly from earlier services. 'Mr Russell, a word if I might,' she says. And she tells him of their trouble and what she has planned. If the minister approves, she would like it announced that she will be standing at the door collecting signatures to send to the New Zealand High Commissioner in London, appealing for clemency for her son who, so far as she knows, has never done a worse thing in his life than lose his father's prize marley up until the day he acted to protect himself from a violent attacker. This is what Albert told her in his first letter from the prison after he was arrested, and she prays to God that this is the truth he has told her.

The vestryman says that he will have a word, and it is all a little unusual but a mother's affection and wish to protect her child is a very Christian attitude, so he will put her case to the minister and it might well be that her petition will get the church's blessing. As she kneels at the communion rail, she thinks that the minister pauses for a longer moment than usual, murmuring the familiar words *the body of Christ*. She lets the wafer rest on her tongue, swallows, and then, after the cup has been passed, rises unsteadily to her feet and makes her way back to her pew. The church seats five hundred and today it appears full.

Then the minister addresses the congregation and, in a blur, she hears him speak her and her husband's name, and more than that, speak well of their son who had gone to seek the new world and found himself betrayed by it.

At the door, she and her husband stand side by side, and Daniel, looking like one of the choirboys, with his white shirt collar and scrubbed face, stands beside them. He knows, after all, she thinks. She can see it now, the startled child's expression, wide-eyed and growing serious. Kathleen holds out the pad with the pencil attached by a string.

'Mrs Black, a sad thing, we've read it in the newspaper. Terrible, what they do out there, New Zealand's a savage place,' a woman says, taking the pad from her. Soon the congregation is queuing up, so that the minister is getting lost among them as he stands to shake hands with the departing flock.

'You need to get more pads,' a man says. 'I'm going out to Antrim tomorrow, to the market at Ballylagan. Sure and I can gather some signatures there. I'll pick up a pad at the stationer's on my way out.'

'The market, that's the story,' another says.

And before they know it, the pad is full and promises are being made, and someone has put in a pound for the purchase of more pads and pencils.

When they get home and Bert puts the kettle on, because he can see that his wife has started something and needs all the help she can get, she counts the signatures. Over four hundred, and the minister's signed too, as well as Mr Russell the vestryman. She counts out money that has been pushed into her hand: there are twenty-two pounds.

'Perhaps I could go to New Zealand after all,' she says, wistful. 'Not that it would take me far.' And besides, she knows that it is a country where she is not wanted, a place where Albert should never have gone.

'You should have a rest,' Bert says.

'Well, no,' she says, 'because I've decided to write to the Queen. I'm going to ask her, mother to mother, to exercise the royal prerogative of mercy.'

'You can't do that,' he says. 'The Queen has enough troubles of her own right now.'

'Her sister? Poor girl. But that's all fixed now that Margaret's said she won't marry Townsend.' The princess had renounced marriage to her lover just days earlier.

'Only because the Archbishop of Canterbury came down so hard on her. There are a lot of people who feel very upset with the Queen and her lot.'

'All the more reason for her to show some mercy to our boy.' Kathleen's face is set with determination. 'It will show she has a heart.'

'I'd be surprised if she got to see the letter.'

'Bert, we can't give up now. You're not giving up our boy, are you?'

'No, of course not,' he says, his anguish raw again. 'Write the letter, Kathleen.'

Chapter 21

November 1955. Since Paddy's death sentence, Des Ball has disappeared. Paddy is surprised to find that he misses him. He had got used to Des and the meanness of his tongue. It is almost as if they had got to liking each other. At least, they understood each other. Wherever he goes inside the prison walls now, Paddy is watched. A man called Knowles has taken over his hourly supervision. Whereas Des was small and wiry, Knowles is a heavy, burly man, thick meat round the back of his neck, and fingers coated with fur. Knowles is different in every way, not so much mean as a bit of a sleeveen when there is nobody listening. 'I'm supposed to keep you from topping yourself,' he says the first day they're together. 'We can't let you escape the noose, that's not justice.'

'I'm not dead yet,' Paddy says. He and Knowles will have to get along. He'd heard that it was Knowles who stuck his fingers in Frederick Foster's eyes when he tried to resist his hanging, the one who had fought to the last. He vows, inwardly, that he won't give Knowles the same satisfaction. There is no explanation for Des's absence, although Horace Haywood muttered something about him needing time off. 'We don't like our warders to carry the burden of your sentence,' he'd said, as if in some way Paddy were responsible for Des needing a rest. Not, apparently, that this burden applies to the prison superintendent, whose task it is now to counsel and console the prisoner. It is Haywood who arrives at Paddy's cell bearing a telegram.

'At your service,' he says, trying to make light of his visit, 'now that I'm your delivery boy, your postal service as it were.' He hands over the buff envelope.

'Perhaps I should tip you, sir,' Paddy says. 'But at the moment I'm clean out of cash. Next pay day, if you can wait that long.'

'Ha. Ball always said you had a quick tongue in your head. Lie down with the knives, did you?'

'No good making a fuss, sir.'

'Seriously, lad, you know what's ahead, don't you?'

'I don't need to be reminded, sir.'

'All right then. You're seeing the priest now, I believe?'

'I am, sir, his visits are a great benefit to me. Thank you for arranging for me to see Father Downey.' He glances at the envelope he's been handed, anxious to view its contents.

'If there's anything I can do.' Haywood stands on one foot and then the other, as if it were he who is in trouble. 'Well, I'll leave you to it.'

Paddy is momentarily disappointed. The telegram might have been from the girl, but it's from Peter Simpson: 'Albert, I am so dreadfully sorry to hear about what has happened and the family here in Naenae is very upset. I am going to try and get some time off work so that I can come to Auckland and see you. Your friend always, Peter.'

It comes flooding back to him then, the days high in the hills above Wellington, blue days when the sun shone, high winds and rain that had sometimes scared him up in the pine trees as he watched the distance between him and the ground, the children at the little state house and kind Rose who had fed and cared for him and with whom he had been almost in love, or would have if she had been more a girl than a woman growing into middle age. More like a mother, he supposes. Thinking about them all, he is filled with shame and sudden self-loathing, the emotion he has been holding at bay. It is true he has killed a man, never mind whether he meant to or not. They were good people who had housed a convicted murderer in their midst. They will be ashamed, and so is he. Perhaps this is what religion does to a man.

This is not the first letter Haywood had delivered. Earlier, one morning, he had appeared at the door bearing another. Paddy was surprised that he would perform such a menial task.

Haywood had handed over a pale-mauve envelope bearing small neat handwriting. 'You'd better read it,' Haywood said, averting his face. All the mail was read before it was delivered to the prisoners to make sure there were no plans for escape outlined in their contents.

Paddy read it through, and then again, the girl's message short and plain, but he trembled as he absorbed it. He thought he could catch her scent from the paper, but his imagination played all kind of tricks on him these days. He understood now why she had sat there at the back of the court and wept when his sentence was passed. He understood in a terrible way why she had not spoken to him that night he flirted with Rita. It was coming at him. He saw so much, how things might have been, the way they could have been different.

'Do you want to talk about this, Black?'

He had shaken his head. 'Not really.'

'She says she wants to come and see you.'

233

'Yes sir, I see that.' There was nothing at all he could do for her. 'I suppose I should see her.'

'You don't have to if you don't want to. Did you like this girl?'

'Oh yes sir. I liked her very much. I'd have married her.'

'You were planning to marry? You're very young.'

'Oh no, I hadn't proposed, nothing like that.' He held up the letter. 'But I would, if you see what I mean. And I'd have been glad about it.' Catholic, she was a Catholic, he remembered that.

'So why don't you want her to come and see you?'

'She's too good for this place, I can tell you that. She's beautiful and, well, what can I do but make it worse?'

Haywood had become agitated too. 'You could talk to her, be kind to her at the very least.'

'Sir, I would like to see a priest if I may.'

'A priest? You're down as a Protestant.'

As if Paddy didn't know that and more. His whole life he had understood that the two were like water and chalk, they wouldn't mix. You could speak in a civil way to a Catholic girl, but that was as far as it went. You couldn't smile with a glint in your eye, you couldn't kiss, you couldn't fondle, you couldn't marry. His parents had reminded him of this, that last Orange Day Parade. There were stories of girls from the Shankill who had mixed it with the boys over in the Falls and they led their whole lives not spoken to by their mam and da; they had wheeled their prams up and down the edge of the street and nobody had turned to speak to them. He could see it for what it was, just plain wrong.

'It's a priest I need, sir. Isn't there a Father who comes to see some of the men?'

'Father Downey? Yes, if you're sure.'

The priest, when he arrived, was a dark, middle-aged man who shook Paddy's hand as if it were the most natural thing in the world.

Paddy half expected to feel scorched, never having shaken hands with a priest before. He found the hand warm, holding his a moment longer than he expected.

'I'm about to die soon, Father,' he blurted.

'So I've heard, lad. That is a cruel thing.'

Paddy didn't know what to say next. He had an idea that death looked different the Roman Catholic way. When his grandparents died — his mother's parents, that was — there were simple closed coffins with flowers placed on top, his mother and aunts sniffing tidily into their handkerchiefs, and a service with a plain-speaking eulogy. Afterwards, there was a cup of tea and nicer cakes than they had as a rule, at the house of one of the aunts. He remembered that he had been considered too young to go to the burial, and so he had stayed home to be comforted by Clodagh.

He'd been to Clodagh's house in Sandy Row when her father died, and that was another thing altogether. Paddy's mother had been called by Clodagh in the desperate minutes after the unexpected passing. (Well, Clodagh should have been prepared, Kathleen told Paddy, he was a very old man, but Clodagh wasn't ready, she just wasn't.) Paddy tried to explain this to Father Downey. 'All the clocks in the house were stopped at the exact moment our neighbour's da died. They drew the blinds and covered the mirrors with white cloth. There was black crêpe paper taped across the front door and the windows were left wide open in the first hours.'

'Why did they do that, Paddy?'

'I thought you'd know that, Father. Clodagh told my mam the window had to be left open for her father's spirit to make its way out. It was a right freezing night, the wind whistling through, but Clodagh said it would take four hours at least before it was safe to close. When my da and I were called on to pay our respects at the house, I saw Clodagh's father, lying for all to see, and he was dressed in a sacred robe. A great noisy sobbing there was going on.' He stopped, remembering his father's face, long as a Lurgan spade. 'You should have seen my da. It was as if he were expecting the Devil to appear any moment. Everyone crossing themselves and all, he couldn't get out of there fast enough.'

The priest had sat in silence, waiting for him to finish. 'Well, there may be some who have brought their ways from the old country. I haven't seen it quite like that here. Maori people are more eloquent in their expressions of grief when a person dies.'

'I know,' Paddy told him. 'I was here when Te Whiu died. I heard his people crying, it was something terrible. The end. But I can't imagine death, it doesn't seem real.'

'It is a modest end, here in this prison.' The priest hesitated.

'We're buried within the walls, I know. We're not allowed in the yard where the other ones lie.'

'Aye.'

'I would have liked to see my mother once more.' Paddy bit his lip. He had resisted tears up until then. His father would have told him that a decent Ulster spud didn't cry. 'And what happens afterwards, Father? Can you tell me that?'

'We can talk about that,' Father Downey said. 'We will need to talk about it, if I'm to minister to you. But I don't think that is why you wanted to see me today.'

'I'd like to become a Roman Catholic. If the Church would take a sinner like me.'

'That is a big step for a Protestant lad. There is a reason?' It was as if he knew already. Well, he probably did; there were no secrets in the prison when it came to the contents of a letter. Haywood would have told him.

'There's a girl,' Paddy said. 'It seems I'm to be a father. Well, if I were alive, that is.'

Father Leo Downey nodded. 'You will be the father, for all time. That can't be taken away from you.'

'So she's a Catholic girl. Can you forgive her for sinning with me?'

'Only God can forgive sin, and she must ask that for herself.'

'And truly repent?'

The priest sighed and folded his hands in front of him. 'Who are you asking this for, Albert? The girl or yourself? This girl will suffer, regardless of what I or any priest says. Perhaps God will see this. Her suffering will be absolution in itself.'

'It would be like a gift for her and the baby if it were to have a Catholic father.'

'What about you? Converting to another faith needs to be for oneself as well.'

'Ah Father, you'd have to be joking about that. The girls in Sandy Row who've had to turn in order to give their children a daddy. Protestant girls, they have to turn if they're to be wed. Your Church collects them up fast enough and not too many questions asked.'

'I'll overlook that.'

'Apologies, Father, no offence meant. I want to do this thing. It's all I can offer her and the baby. Like a blessing.'

'Well then, you have some time on your hands. You'll need to do some reading, starting with the Catechism. Will you tell your parents about your conversion?'

'I will tell them that I am to change my religion, yes. My mother will pray for me, no matter what. My father? I don't know, he has always held me in some suspicion. I lost his best marley once, the one that stood for him being in the war. There are so many things I don't know, so little time.'

So it has been a while now; the trial has been and gone, he

has learned the Catechism and soon he will be received into the Church.

Haywood turns up one morning when Albert is not expecting him. Well, he never does. The routine of prison goes on the same day in and day out, and any break in it is bound to be the unexpected. 'I've to tell you there is going to be an appeal,' he says. 'And Paddy, I pray it succeeds. You're not a bad lad. I can't bear to think you'll swing.'

'I don't think you're supposed to say that to me, sir,' Paddy says. He has a strange light-headed desire to laugh.

'This system, lad, it's intolerable.' Haywood's nose is covered in fine purple veins. Paddy can smell musty Johnnie Walker on the superintendent's breath.

'Thank you, sir,' he says. And without his bidding, hope comes flooding over him. He thought he had conquered that. 'What do I have to do?'

'Your lawyer has an appointment to see you tomorrow.'

When Haywood leaves his cell, Paddy sits down and writes two letters, the first to the girl. He has written four letters to her since hers first arrived, but so far she hasn't replied. Just given him the biggest bombshell and retreated to wherever it is she has gone. The address she had written from was that of her parents' farm in the south but she wouldn't be staying there for long; soon she would be living in a home for people like her, unmarried mothers. She had said she wanted to see him, but now she has disappeared.

'Bessie,' he writes, 'I would so like to talk to you about the future. Please contact me if you can. I don't know whether there is hope for me, but if there is I want to make things right for you and the baby. And for me. I know my mam had our William, my brother who died, soon after she married my da. I will do the same with you if it's what you want and I'd be happy about it. Think of it as a proposal if it comes to pass that I am free.'

His second letter is to Peter in Naenae.

'Thanks a million for your telegram, to be honest it was quite a surprise, I was going to write to you sooner, but you know so much has been happening to me these last few months, I am really in a bit of a dither, or should I say I was, as everything is just about over. Well Peter, I guess I have come to a one-way street. I need not explain because you have probably read all about it in the paper. I would honestly like to see you Peter before I go, if my appeal fails, although I can't pin too much hope on that, as we have quite a few things to talk over I should imagine. Well Peter, I shan't write too long as every word means a moment gone. Incidentally, if you do manage to get time off to come to Auckland the visiting hours are 9–11 and 2–4 weekdays and weekends. So cheerio for now Peter, as they say in Liverpool. Your Old Mucker, Albert.'

Chapter 22

Paddy has begun to feel lighter in himself since beginning his sessions with Father Downey. When he writes his name at the bottom of a letter, he is back to signing himself Albert, his true name, and he is proud of it, although in prison they still call him Paddy. But Albert is who he really is. He doesn't recognise the fellow Paddy Donovan who hung out in the boarding house in Wellesley Street. He has seen his day of judgment come and go, and when he looks back on it he cannot believe it happened. All that pomp and ceremony, the wigs and gowns, the bowing and scraping, all on account of him; he couldn't relate to any of that. The girl in the witness box; the parade of youths who he had temporarily thought were his friends but turned out not to be after all, just a bunch of muddled young men who had been too addled with drink to get their stories straight; the sombre judge with his tight mouth; the jury with their closed faces. Or most of them. When he looked at them out of the corner of his eye he had sensed that he didn't stand a chance. Only his fleeting glimpses of Bessie Marsh had registered as reality, and with it a profound sense of connection, some inevitability, as if their souls rested together. The real day of judgment is yet to come when he is face to face with God. He believes that he will see Him, though exactly how and where he is yet to understand. When he asks Father Downey what he thinks about this, the priest answers in an oblique way, saying, *Who is God, and where is God, and where His dwelling?* It is something an Irish priest had said to him once, and it came from an old chant or song or poem, he isn't sure which, but it is the universal question that everyone who believes asks in one way or another, he had said.

On the other hand, since his conversion, Paddy's dreams have been haunted by the sound of the passing bell. The passing bell warned of impending death, the first of three bells that complete the death knell. His soul is already preparing for flight, and it will be on its own, without the girl to encourage him. He had all but given up hope of seeing her the morning the superintendent brought news of his appeal.

In writing to Peter and, yet again, to Bessie, he has allowed himself faith that he'll be in the world long enough to see them again. It is only a matter of days before he hears from Peter. He is coming to Auckland the following week, having arranged for time off from his new job at the hospital in the Hutt. Well, Paddy thinks, his must be a dire story Peter has told his employers if they have given him the time so soon after starting work with them. About his dying pal, perhaps. So maybe Peter doesn't have much hope for him, given that he is hurrying north.

Peter hasn't been to Auckland before, but Paddy reminds himself that his friend is a person who knows his way around. After all, he comes from Liverpool.

In his next letter, Paddy writes: 'I hope you don't get lost, though, as one should imagine Mount Eden prison is easy to find, as it is quite a popular place. Our Naenae days seem a long way off, though I did not realise how long until I started thinking back. Since we parted, oh well, you know life has just seemed one big whirl. Guess I have stopped spinning now, for a while anyway ha ha. I'll finish, until I see you, for there is nothing like a good heart to heart natter in person.

'Cheerio for now,

'Your pal, Albert.'

In the exercise yard, the man called Horton slides over to him. 'Cigarette, mate?'

'I never used to smoke until I came in here,' Paddy says, taking one and coughing as he lights up. 'Bad habit.' They keep walking, six rounds of the yard and it will be time to go inside again. The sky looks a long way off.

'It won't last long,' Horton says.

'Meaning?' Only he knows what Horton means: he'll be dead soon, however much he protests that he is still alive.

'Did you enjoy it?' Horton asks. 'Killing the bastard.'

'I don't know what you're on about.'

'Ah ha, you do though, don't you? I killed an old biddy in Wellington, after I'd got into her. It was all right, you know. She was English and as prissy as they come, and I wiped that look off her face.'

'I wouldn't force a woman. I wouldn't kill one.'

'You didn't plan to kill your mate either, did you? Don't kid yourself — you're a killer too, just like me.'

Paddy draws in a lungful of smoke, holding on to it. It is the only thing he can do to stop himself hitting Horton. 'You've no regrets?' he says, when he is ready to speak, letting out a plume of smoke into the still air above the yard. He watches it rise lazily to freedom.

'Oh well, I've only got the memories now. And I'm sick of this place. I'll tell you, if I could get out I would.'

'Why didn't they hang you?'

'You're shocked, eh? Look at you, as if butter wouldn't melt in your mouth. Well, you see, I've got the laugh on you, boy. There wasn't a death sentence then. It was because I was such a bad bugger they brought it back, but it was too late to do anything about me. You could say you're headed for the gallows thanks to me.'

Paddy stops in his tracks. 'I'd like to drop you.'

'Go on then. Only I'd heard you weren't a fighting man. Just a lad with a bit of Irish temper, that's what they say. C'mon, have a go, they can only put you in solitary.'

Knowles saunters over. 'Break it up, you two.'

'No bother,' Paddy says. 'There's no trouble.' Because sooner or later the warder is likely to turn his back, and Horton will deliver him two black eyes and not a thing he can do about it.

'Time for your band practice,' Knowles says to Horton. 'You'd best be getting along.' There is a brass band in the prison; when Paddy first heard it he closed his eyes and the Twelfth of July spooled before him. The band isn't as good as the ones that cross Boyne Bridge on Orange Day but it's galling that men he considers no better than himself can make their own music.

Paddy holds his hands to his sides, fighting the anger inside him. If he gives in to Horton, he won't see his friend. The screws are friendly enough towards him, but only because Haywood tells them they have to be; he thinks he is one of the superintendent's favourites. A dose of solitary would take him right back to where he was when he first came into the prison. He reminds himself that Horton has nobody visiting him, just the attention of poor Mrs Haywood. Deluded, Paddy thinks, if she believes she can make Horton a better man. Then he catches himself, because who is doing the judging now? He had judged Alan Jacques and it had got him nowhere but here.

Peter looks much the same when he arrives, the broad planes of his cheeks a little flushed at the whole experience of getting through the prison security system, his Liverpool accent as thick as ever. He has never been in a prison before. Rose has given Peter fresh eggs to give him, and he had brought a carton of cigarettes, which he considers the most useful thing to bring, as well as a bunch of magazines. He had had visions of handing them all over to Paddy, he tells him, and watching his eyes light up. Instead they had all been taken from him at the gates. They would be inspected and it would be decided what Paddy was allowed to have. The eggs could be a problem, although it wasn't explained why. This was particularly annoying, Peter tells Paddy, given that he sat up all night in the train holding them in his lap so they wouldn't break.

'Lucky they didn't hatch into chickens,' Paddy says, and in a minute they are having a laugh, and it feels good, the first laugh he can remember in a long time.

'The guards mightn't like the centrefolds in the magazines.'

'They'll like them too much. I'll probably never see them.'

They sit in cubicles separated by clear unbreakable Perspex that reaches up to the level of their faces. The visiting area is at the back of the chapel, a whole line of booths side by side. Peter has got a job as a laboratory technician, he tells Paddy. No more swinging through the pine trees for him, this is the kind of job he's always hoped for. The nurses are great and he has a girlfriend.

'You came out for a better life,' Paddy says. 'I'm glad it's paying off.' Peter falls silent. 'It's all right, my old mucker, you don't have to feel guilty because you're making something of the opportunity. I blew my chance all on my own. It doesn't make much difference whether I meant to kill Johnny or not. He lost his chance of making something of his life, thanks to me. I don't have the right to expect anything better.'

'You might still make it out of here.'

'I'm hoping so. Don't be gloomy about it. I've accepted it one way or another.'

'That sounds like a death wish.'

'No,' Paddy says. 'I've plenty to live for. But I need to make my peace.'

Peter shakes his head. 'I don't understand.'

'It will come to you,' Paddy says. He has done talking about it.

Peter has arranged to stay in Auckland for three nights so that he can see Paddy again. When he leaves, after the first visit, Paddy asks his jailer for his eggs.

'No way,' Knowles says.

'So why would that be?'

'Your diet, you know you have to stick to it.'

'I haven't seen an egg in nearly four months. I can't see how a few eggs are going to make a big difference to the hangman.'

'Who said anything about the hangman?'

'You think I don't know why you weigh me in every day? How heavy is a bag of sand? A bag of sand that weighs exactly the same as me, so the hangman can practise dropping me from the gallows. You can't string me up this week. I haven't had my appeal yet.'

'You're full of fancy talk, Black.'

'Eh? I'm right aren't I, Mr Knowles? How heavy is an egg? You could balance it on a feather.'

'I'll ask the superintendent,' Knowles says.

As he speaks, the shadow of the superintendent himself falls at the door, another unexpected visit, and they ask about the eggs there and then. Haywood frowns and rubs his chin. 'Just once,' he says. 'I'll get some cooked for you tomorrow.' But his visit isn't about eggs; this time he has news of a different kind. 'You're to have a visitor.'

'Yes sir, it's my friend Peter who's come all the way from Wellington on the train.'

'Another one.' Haywood waves Knowles out of the room, dismissing him. 'It's the girl,' he says. 'The one who wrote to you. She can be here the day after tomorrow. I've given her half an hour after Mr Simpson's scheduled visit.'

'Just half an hour?' He feels blood rushing to his head. 'Peter won't mind if I cut his time a little short. I need to see her. I must. Just half an hour, is that all you're allowing her?'

'That's all she can stay.'

'Perhaps she could stay longer next time?'

'I doubt that. She is being brought here by the matron of the home where she's living at present.'

'The home?'

'For fallen girls.' The superintendent waits for the words to sink in.

Paddy drops his head in his hands. 'Sir, I'm all of a muddle.'

'Her visit is arranged. The time's set in place, regardless of your friend. Just make sure he leaves sharp on three thirty.'

She is coming to me, Paddy thinks, and his heart swells with longing. He will see her again. He begins to count the hours.

So once again he will be saying goodbye to Peter, and he doesn't know whether or not it will be the last time. Peter looks settled in for a long visit. They have talked again about the times spent together, reminding each other how they used to pin their shirts up over the window to keep the sun out of their hut that first summer at Trentham, the beers at the pub, and how Rose's children are doing at school; Peter shows Paddy the picture of them again, pointing out how much Evelyn has grown and Harry is already taller than his mother. And signed up to play soccer, so that's a bit of an achievement, and he's been made team captain, and that's shut the rugby kids up. But, all the time, Paddy is glancing at the clock on the wall. 'I think we should call it a day now,' he says.

'I'm not in a rush,' Peter says. 'The train doesn't leave for a few hours.'

A silence falls between them. It is quarter past three. Paddy wants to tell Peter about his girl and the baby, but it doesn't seem right because it might not turn out well when he sees her, or Peter might get the wrong idea about the kind of girl she is. To look at him, Peter would be described as a square at Ye Olde Barn cafe, wide grey slacks, a buttoned-down collar and knitted jersey. How could he explain in five minutes what Bessie was like, that the two of them would get along famously, her a teacher and all and quite serious. Well, his imagination comes up short, because he guesses that now she may not be able to become a teacher after all.

'I'm a bit done in,' Paddy says, and it sounds lame.

Peter is nodding, and Paddy sees that although he hadn't thought he was ready to leave, he is now.

'You need to escape before they lock you up with me,' Paddy says. 'I'm giving you the keys, my friend.'

There's not much more to say and they can't shake hands and they're not like the girls who blow kisses to men as they leave. Peter puts his hand out on the Perspex, holding his palm against it, and Paddy puts his there to meet it, and for moment they sit there like that and Paddy finds himself blinking away tears as Peter stands and leaves without saying another word.

And in a few minutes the girl is there.

She takes the seat that Peter has so recently vacated, and looks at him wordlessly. He sees the small bulge around her waist. If he didn't know, he wouldn't have noticed it.

'When?' he asks.

'In March.'

'Are you keeping well?'

'I'm all right.'

'I wish I could look after you. You know that, don't you?'

Bessie bites her trembling lip and nods.

'That girl who gave evidence. She was nothing.'

'Don't,' she says. 'I don't want to talk about her ever again. Not now, not ever.'

'What I said in my letter, I meant it.'

Instinctively, she touches her ring finger. 'Oh Paddy,' she says, 'what have we done?'

'We've made a life.'

He leans towards what passes for glass. 'Listen,' he says. 'Come close as you can.' He begins to sing so low that nobody but she can hear him:

> *I will twine thee a bower*
> *By the clear siller fountain,*
> *And I'll cover it o'er*
> *Wi' the flow'rs o' the mountain.*
> *I will range through the wilds,*
> *And the deep glens sae drearie,*
> *And return wi' the spoils*
> *To the bower o' my dearie.*
> *Let us go, Lassie, go.*

'My mam used to sing that to us we'ans when we were going to sleep of a night. Will you sing it to the little one?'

Her shoulders are shaking and she can hardly speak. 'Paddy,' she says, 'don't you get it? They take them away as soon as they're born.'

'No,' he says, 'oh no, they can't do that.'

'The baby will have to be a secret. Our secret.'

'Of course,' he says, recalling the way things were back home — either marriage, which he cannot give her now, or a baby whisked away to grow up not knowing its true mam or da. 'I hadn't thought of that.'

'But I'll remember the song. Just in case.'

'You promise?'

'I promise. I have to go now, Paddy.'

As Peter has shown him, he puts his hand on the Perspex, palm flat, and she copies him. Her fingers are long and slim, so that they almost match his in length. They hold them there so long that the guard steps forward to separate them, as if they were touching.

'I love you, Bessie Marsh,' he says.

She takes a huge breath. 'I know,' she says, 'I know that, Paddy.'

Then she is gone. She hasn't said whether she loves him. He hopes that she does.

Chapter 23

November 1955.

'Dear Peter,

'Your most welcome letter came today and I was certainly glad to hear from you so soon. Now Peter, old chap, I hope you don't think I was getting bored with your company when I asked you to go the last day you visited. You see my girlfriend was waiting to see me, and I only had until four o'clock. I do hope you will understand. Well my appeal comes up on Tuesday, so here's hoping. Yes, prisoners come and go but I guess I stay on for ever. Ha ha. Well, I see you went to my happy hunting grounds. I'm sorry that you did not like Ye Old Barn cafe.

'You ask me what I would like to do for work. I have not thought much about a trade though I may take up plumbing if I get a chance. Time seems to go ever so quickly for me, it seems only yesterday I booked into this hotel.

'God bless you, Peter. Your friend, Albert.'

This time there are five judges sitting on the bench, but Albert Black is absent.

'Do you mean they all get to talk about me behind my back?' Paddy asked Buchanan when he outlined the procedure to him.

'There's nothing more they'll allow you to say, I'm afraid. The discussion is all on points of law.' All the same, Paddy was excited when he heard the arguments to be presented on his behalf for the appeal. He'd hold his breath all day, he promised. Buchanan had to explain to him that it wouldn't all happen on the same day. The judges would have to go away and think about it.

A fly circles around the courtroom, and some of the esteemed judges try to swat it away. It is almost as if the defendant had sent the essence of himself in the form of a small malevolent insect, Oliver Buchanan thinks, an irritant in the room that had to be dealt with.

Pearson rises to his feet. The learned judge who had presided over Mr Black's trial, he respectfully submits, failed to direct the jury adequately that, apart from the question of provocation, they could still bring in a verdict of manslaughter if they considered it appropriate. 'I submit, your Honours, that apart from the intent to kill, the jury could properly have found manslaughter if they thought the accused did not intend to inflict bodily injury of a type likely to cause death.

'Equally, the jury could have found manslaughter if they thought that, whatever Mr Black's intention, in fact the bodily injury he inflicted was not likely to cause death. The evidence put forward by the pathologist Mr Cairns suggests that it was extremely unlikely he intended to sever Alan Jacques' spinal cord and something of a fluke that he did. So, if he didn't intend to sever the spinal cord but only to stab the victim in the neck, it's extremely unlikely that would cause death. I suggest that a verdict of manslaughter was not only open to the jury but quite possible, and the judge should have directed the jury accordingly.'

Mr Justice Gresson, the presiding judge says, 'I'd have thought a stab in the neck was most likely to cause death regardless of where it landed.'

There is a general murmur of assent among his colleagues, a nodding of heads in unison. Because this is the Court of Appeal, the judges do not wear robes, for all the world like businessmen about to head for the stock exchange or a company board meeting.

'Frankly,' says the judge sitting on his left, 'I thought the summing-up was benevolent to the defence. It's difficult to see how defence counsel can seriously question the summing-up.' The lazy fly traverses the tip of his nose; he swats it with mounting irritation. Buchanan thinks then, this is what it may come down to, a fly distracting the judges. He wishes he had a handy fly-swatter in his pocket. How ingratiating would that be? His heart is sinking; he sees little sympathy in the faces of the men on the Bench.

It is his turn now to speak. 'That is not the only grounds for notice of appeal,' he tells them.

'Yes, yes,' says Gresson, 'we're aware of that.'

Buchanan traverses the grounds again. The second ground in the notice of appeal was that a miscarriage of justice had occurred because certain statements had been published in the press during the trial, both in morning and evening newspapers, reflecting the judge's opinion of the accused before the verdict had been delivered, in fact, before the case had even begun, and that that opinion was prejudicial to Black's case. 'Listen,' he says, quoting from a newspaper cutting, 'May I remind you of this: "He" – meaning Black – "belongs to a peculiar sect, if you could call it that, or a peculiar association of individuals whose outlook on life varies from the normal." It goes on to say that he's not needed in this country, and that it's premeditated murder. If that's not prejudicial, what is, your Honours?'

Although these comments had been made to the Grand Jury six weeks earlier, he reminds them, they had been released in the newspapers to coincide with Albert Black's trial. The common jury had received copies of these newspapers and, Buchanan tells the Bench, the comments were likely to influence the outcome of the trial.

'We have the affidavit of a witness,' Buchanan says. 'Mr Rabone was the assistant manager of the Station Hotel, and his evidence will be that, on instruction, he distributed copies of the *Auckland Star* and *The New Zealand Herald* to members of the jury while they were domiciled in the hotel.'

Mr Justice North asks, with some impatience, 'Well, is this about what the judge said, or is it about what was published?' He appears to have taken charge of the line of questioning.

'Your Honour,' Buchanan says, choosing his words with care, 'it's immaterial whether or not it was a correct transcript. I'm in no position to know whether the report was a verbatim account of the judge's direction. What I do know is that the character and reputation of my client was effectively destroyed when the jury read the comments by the judge.'

'The judge was addressing a Grand Jury on depositions from the Magistrate's Court. It didn't disclose the defence. You need to be careful of what inferences might be taken from your comments, Mr Buchanan.'

It goes through Buchanan's mind that his own reputation is being monitored. Then he sees Paddy's young face swimming before him, the unquenched hope that his life might still be handed back to him. He takes a deep breath and continues as if the judge hadn't spoken. 'There is nothing wrong, your Honour, with the judge speaking as he did, but with the publication. It's one thing to say something to the Grand Jury, which is only concerned with deciding about a true bill and not with questions of defence, but it matters if what is said could gravely prejudice a trial jury.'

'Well, really,' the judge shoots back, 'doesn't the whole thing come down to a question of whether the publication of proper remarks by the judge to the Grand Jury could ever be regarded as prejudicial?'

'In essence, yes. The judge is entitled to say whatever he likes, provided he directs that the common jury doesn't hear what he says.'

'So how do you screen a jury once it's been empanelled?' the judge asks. 'Who's supposed to do that?'

'I'm not in a position to answer that, your Honour. At the very least, it would have been advisable if the newspaper reports had been kept from the common jury.'

'So the effect of your submission is either that judges should refrain altogether from making any remarks even remotely approaching these, or that newspapers should in some way be prevented from publishing these remarks?'

'That might be the result,' Buchanan says. He thinks he may be getting somewhere but he's not sure.

Mr Justice Gresson starts to pay attention, as if he had been drifting away into some personal reverie and had suddenly reminded himself where he was. 'It's inconsistent with the whole basis of the administration of justice if a Grand Jury must be addressed in secret,' he says.

Buchanan sees the case slipping from his grasp. It is the fly, he thinks, the bloody fly.

Timms, for the Crown, weighs in. 'For this submission to succeed the appellant must show that there's been a miscarriage of justice — in the sense that, on fair consideration of the whole proceedings, this court must hold that there's a probability that the newspaper publicity turned the scale against the appellant. There's no justification for suggesting that members of the jury could be so influenced by what they may have heard or read that they cannot be relied upon to do their duty as a jury.'

'Your Honours,' Oliver Buchanan says, 'be that as it may, we are talking about putting a man to death. The death penalty may be enshrined in the law as it now stands, but it has not always been the case. In fact, the law has changed several times over the past two decades.'

'Are we now to be treated to the crusade for abolition?' the judge on the left of Gresson says.

'I'm aware of campaigns for abolition,' Buchanan says. 'But I speak from the heart. The famous writer, Victor Hugo, whose name I'm sure is familiar to you all, conducted a life-long crusade against the death penalty. He wrote these words — *Look*, examine, *reflect*. You hold capital punishment up as an example. Why? Because of what it teaches. And just *what* is it that you wish to teach by means of this example? Thou shalt not kill. And how do you teach that "thou shalt not kill"? By killing. Hugo goes on to explain that he had examined the death penalty under each of its two aspects: as a direct action, and as an indirect one. What did it come down to? Nothing but something horrible and useless, nothing but a way of shedding blood, that is called a crime when an individual commits it, but is called "justice" when society brings it about. Make no mistake, you judges and lawmakers—' and here Buchanan pauses long enough for the judges on the Bench to be clear that he is reciting Hugo's comments for their benefit '— that *in the eyes of God as in those of conscience, what is a crime when individuals do it is no less an offence when society commits the deed*.'

'Have you quite finished, Mr Buchanan?' asks the presiding judge.

Chapter 24

And still the notebooks pile up in the Blacks' front room. Kathleen can estimate the number of signatures by multiplying the number of notebooks by the number of pages by the lines in each notebook. Notebooks × pages × lines = 12,000. More and more just keep arriving. Signatures from the church, from the marketplaces where they ran a book, from the pubs, most of all from the mills. There is her own Jennymount Mill, but her fellow workers know others in different mills. Inside of a week these twelve thousand signatures have arrived, supporting the petition seeking clemency for Albert Black.

In the night, Kathleen lies awake, her eyes scratchy from tiredness, until she can't stand it any longer, and she inches herself out of the hollow of the bed. Bert groans in his sleep and throws an arm out as if to stop her, but she's hell-bent on counting the notebooks again. She needs to check through and see if any have been crossed out, or lines missed, or someone hasn't put their address. It feels the same as if she were counting votes in an election. Every vote for the life of her son must count. They are running out of time. The notebooks have to be delivered to Mr Clifton Webb who is about to visit Belfast.

She wonders, over and again, what is happening inside the head of her boy. He has written her the strangest letter, telling her of his conversion to the Roman Catholic faith. There must be some reason for it, but she hasn't worked that out. Or maybe this is to do with the state of his mind that he is talking guff. She hasn't told Bert about this letter.

In New Zealand, a railway worker called John Vermeulen stabs another man by the name of Dick Lucas on a Hamilton dance floor, enraged because Lucas is dancing with his girlfriend. He inflicts four knife wounds. Lucas doesn't die. But he might have, people mutter, and there is an unease in the air. Vermeulen is required to take out a prohibition order, and undertake not to attend a dance for a period of time, and not to carry a knife. Otherwise, he goes on with the business of keeping the trains running on smooth track.

In London, the colourful and passionate-hearted publisher, Victor Gollancz, heads a four-thousand-strong rally in Hyde Park, demanding the abolition of the death penalty. He tells the crowd that it is unnecessary, morally unjustified and inconsistent with the self-respect of a civilised and Christian country. YES, the people shout in unison, ABOLITION. He quotes the words of an American abolitionist who has declared the penalty arbitrary, haphazard, capricious and discriminatory. DOWN WITH THE DEATH PENALTY, shout the crowd, as they strain to shake the hand of Gollancz. He is hoisted high on shoulders.

Kathleen thinks that Mr Gollancz probably doesn't know about her Albert, but Mr Webb will surely know about Gollancz. Will it make any difference? When she thinks about it in her terrace house, in the fastness of the Belfast night, it occurs to her that Mr Gollancz is a Labour man, and she thinks Mr Webb might not be sympathetic to his views. She has never thought much about politics, she hasn't had the time, what with working in the mill and caring for her sons and their father and making ends meet and all of that. It's more a case of who kicks with which foot, the left or the right, and the distances between the Irish people in general that have preoccupied her, not the goings-on in places across the sea. Now she is doing her homework. Since she has been told, in effect, not to go to New Zealand, she has asked a lot of questions, called on the editors of the newspaper, and asked them what they know of who's in and who is out in New Zealand, what attitudes are held and by what parties. What she hears is not encouraging. Why is she not surprised that Mr Webb has been and gone without seeing her? But she cannot be ignored, she believes. For by now she has delivered the letters to Mr Warnock, who, she understands, has passed them on to the New Zealand High Commissioner. And there is the letter she has written to the Queen. Surely someone will take note of that.

In Wellington, Ralph Hanan is meeting with Jack Marshall. Hanan, the draper's son from Invercargill, and Marshall, a Wellington man through and through. He knows how the city works, its intrigues and secrets. He is also a chess player. The two Honourable Ministers of the Crown sit discussing the implications of hanging. A secretary has brought in a tray bearing a silver teapot, cups and saucers, a plate of scones and a little Royal Albert dish of raspberry jam. There is a choice of butter or whipped cream. 'A special little treat I asked Bellamy's to provide,' Marshall remarks. Hanan has waved away the scones, and perhaps this is a mistake. He takes a cup of tea with a dash of milk. Marshall drops jam thoughtfully on his scone.

'Jack, you know why I'm here,' Hanan begins. 'I've just heard the news about Black's appeal.'

'Well, not good news for him, I'm afraid.' Marshall's voice is as smooth as the butter in its dish. 'I've sent a telegram to Webb this morning so he can let the mother know.'

'We still have the chance to do something for Black when the Executive Council meets. As a government we can advise the Governor-General to stop this going ahead.'

'Really, Ralph, we've gone over this more times than enough. Why on earth should we overturn the views of five judges? Our very top men.'

'Your men. Mr Holland's men.'

'That's enough. I won't listen to this.'

'Look, you must know as well as I do the arguments being made abroad. Surely you can't deny that the death penalty in this country is haphazard. You've got Horton locked up for a truly vicious rape and murder alongside Black, who might or mightn't have intended to kill his victim. You can't hang Horton, because there wasn't a death sentence in play, but you can hang Black. It doesn't make sense. The penalty in this country has been enforced and suspended, then abolished, then reinstated and suspended again. All since 1935. It depends on which government's in power. It's too important to be decided on a whim.'

'I resent that,' Marshall says. 'My beliefs are not a whim. In fact, Horton's situation is surely worse than that of Black. It seems inhumane to me that a man be locked up in Mount Eden prison for the rest of his natural life. That seems like torture.' His voice is quivering with anger.

'I see. Well, Jack, if you mean that, I guess we're looking at what's humane and what's not from different points of view. I'm ready to respect that, but it doesn't change where I stand.'

'We must have deterrents to murder in place.'

'But the hangings that have happened over the past five years haven't deterred the more recent murders.'

'So we should have hanged Horton?'

'No, that's not what I said.' Hanan's voice is impatient. 'Look, murderers are often indifferent to death. Look at those who kill themselves before their sentence can be carried out. And there's some murderers who simply don't think of the consequences between their action and what will happen later.'

'Like your Mr Black?'

'He's not my Mr Black. Although I'm not convinced he's a murderer. But yes, I'd say that the death sentence was the last thing he had in mind in that cafe. I believe that essentially he is a young man of good character.'

'What is character, Ralph? It's been said that character is the sum of a man's habits. Have you studied this man's habits?'

Checkmate. Hanan pauses, gathering himself for a fresh argument.

'I don't agree with anything you're saying, Minister,' Marshall says, 'but perhaps you'll be happier if I tell you that I've ordered some evaluations of Black to see whether or not he's a suitable candidate for the hangman's noose. Well, there are certain pressures. As you know very well or you wouldn't be here. It might illuminate the discussions we have when the Executive Council meets. The Governor-General has to be able to account for our decisions when he next meets Her Majesty.'

Hanan walks out of the room, along the pale-green corridors of Parliament, beneath its archways and cornices, its stained-glass windows and high ornate ceilings, until he comes to the public gallery that looks down on the debating chamber. It is empty now, but in the afternoon it will fill with Government and Opposition members. He will take his seat there in one of the high-backed chairs that stand in rows on the dark-green carpet with its fleur-de-lis pattern. He is looking down at that space and wonders what he would be thinking if he were a member of the public sitting here later in the day. What would be expected of him? And he knows the answer. He would expect the politicians to be honest with one another, but most of all to their own selves. He is not sure how long he will live. The old war wound haunts him, his lungs fit to burst some days. Whatever happens, however long he is given, he must find a way to change those things that he believes to be wrong.

'Dear Peter, Here I am again as happy as can be. "Oh Oh!" What jolly good company. Sorry Peter, I hope you will forgive my sudden burst of enthusiasm. One goes a bit potty in here now and again so I guess I just write how I feel. I say, you have not told me much about your girlfriend — I mean, is she tall, fat, thin, strong, or something out of a vision? Oh sorry, I apologise for all that trash, my pen has a habit of running away sometimes. But I do want to know.

'I am pretty busy at the moment, getting visits from psychologists, psychiatrists and what-not from the Department of Justice in Wellington. Of course, all this comes up in the Executive Council that is, or should I say, my last thread of hope. I expect that is why they won't let you visit me till that lot pushes off. I think they will be finished with me by Saturday. I shall write after that and let you know what's cooking. It was no great shock to me when my appeal failed, for I sort of expected what the verdict would be. As you probably know, Peter, I have never taken religion more seriously since I came in here. I can tell you, it has helped me to get through this without cracking up under the strain. I owe a lot to you, too, for having given me the strength to keep my chin up.

'Another thing, some people don't know when they are going,

but me, I have a firm pointer. Maybe I should be afraid, but for the life of me, I can't. I guess that's God's comfort to me.

'I will write again in a couple of days' time. God bless you, your friend, Albert.'

Chapter 25

The psychologist who interviews Paddy is determined to be friendly, a small man with a short-back-and-sides haircut and a very straight parting. He holds out his hand to shake Paddy's, as if they were on the outside, not sitting hunched in a cell. Paddy sits on the bed while the psychologist, whose name is Ramsey, perches on the chair.

'I asked to see you in here,' Ramsey says, his voice earnest, 'so that we wouldn't have guards watching us in the visiting area. I want to connect with you, Paddy. You know, really get to know you. I want to know what makes you tick, your thoughts and your *feelings*, to open up your heart to me.'

'Well, some people would say I don't have one of those. A heart, ha ha.'

'This isn't a laughing matter.' Ramsey is wearing a lime-green merino jersey with a diamond-checked red and brown panel down the front, as if to show that he is really quite a casual person and not a bureaucrat. 'It's your life, young Paddy my lad. Believe me, I know the value of life, I was a fighter pilot in my war days. Flew Spitfires over the Pacific. Did your father serve in the war by any chance?'

'He was a soldier, yes.'

'Hmm. And what did he tell you about the war?'

'Not much, sir.'

'Please call me Ramsey,' the psychologist says. 'I want to be your friend.' He has very bright blue eyes, as though he were wearing the sky in them, but somehow they contain a blankness, as if he wouldn't recognise a cloud if he bumped into it.

'My da said that it was best put behind us. The war, sir. Uh, Ramsey. He had a marley that he took off a German, but I lost it.'

'What is a marley?'

'A marble, sir.'

'A marley, well now isn't that interesting? I've learned something. Language is so fascinating.' He seems to have given up on Paddy calling him by his name. 'I'm interested in the meaning of bodgie. You don't happen to know that, by any chance?'

'I did hear. I had a friend called Henry, he stayed with me now and then and he was a Teddy boy. He was a pretty smart guy, was Henry, and he wore the best clothes — really smart Edwardian gear, if you know what I mean, the long coats and shiny shoes.'

And talking about Henry reminds him of something that has hovered alongside him, the shadow of something or someone he hasn't been able to recognise. It's Henry's face swimming before him, and he is in Ye Olde Barn cafe the night Johnny McBride died. Or that's what he thinks, even though it's improbable and wasn't Henry away at sea that night? The Henry he is seeing is wearing a dark heavy jersey, not his Teddy boy clothes. He shakes his head; he must be dreaming.

'So the bodgies? We were talking about the bodgies.' Ramsey's voice is insistent, persuasive.

'Yes, sorry. Bodgies, the way I used to dress after I got to Auckland, we're a bit more casual. You know, sweatshirts and bomber jackets, that sort of thing. Anyway, Henry told me that bodgie comes from budgerigar, which is an Australian love-bird. We're the down-under types.'

'But you're not a down-under man.'

'I'd like to have had gear like Henry's, but it costs, you know, all tailored stuff. The stewards and seamen who come off the ships, they've got money for it. I might have got round to it, but I was kind of saving my money for other things. Well, I was going to start saving.'

'Like? Like what other things?'

'Going home perhaps. I don't know.' His voice is wistful. Everything is floating before him now. The girl, his mam and da, the little boy Daniel, all of them.

Ramsey is busy scribbling down notes. 'So why do you people want to dress like this? These hair-dos and all this sort of thing?'

'It's a bit different, isn't it? No offence meant, but everything's a bit grey here, isn't it, sir? I mean, why does everyone have to look the same?' Paddy is trying to pull himself back into this strange exchange.

'So everything in Northern Ireland is different from here, is that what you're saying?'

'No, it's pretty plain living in Ireland, sir. There's not all that much money there, I can tell you that. But we get dressed up for the Orange Parade — you know, sashes and things.'

'Ah yes, groups of Loyalists, hmm? So you like going round in gangs?'

'We stick together. All the crowd at Ye Olde Barn cafe were like mates. Well, most of us, until things went wrong. As they did for me. You get a bad egg or two.'

'But, on the whole, you'd hang out together and make yourselves very obvious? Quite provocative to passers-by. Would that be fair comment?'

'Not intentionally. Some of these Kiwi blokes want a punch-up sometimes, they don't like that we all have girlfriends.'

'Your lot carry knives?'

'Some of them do.'

'You did.'

'That night. Not as a rule. If you got cornered alone in a back street and someone took against you, you needed to protect yourself. Some of the boys used their boots and broken bottles. Like Johnny McBride.'

'But the witnesses say you had a broken bottle the night of the party at 105 Wellesley Street.'

'Did they say that? I don't really remember. I forget what happened that night. Does it matter now?' Paddy feels very tired.

'So let's move on to the girls. Everyone had girlfriends, I gather?' The voice of the psychologist is inexorable, the blue eyes shining with something like excitement, his first real sign of emotion. 'The widgies. Do you know what a widgie is? Any idea where that comes from?'

'No.'

'Widgeons, I'm told. A kind of duck. That's what I've heard. Ducks, I tell you. Now there's a bit of information for you.'

'So you knew where bodgies came from before you asked me?'

'Don't go smart arse with me, Black. Of course I know the answers. I think I know the answers to most things about you.'

'If you say so.'

'This conversation isn't going anywhere much. You'll have to be a bit more cooperative than you're being now. How come this girl Rita was so quick to go to bed with you?'

'Well, the girls, you know, they're willing. They enjoy sex. So do I.'

'So you had plenty of girls at your disposal? How often did you have sexual intercourse?'

'Oh, four or five times a week.'

'With the same girl?'

Paddy has had enough of this. The man is writing away with feverish enthusiasm as if he were getting kicks out of the conversation. 'Nup, not always. I liked a bit of variety.'

He hears himself in his head and feels slightly sick. 'That is, until—' He stops. But no, he is not going to tell the psychologist about Bessie. This is a grubby little game at best.

'So it was all right if you double-crossed your own girlfriend?'

'It wasn't like that.' But what was it like? He hopes the man doesn't ask him that.

'Did you take precautions against venereal disease?'

'No, I didn't, and so far as I know I've never had the clap.'

'What about pregnancy?'

Perhaps this Ramsey knows about Bessie anyway, but he won't find out anything about her from him. 'I guess some girls get pregnant,' he says, in what he hopes is an even tone.

'So these gangs of youths you hung out with, they don't work regularly?'

'I didn't at the time. But I did have the same job down south for a year and a half or thereabouts. I earned enough to get by.'

'So really, you were a defaulting assisted immigrant picking up a bit of work here and there until you ran out of money again?'

'Something like that.'

The interview is over, the notebook snapped shut. 'Well, thank you, Mr Black, you've been helpful after all.' The psychologist doesn't offer to shake hands this time.

What was all that about? Paddy wonders. The man hadn't wanted to get to know him at all; it seems he just wanted some gossip as juicy as possible. Paddy can hear it going down a treat in his office. It occurs to him then that this is what the Executive Council will hear. Well, hadn't he known that from the beginning? This was his chance to grovel and he's messed things up again. There is no taking any of it back.

Chapter 26

30 November 1955. After the weekly Cabinet meeting of the ministers of the Crown, the Executive Council meets to decide Albert's fate. The Council is the highest formal authority of government, and its members also comprise the ministers, the institution through which the Government collectively advises the Governor-General. The Governor-General of the day is Sir Charles Willoughby Norrie. An Eton man, he has fought in both world wars; he plays polo and hunts foxes when he is at home in England. According to his reputation, he is a man averse to sentimentality.

It's a short meeting. The Prime Minister, Sid Holland, remarks again on the undesirability of men like Albert Black in New Zealand. If they can't be sent back to where they came from, they have to be prevented from pursuing further crime in New Zealand. The reports on him suggest a highly immoral lifestyle, something that he and his friend Mr Mazengarb aim to stamp out. It will not just punish the crime that has been committed but serve as a short, sharp reminder to those who follow reprehensible modes of living and are sexually promiscuous.

Ralph Hanan says, 'So Black is to be made an example in respect of the Mazengarb Report?'

'None of them were up to any good. The youth who was killed had been reading banned books. He even modelled himself on one of Spillane's characters.'

'So two men die, thanks to Mr Mazengarb. Are we, as a government, not succumbing to lynch law?'

The Attorney-General rolls his eyes, and the rest of the Council members sigh and look away.

The Prime Minister says that unless there are any further objections, it will be recommended to the Governor-General that Black's execution take place forthwith.

There is a time frame for the procedure. Once the Council has made its recommendation the penalty must be imposed within seven days. Hanan looks at his colleagues one at a time, until they look away from him and drop their eyes.

4 December 1955. She knows it cannot be long now. Kathleen feels like stone. She cannot move, she cannot cry, so removed does she feel from reality. The winter is closing in. She should have lit the fire, but it can wait. At last, hearing Daniel coming home from school, and throwing his bag down, she stands up from where she has been sitting on the edge of what used to be Albert's bed. Like an automaton, she moves to the wardrobe. It is mostly Daniel's clothes that hang there now, but there is still a jacket that his brother left behind him when he left for New Zealand. He wore it in his last year at school; she had saved up the money to buy it for him. Now she slides her hands into its pockets and holds them inside. His hands have been there. In a pocket she finds a piece of chewed gum rolled up in its wrapper, an unused matchstick, a small twig that he might have pulled carelessly from a hedgerow. She puts her face against the fabric, inhaling, as if she might catch his scent.

'Mam,' Daniel calls, 'are you there?'

He is hungry and she needs to tend to him, to still be the best mother she can. When he is sat at the table with a piece and a cup of hot milk, she says, 'Would you like to look at the photographs?' She rummages in the bottom drawer of the dresser and there it is, the little album where she has kept the pictures.

He pulls a face. 'Andy is waiting for me, can I go over to his house for a bit?'

'As long as you're not late,' she says. And the fact is, she would rather be on her own.

As the door closes behind him, she opens the album. First up, there is a studio picture of wee William, his baby face pinched. It was an extravagance but she had wanted the picture so bad, as if she knew he wouldn't make old bones. And here is a picture of her with Bert, and she is holding Albert in the doorway of their first house in Tate's Avenue. She is wearing a summer dress, her arms bare. The baby is swaddled up in a shawl, just the top of his downy head where the caul has been and the tip of nose showing. Her mother must have taken that one, because all three of them are there, and she remembers now that her mother, who did not have so long to live after that, had come round to greet her when she came home from the hospital. And there Albert is again, in his little cotton hat, holding her hand. It is one of those street photographs, and he is pointing with his free hand and laughing at something beyond the edge of the picture. She wishes she knew what he was looking at then. Now, there they all are in this next one, her and Bert and Albert and Daniel, on their holiday at Ballycastle, the headland rising from the sea in the background. Oh, wasn't that such a nice time? Who took that picture? A passer-by, she thinks. Bert had dug out his old Box Brownie his parents gave him when he was a we'an and his family still had the money. Perhaps they'd asked some stranger to point and click in their direction? In the next one Albert is on board the *Captain Cook*, his springy hair that resembles her own like a dark halo round his head, riffled by a breeze, his hands crossed and loose before him, and again the sea's horizon at his back. Peter Simpson has sent her this, as he has the two remaining ones of Albert. These last two have been taken in New Zealand. In one there is Albert, holding a cat and surrounded by children, on Rose Lewis's lawn. It's Christmas Day, the past year. She had felt a pang of envy when she took that one out of its envelope. It was like Albert had another family in New Zealand. The last picture is more formal and it's not a true photograph at all but a newspaper clipping. Albert is dressed smartly, his hair tamed and stylishly cut. His tie has a jaunty diagonal stripe, and the white shirt looks like the one she sent him for his birthday. He is looking a little away from the camera, not towards her.

Horace Haywood is drunk and entirely on his own. He wishes he had some company, is nostalgic for the presence of Des Ball. But Ball doesn't work here anymore. He thought he knew Ball, but it seems he was wrong. He wonders, in moments like this, when his head is floating and his thoughts off their tether, if it is the killings that have done it for Des. Some men have more fragile hearts than they let on. He wishes he could have helped him. For that matter, he wishes he could help himself. Tomorrow there is a job to be done.

Why is he not at home with Ettie? He is as guilty of neglect in his own way as the other man. But she will be busy with her plans for the men's bowling trip on Wednesday morning. Ettie always has a plan.

Oliver Buchanan is so restless his wife is becoming irritable. No, that's not fair. She knows what is going through and through his mind. There is nothing she can say to calm him down. He can't look at her or the boys. He has decided to go for a walk, he tells her. It's a warm night and he doesn't take a jacket, leaving the house with his tie loose and his shirtsleeves rolled up. It is a Sunday night; he knows that the execution must take place very soon. He has been expecting the news every morning.

He walks for a while around the wharves, watching ferries come and go, the evening light dropping over the sea. Don't worry, I might be a while, he'd said as he left home. The streets are almost deserted. He takes the route along Queen Street, and almost decides to cross Albert Park, but something makes him keep walking, on and up past the turnoff to Wellesley Street, on further until he comes to Ye Olde Barn cafe. He expects it to be crammed with young people, but it too is nearly empty. Perhaps people have stopped coming, or perhaps the weekend has taken its toll; he wouldn't know. The last time he was here, to study the scene of Johnny McBride's killing, music spilled forth and the cubicles were full, as if nothing untoward had happened here at all. At any rate, there is just one man sitting by himself on a stool at the counter. He's a Teddy boy, turned out like a male model, a mannequin in a shop window, so perfect his grooming.

'Do you mind if I sit here?' Buchanan says. Silly, really, he thinks, when he's not seeking company. There is something about sitting down in one of these empty cubicles that makes him uncomfortable. He orders his coffee from the man he recognises as

273

Laurie Corrington, the man who had run down the street to find a policeman, blood splattered all over his apron.

The young man grins, offers his hand. 'I'm Henry,' he says.

'Oliver Buchanan,' he says, offering his hand.

'I know you,' Laurie says from along the counter. 'Can't keep away from the scene of the crime, eh?' He turns to Henry. 'He's Paddy's lawyer.'

'One of them.'

'You haven't saved him from the noose, have you?' Laurie hands Buchanan the coffee and walks away. As if to liven the place up, he takes a coin from the till and wanders down to the jukebox. The Ink Spots are singing 'We'll Meet Again'.

Henry says quietly, 'I've been at sea these past months. I heard what's happened to Paddy.'

'It hasn't happened yet,' Buchanan says, sipping the scalding treacly liquid. 'Tomorrow, I expect. You knew him?'

'He was my friend. I stayed with him a time or two.'

'You did? How did you find him?'

'Paddy? He'd give you the shirt off his back. He was a good bloke, kind-hearted. I was in here the night McBride was killed. I was sitting just near Paddy. He didn't see me when he came in. I was supposed to have gone to sea the night before, the night he had his party. I went down to the ship, but sailing was delayed for a couple of days. It was too late to go to the party, so I turned in for the night. Next day, we did some work on board ship and then I came up here for a coffee before we sailed. I was in my seaman's clothes, so perhaps it didn't occur to him to look my way. He was in a state, I could see that, and Johnny was rarking him up something awful, so I thought just let them sort it out.'

'In what way was he rarking him up?'

'Oh, you know, Paddy was trying to play "Danny Boy" on the

jukebox over there. You can override that Wurlitzer, so when Paddy put his money in Johnny keeps wanting to play "Earth Angel" and cuts him out.'

'Nobody told me that. There were other witnesses. That's not what they said.'

'Well, it's what I say. He cut him out two, maybe three times. Perhaps his mate Jeff saw it too. Jeff Larsen, that is, though I wouldn't know. I haven't clapped eyes on him again.'

Buchanan stirs his coffee, pausing before he speaks. 'Why didn't you tell the police?'

'They didn't want to know. We stood there, there were three of us who saw it happen, the whole thing, eh Laurie? You saw us.'

Laurie busies himself with folding some tea towels, as if he hadn't heard.

'We waited. The police came in. We said we were here when it happened. They told us they were busy, it was a crime scene, and we should get on out of it. Perhaps it was our accents that put them off. I'm a Pom, you know — well, I guess you've worked that out. They'd rounded up plenty of good Kiwi blokes. They must have thought they had enough witnesses.' His tone is bitter. 'Later that night my ship sailed.'

'Did you see Johnny hit Paddy?'

Henry sits thinking, tracing a muddy pattern in spilled coffee essence on the counter. 'I didn't, to tell you the truth. I've heard since that that's what he said to Larsen on the way to the police station. But I didn't see that. Things happened too quick. Paddy sat down, then got up again, and next thing Johnny's dropped against that post, and Laurie here is yelling blue murder and there's chaps rolling him over on the floor. I reckon that wasn't the best thing either. All they did was stick the knife in deeper.'

'But you did say Johnny was provoking Paddy?'

'Oh yes. You know, I think Paddy was sick of getting hidings. He wasn't a big guy, not a fighter. Look, would it have made any difference to Paddy if I'd spoken up more? Not gone to sea that night?'

'I don't know,' Buchanan says. 'It might have made a difference to what the other men said. But perhaps they were all telling the truth the way they saw it. In which case I doubt it would have made much difference. The thing is, your story is closer to Paddy's than that of the others.'

Henry's face pales. 'I could have done more. I'm sorry.'

'You're not on your own there. But thank you for telling me.'

'If he hangs, it'll haunt me the rest of my days,' Henry says, 'I can tell you that.'

'I fear that's a fate we're bound to share,' Buchanan says, offering his hand.

And so the night passes. It's lights out as usual. Paddy stays awake so that he can savour the minutes, one by one. He has been shifted to a ground-floor cell near the kitchen. It is also alongside the courtyard area where the gallows stand. Knowles watches over him, or at least he is supposed to, although now and then he dozes off.

Before Paddy left the upper cell he wrote two letters. When Peter Simpson gets his, he will see that the ink is smudged over his name and above it there is a mark that looks like the shape of a teardrop.

'Dear Peter. No doubt you have read in the press of the Executive Council's final verdict and have guessed what my fate is to be. I should like to take this opportunity to say goodbye, and to wish you many years of future happiness. You have been a very staunch friend of mine.

'I look back to many days of good fun we had together. Ah yes, one always thinks of happiness never the unhappiness. I too remember our first Christmas together in New Zealand. You know Peter, I always thought you would outlast me in life. I did not take the latter seriously enough, but Peter, I guess this is God's will that my time is up and I have come to accept that. Well, I always believe the shortest goodbyes are the best, so I shall close forever, always remembering our friendship. I guess it's goodbye.

'Your friend always, Albert.'

When it came time to write to his mother, the letter he had left for last, he found there was nothing to say. Mam, he had said in the silence of his cell. Oh, Mam. How could he explain to her that which he could not explain to himself? Instead he had written some lines of the song she had sung to him so many times, the one about the wild mountain thyme on the moorlands. When he came to the lines *Let us journey together, Where glad innocence reigns* he faltered. Had there ever been a time of innocence? The two of them together perhaps, picking berries in the sun, not knowing what was coming, before the bombs and the blazing streets and the wartime shelters. Or that time at Ballycastle when the four of them stood side by side, one happy family. The face of his brother Daniel swam before him, trusting and innocent, believing that he would always be there, the big boyo who would look out for him. Well, Daniel would know better now. He couldn't write the last line, his Mam knew it anyway. He hesitated before writing a p.s. 'Love to my da.' He put the sheet of paper in its envelope, wrote the address and put it with his letter to Peter to be posted.

Chapter 27

5 December 1955. The Sheriff of Auckland who is also the Registrar of the High Court is designated to conduct the hangings in Mount Eden prison in an orderly fashion. He is the man who will give the signal for the release of the trapdoor through which the prisoner will fall. Only, when it's Albert Black's turn, the registrar is absent because the last two hangings have precipitated a nervous breakdown. It's over to his deputy this night.

Albert has been offered a sedative in the morning but has turned it down. Likewise, he has turned down the offer of a meal of his favourite food. 'The asparagus season is over,' he had said. 'But thank you.' Up until around four in the afternoon, he has spent the day playing draughts with Knowles or one of the three other guards assigned to assist in rotation. He feels sorry for them, because he beats all of them and he doesn't want them to think that he sees himself in any way superior; he's just no good at losing. He would have preferred to sit in silence, left to his own thoughts, but it doesn't work like that. His mind must be kept off what lies ahead. It worries the guards that he has turned down the pill to make him oblivious. You never know how the condemned man might behave on the gallows. Think of Frederick Foster, fighting for his life at the last.

At five o'clock Father Downey comes in to anoint him before he is prepared for death. The priest asks him if he has any special words for those he will leave behind.

'I have said all I have to say, Father. And thank you for everything. I'm at peace.'

'I sense that.'

'If only I had known what I now know, things would have turned out differently. But it's too late for regrets.'

'The love of God will keep you safe, Albert.' At this point he had to leave Albert and retire to the superintendent's office to await the formal proceedings.

Father Downey joins the procession of witnesses making their way to the yard. A fellow priest, a justice of the peace, a doctor, a coroner and a variety of lay people that includes a newspaper reporter have joined him. They have been advised late in the day that the execution will happen that evening, so that there isn't time for word to get around. The party is warned to walk quietly in single file through the long stone corridor, keeping to a strip of coconut matting laid in the centre to muffle their footsteps. On each side of the corridor stand a line of boots and shoes outside the cell doors. The Judas holes have been covered over. They proceed down a short flight of stairs, gripping the steel railings that protect it. The execution yard, when they reach it, is covered with wire netting, over which canvas has been laid.

The party assembles along one wall, facing the scaffold. There is a wind that evening, a noisy buffeting wind that lifts the canvas like a ship's sail in a storm. The scaffold is a high steel structure, with a platform reached by way of seventeen steps.

Around the supports at the bottom of the gallows canvas has been lashed to conceal the space beneath. The whole scene is lit by a powerful electric light. The light shines on the white rope coiled beneath the gallows and on the noose hanging over the trap. The hangman stands waiting at the back of the platform, his back to the observers.

Albert appears, led by his guards. He doesn't walk along the polished corridor; rather, he shuffles because his body is harnessed by broad leather straps. The straps are crossed around his arms at the elbows, his crossed hands strapped in front of him, and his legs pinioned above the knee. In some ways he resembles a log of wood, or a five foot eight tree stump. To further ensure that his body is as rigid as it can possibly be made, he wears a stiff canvas coat and a pair of heavy boots provided by the prison.

He ascends the stairs slowly, and the hangman turns to meet him. In the bright light Father Downey sees that the hangman is dressed in a felt hat pulled low over his brow, sunglasses hiding his eyes. His chin is sunk in the collar of a long topcoat buttoned all the way up the front.

Albert is facing Horace Haywood. 'Have you anything to say, Black?' Haywood asks.

Albert turns and looks down on those assembled beneath him. In a grave voice, he answers: 'I wish you all a merry Christmas, gentlemen, and a prosperous New Year.'

His legs are quickly pinioned, the noose dropped around his neck, and Haywood slips a white hood over Albert's head, which a guard tucks in beneath the noose. Haywood and the guards move aside, and for a moment Albert stands there alone in the blinding overhead light, while the canvas above them bangs and thumps and strains to rise from its mooring into the wind. The deputy sheriff raises his hand, the hangman releases the trapdoor and Albert has gone. The rope goes taut, skips for a moment like a child's rope, there is a thud.

Two minutes and seven seconds have elapsed between Albert leaving the door of the death cell and his exit from the top to the bottom of the gallows. The wind continues to rise, and blows hard in the courtyard, lifting the bottom canvas. Only Horace Haywood approaches the body to check that death has occurred. As is the law, the body must lie for an hour before it is moved. Father Downey and his fellow priest begin to pray. *Lord, those who die still live in Your presence, their lives change but do not end.* Father Downey's voice is so cracked and sad the words come out as little more than a whisper. In the corner of the yard the gravedigger stands, shovel in hand, ready to begin his task. The crowd is ushered quickly away, lest they catch sight of the dead, the glimpse of a boot now showing.

At the door of the recently vacated cell stands a pair of empty shoes like those outside all the other doors in the prison.

'He died game,' the justice of the peace says.

There is a murmur of assent from those around. Yes, he died game.

Chapter 28

A telegram comes in the early morning to the house in Gay Street off Sandy Row. Kathleen has stayed home from the mill every day this week, waiting for it to arrive. To hell with the money, she has said to Bert. Who cares? The telegram boy cannot look at her as she opens the door. She takes the envelope slowly and offers the boy a sixpence, but he shakes his head.

Her neighbour Clodagh has seen the boy too. After a decent interval she will come over and put the kettle on.

The husband has already left for work and the small boy, Daniel, for school. 'You should find Bert,' she says.

Kathleen shakes her head. 'It's all right,' she says. 'I'll be all right after a bit.'

Later that day she puts on her coat and sets off for a walk. It's a very cold day.

Bert will find her, as he has always done, sooner or later. She is sitting in the Botanic Gardens, on a bench near an archway. She sees her son, the one that went to New Zealand. He is small and playful and he puts his arms up as he runs towards her. The beds of pruned roses are mounded up. When spring comes, sometime next year, although right now she can't think that far ahead, the roses will bloom, and out on the downs the heather will turn purple again. Light snow falls in flurries around her.

Her husband gives her his hand and draws her up, putting his arm around her waist. There they are, the two of them, walking off into their own history of sorrow.

And what of Bessie Marsh? Well. Ready or not, she is moving into the story of women's lives. Where there are women there are usually men. There is always the chance then of love, its possibilities, and its anguish. For a time, after her baby has been given away, Bessie will be alone. But not always. Bessie is a steadfast woman, one of the strong ones. She'll survive on her own terms.

She won't forget. Not ever.

Sometimes in nights to come she will see the face of the Irish boy, and she will say his name to herself.

Albert Black.

Afterword

The Hon. J.R. (Ralph) Hanan continued to campaign for the abolition of the death penalty. A tide of disgust against the penalty overtook public perception after the hanging of Albert Black. One more person was hanged before the election of the 1957–1960 Labour Government. During that term all death sentences were commuted to life imprisonment. In 1960 a National Government took office again. In 1961 Hanan, by then the Attorney-General, introduced legislation to withdraw hanging as a punishment. The Hon J.R. Marshall put forward six reasons why it should be maintained. The Bill was debated on non-party lines.

Hanan said, at the end of the debate: 'Justice is due to all men, murderers as well as the rest of us, simply because we are men. The situation through the vagaries of party politics in New Zealand for the last twenty-five years has, therefore, violated justice.'

Ten members of the National Party voted with Labour to abolish the death penalty for murder.

Hanan died suddenly in 1969. He was sixty years old.

Acknowledgements

This book could not have been written without the generous gift of research material by Redmer Yska. Redmer not only provided trial transcripts and notes of his own earlier interviews with now-deceased figures associated with Albert Black, but also gave practical support and advice throughout the writing of the book. I cannot thank him enough. I wish to acknowledge that chapter 27 is based on a searing eyewitness account of Albert's death written by *Truth* reporter Jack Young, and that some of the phrases used are his. Although the account appeared without a by-line, Young's identity was later revealed. His story stirred the public conscience and made a significant contribution to the abolition of the death penalty in New Zealand.

The Quintal brothers, Rainton Hastie and Laurie Corrington were real people, but the names of other trial witnesses, and their personal circumstances, have been changed, as have those of the lawyers and all of the jury. Although events unfolded around the Black family in Belfast as they are described, the background to their lives is imagined.

I thank many people who have provided information, advice and assistance with research. They include Ross Brown, Richard Douglas, Peter Farrell, the late Ian Kidman, Joanna Kidman, Peter Larsen (author of the play *Albert Black*), Nana Matenga at the Auckland High Court, Greg Newbold, Jill Nicholas, Vincent O'Sullivan, Sir Geoffrey Palmer, Pete Smith and Desley Watkins of the Department of Corrections Ara Poutama Aotearoa, who arranged my tour of Mount Eden prison, and also staff at Ngā Taonga Sound and Vision (the New Zealand Film Archive). Thanks to the several people who provided me with copies of Albert Black's letters to Peter Simpson. Some contributors have requested anonymity: I am particularly grateful to E.H., Albert's daughter, who was born in March 1956, and also to a member of Albert's Naenae 'family'. I acknowledge many hours of assistance provided to me at Births, Deaths, and Marriages in Belfast, and at the Linen Hall Library, Belfast. I was a guest of the Belfast Book Festival in 2016, and thank the organisers for their hospitality. My publisher, Harriet Allan, contributed local knowledge of Belfast, and also travelled with me to meet some informants. I am grateful to her, Stuart Lipshaw and Jane Parkin for their editorial skills and warm encouragement.

Last, but never least, thank you to Creative New Zealand for a grant to assist with the writing of this work.

During my research the following books and texts were invaluable:

Jerry Adams, *Falls Memories: A Belfast Life*, Roberts Rinehart, 1993.

Geoffrey Beattie, *Protestant Boy*, Granta Books, 2005.

Department of Justice, *Crime in New Zealand: A Survey of New Zealand Criminal Law Behaviour*, Government Printer, 1974.

Greg Newbold, *Punishment and Politics: The Maximum Security Prison in New Zealand*, Oxford University Press, 1989.

Rt. Hon. Sir Geoffrey Palmer QC, *Law and Life*, New Zealand Centre for Public Law, Occasional Paper No. 21.

Redmer Yska, *All Shook Up: The Flash Bodgie and the Rise of the New Zealand Teenager in the 1950s*, Penguin, 1996.

Various Radio New Zealand transcripts, including *Spectrum* documentaries.

Papers Past at the Alexander Turnbull Library.

The quote attributed to Victor Hugo on p. 255 comes from his novel *The Last Day of a Condemned Man*, 1829.

Reading Group Guide

- Fiona Kidman is campaigning for Albert Black's murder conviction to be overturned. Having read her account of the story, do you believe Black received a fair trial?
- What does the novel have to say about the death penalty? Would you describe the book as a political novel?
- What impression did the book give you of 1950s New Zealand? Why do you think Kidman chose to base her novel around real events?
- How does the novel compare to other books and films that revolve around court cases? There is currently huge interest in true crime and potential miscarriages of justice, with podcasts such as *Serial* and TV series like *Making a Murderer*. Why do you think we are drawn to this type of story?
- At the end, we are told Bessie Marsh is 'moving into the story of women's lives'. The majority of Kidman's previous novels have focused on female experience. How do the central women in *This Mortal Boy* – Paddy's mother back home, and Rose, Rita and Bessie in New Zealand – shape Paddy's life?
- What is the effect of the inclusion of snippets of folk songs in the narrative?